HIGHLAND HEART

BRIDES OF THE HIGHLANDS
BOOK 1

KIRSTEN OSBOURNE

ARE YOU SIGNED UP FOR DRAGONBLADE'S BLOG?

You'll get the latest news and information on exclusive giveaways, exclusive excerpts, coming releases, sales, free books, cover reveals and more.

Check out our complete list of authors, too!

No spam, no junk. That's a promise!

Sign Up Here

www.dragonbladepublishing.com

Dearest Reader;

Thank you for your support of a small press. At Dragonblade Publishing, we strive to bring you the highest quality Historical Romance from some of the best authors in the business. Without your support, there is no 'us', so we sincerely hope you adore these stories and find some new favorite authors along the way.

Happy Reading!

CEO, Dragonblade Publishing

CHAPTER ONE

The Highlands, 1555

F IONA MCAFEE NOCKED another arrow to her bowstring with a practiced ease that one would never expect from the statuesque blue-eyed blonde. The morning air, crisp and cool, was filled with the muted rustling of leaves.

She drew back the string, the familiar pressure comforting against her fingertips. Her world narrowed to the target, a distant point awaiting the destruction of her arrow. Fiona sighed. Between one heartbeat and the next, she loosed the shaft.

It soared and struck true, piercing the center of the target with a satisfying *thunk* that resonated through the stillness. A small smile twitched at the corners of Fiona's mouth, but it was a fleeting thing, for there was no time to bask in satisfaction—not when there was yet more to prove, more to perfect.

Fiona set to work, the rhythm of her movements as fluid as the waters of Loch Lomond, each motion a graceful dance honed by years of disciplined practice. Her arrows found their marks unerringly, a cascade of whispers against the targets.

She stood regally as she sighted down the arrow. The archery yard of Clan McAfee had become her court, the thrum of bowstrings her decree.

Yet beneath the serene surface, a storm of considerations and strategies brewed within Fiona's mind—matters not of the heart but of duty, the weight of responsibility pressing upon her shoulders. Her father had invited men from all over, and unbeknownst to the men, he planned to choose her future husband from among them.

After much arguing, she'd gotten her father to listen to her opinions of the men. Yet deep down, she craved true courtship. She desired a man who would take her for walks and get acquainted with her for more than just a political alliance.

And though none could hear her, Fiona was far more than just a skilled archer. As Laird Duncan McAfee's eldest daughter, she was a prize to any of the laird's sons her father was inviting—for he would settle for no less than a laird's son to become the future laird of Clan McAfee. Her younger half-sisters would hopefully be given more freedom, though the youngest of the trio, Moira, had declared she would never marry. She loved her freedom too much to trade it for a lifetime of duties and childbearing.

Fiona sighed, her breath misting in the crisp Highland air as she lowered her bow. The anticipation for the upcoming games kindled a fire within her breast, the likes of which she had never felt. This would be the first time she was allowed to compete, and she looked forward to besting the men. Oh, she'd competed with her father's soldiers and her sisters, and she'd beaten them all, but to compete in true Highland Games was something she aspired to. She could almost hear the clamor of the crowd, the clash of steel, and the triumphant cries that awaited at the fields near her home.

She observed the targets, each punctured by her arrows. It was more than mere practice. It was her preparation to be introduced to the world as a warrior of Clan McAfee.

"Let them see what a McAfee lass can do," she whispered with determination.

MEANWHILE, WITHIN THE imposing stone walls of McClain castle a half-day's ride from Clan McAfee's own fortress, Alisdair stood among his brothers. "The Highland Games are nigh upon us," he announced, his voice carrying the gravity of their ancestral halls. "And with them, an opportunity presents itself—a chance to find a wife."

Alisdair had the muscled strength of a warrior. With his dark hair and blue eyes, he was considered a catch by all the women of the clan, but he couldn't marry a McClain woman and still rule. No, he must find a clan who needed a strong leader, so he could marry their daughter.

His younger brothers, Lachlan and Brodie, exchanged knowing glances. The task of finding a bride was no trifling matter, especially for a man like Alisdair, for Alisdair, though he was the eldest son of a laird, would not have the opportunity to rule Clan McClain. No, that honor would go to their youngest brother, Boyd.

Each generation of the McClains brought seven sons, with the youngest inheriting. No one knew why it happened that way, but the elders of the family claimed that it started with a family who came from Normandy and fought with William the Conqueror centuries before.

"Ye seek a woman who will give you the best political alliance," Lachlan remarked, a playful twinkle in his eye. "I ken ye want a lass whose marriage will allow ye to lead a clan—a powerful clan."

"Aye," Alisdair affirmed, his gaze piercing as an eagle's. "She must be strong, wise, and capable of standing beside me through the trials and triumphs that await." His thoughts turned unbidden to the whispers he'd heard of the McAfee sisters—warrior women of unparalleled mettle. The prospect of meeting them on the field of honor intrigued him. He'd never met a woman who could compete with a man on the field of honor, but he'd been told these women could and at this Highland Games for the first time—they would.

"Strength and grace," he mused. "I hear whoever marries the

oldest shall expect to call himself Laird of Clan McAfee. I canna be laird of Clan McClain, as that honor goes to our youngest brother. But if I can find a lady with qualities befitting a future lady of a clan, I hope I will find them in her."

IN THE STONE-CLAD hall of Castle Sinclair, Laird Arran Sinclair convened a meeting with his sons. The air was cool and still, save for the crackling hearth that cast a warm glow on their stern faces. Malcolm stood flanked by his younger brothers, Ian and Callum, each embodying the strength and resolve of their lineage.

"Malcolm," began Arran, his voice deep and steady as the rolling hills that surrounded their land, "our fields thirst for water, and our future requires more fertile ground." His gaze made it clear that they were not to argue with him. "The lands we seek are under the banner of Clan McAfee—our allies, true, but such bonds must be tightened if we are to endure."

With the measured cadence of a seasoned leader, he unfolded his plan, speaking of bonds not forged by mere pacts but by the unbreakable ties of matrimony. "You will journey to the Highland Games hosted by the McAfees. There, you must win the hand of Fiona, their eldest. Through this union, our clans shall become one, and none shall dare challenge our might."

As the gravity of his father's words sank in, Malcolm straightened himself, his eyes alight with a quiet fire. It was more than an order. It was a gauntlet thrown at his feet—the path to elevate his clan and etch his name into history. An opportunity to emerge from the shadow cast by his father's formidable reign, to harness his own ambition and cunning for the glory of the Sinclairs.

"I will do as you command, Father," Malcolm replied, his excitement thinly veiled. "To stand as laird over a domain so vast, to protect and prosper our people twofold—it is an honor I accept with pride."

Laird Arran nodded, his expression betraying a hint of approval. For Malcolm, this was more than a quest for land or power. It was a chance to prove his worth, to confront the gnawing insecurity that clawed at him in the quiet hours. To be deemed worthy in the eyes of the man who had shaped him with expectations as rugged as the Highlands themselves.

And though the path ahead would be fraught with trials, Malcolm Sinclair embraced the charge with fervor, ready to unite two clans and forge an indomitable legacy.

ALISDAIR MCCLAIN STRODE through the corridor of his ancestral home, his boots echoing off the stone walls. The air held a chill, one not entirely born of the draft that whispered through the arrow slits. It was a tangible reminder of the responsibility he carried upon broad shoulders. His family was unique amongst the ruling clans of the Highlands. The youngest would inherit, and that would leave the eldest to find another clan to rule, or be ruled by the youngest. He loved his brother Boyd, the youngest of the seven brothers, but he was the one who was born to lead, not his brother, who was happier playing with butterflies than he was on the battlefield.

It didn't matter though. Boyd was destined to rule, and he, Alisdair, was destined to… do something. He would be a great warrior, and he had to find a clan who was searching for a laird. A man with a level head and great strength needed to be a leader, not a follower.

He found his brothers, Lachlan and Brodie, once more. "Brothers," he began. "The games draw nigh, and with them, the eyes of the clans. We must present ourselves as the formidable force we are." His two oldest brothers glanced back at him.

Lachlan leaned forward, the firelight casting shadows over his features. "Aye, and beyond displays of strength, 'tis alliances we might forge. Each clan brings not just their brawn to the field, but a chance for kinship."

"This is true," Alisdair acknowledged, already contemplating the chessboard of clanship and legacy. "The McAfee lasses, for instance. They are said to possess a skill that rivals even the seasoned warriors of our own kin." His voice betrayed none of the curiosity that flickered within him, a flame piqued by tales of archery prowess and unyielding spirit. In his mind, the eldest Fiona was already his own.

"Have ye heard much of them?" Brodie inquired. Brodie was the youngest of the three brothers who would attend the Highland Games. He was interested in tales of the warrior women.

"Enough to recognize they are not to be underestimated," Alisdair replied, his eyes narrowing slightly. He imagined the eldest, Fiona, her name uttered in reverent tones throughout the Highlands. "Their father has raised them more akin to sons than daughters, each skilled in ways that could benefit our clan... or challenge it."

"Would ye consider an alliance with the McAfees then?" Lachlan asked, tilting his head as though to weigh the prospect himself.

"Perhaps," Alisdair conceded. "If the fates decree it so. But let us not forget the games are more than mere courtship. They will be watching us all and judging the entire McClain clan on our actions." He smirked. "There are already enough tales about the crazy McClain family, but all understand we are warriors."

After his brothers left the room, he thought about what he wanted from the Highland Games. He wanted victory, of course, but he also wanted a wife. For Alisdair, an alliance must come first. He didn't care about a love match. A woman could be ugly as a troll and he would marry her as long as she came with a clan for him to lead.

"Mayhap," he mused, "I will find the perfect lass to marry." His gaze drifted to the window where stars peeked through the twilight, their celestial patterns like the intricate knots of a tapestry yet unseen. "A woman of courage and intellect who can stand shoulder to shoulder with a laird in both heart and mind."

As if on cue, the constellation of Orion, the great hunter, met his eye, reminding Alisdair of the tales of prowess and partnership that filled the highland lore. The thought of such a companion stirred something within him—a yearning mingled with apprehension, for how often did the desires of a man align with the needs of a clan?

Meanwhile, Fiona McAfee stood in the middle of her practice field, her bowstring still quivering from the last arrow loosed. She sighed slowly, her breath visible in the cool air of twilight. The Highland Games beckoned to her like a siren's call, promising a boare upon which to demonstrate her worth beyond the confines of tradition. Aye, she was a woman like any other, but she didn't enjoy thinking about hairstyles or making supper plans. She wanted to be able to fight with her father's men, and he often allowed her to train with them.

She wasn't certain she could ever marry, though her father had been pressing her to choose a husband. Yet what husband would allow her to train with men?

Her heart thrummed with anticipation, not solely for the contest of arms and agility, but for the myriad possibilities it offered. What alliances might be struck? What challenges would arise? And, hidden in the weave of those questions, was the whisper of a deeper query—one of connection, of kinship, perhaps even of a shared destiny with someone she had yet to meet. These Highland Games would change her life in ways she could only imagine.

Fiona collected her arrows. As she stowed them in her quiver, her mind danced toward the morrow, toward the gathering of clans and the spectacle it promised. Her sisters, Ailis and Moira, would surely be abuzz with their own preparations.

All three sisters would compete in the games. Fiona would compete in archery, Ailis in dagger throwing, and Moira in swordsmanship. Moira was the smallest of the three as well as the youngest. Their father had a sword specially made for her when she'd demonstrated ability with the wooden swords he'd had them all wield as practice swords first.

With each step toward her clan's keep, her mind whirled with strategies and visions of the games. The Highland Games were not merely a test of strength and skill. They were the way the mettle of whole clans was judged. And she, as the eldest McAfee sister, bore the weight of her clan's honor upon her shoulders.

Most of the McAfee soldiers would also compete in the games. Fiona looked forward to watching them compete, but she also looked forward to meeting new people. She'd been isolated most of her life from anyone other than kin. After her mother's death in childbirth, her father had married twice more, hoping to find a mother for her, but all three had died. Each had left him another daughter. After he'd lost his third wife, Laird Duncan wouldn't try for another son. It was too difficult to keep losing mothers for his daughters. He concluded that he was not meant to have a son, and he then began training his daughters to be sons instead.

Ailis and Moira awaited her arrival, their faces lit with the fervor that the coming event had ignited in all their hearts. Ailis, ever the nurturer, approached with a furrowed brow, undoubtedly concerned for their unity and well-being. Moira, eyes gleaming with untamed spirit, clutched an assortment of weapons she had acquired—each a small rebellion against the world's expectations.

"Have you honed your aim, Fiona? Will the arrows fly true when the moment of truth arrives?" Moira asked in jest and earnestness. Moira was the true warrior of the family, as she was good in hand-to-hand combat, excellent with a bow, though not as good as Fiona, and she excelled with the sword her father had given her when she was old enough to carry one.

Fiona smiled, her confidence unshaken. "As true as the McAfee name. Our clan shall rise in the esteem of all who gather."

Ailis hummed a tune of quiet encouragement, her melody weaving through the cool air, wrapping them in a shroud of shared anticipation. Her stories, often told by flickering firelight, had a way of fortifying their spirits, reminding them of the legends they themselves might one day become.

"Let us not forget the duty we owe to our name," Ailis counseled, the mischievous glint rarely seen by others flashing briefly in her gaze. "We must compete with the men and beat them. Nothing less will be acceptable to Father."

The three sisters exchanged glances of understanding, each one acknowledging the gravity of the games. It was more than mere competition. It was a display of their clan's resilience, a chance to forge alliances, and perhaps, for Fiona, an opportunity to encounter a destiny long whispered by the winds that swept across the highlands.

"Tomorrow, we show the strength of the McAfee blood," Fiona declared. "For our kin, for those without a family to call their own, and for the future we will shape with our own hands."

FIONA PLUCKED THE last of her arrows from the target. She faced her sisters, a smile playing upon her lips, the weight of the impending games momentarily lifted by their presence.

"Ye think yer aim will be true when the eyes of the clans are upon ye?" teased Moira.

"True enough to best any man—even a McClain—who dares cross my path," Fiona declared, arching an eyebrow in feigned defiance. The McClains were the men who were reported to be the strongest among the Highland Clans. All three sisters had watched them for years. Ailis had always dreamed of marrying one, though Fiona and Moira had dreamed of besting one on the battlefield.

Ailis joined in the jest. "And what if the McClain's gaze lingers less upon your arrows and more upon the archer?"

"Then he shall find himself sorely distracted," Fiona answered, her heart fluttering at the notion. One of the McClain brothers had caught her eye in the previous game as she'd watched from the window, and she was hoping to see him again. Quietly hoping. She would never admit it to her sisters. "For 'tis not a fair maiden they'll meet, but a warrior of Clan McAfee."

THE WARM GLOW from the torches of McClain castle revealed a gathering in the grand hall. Alisdair McClain stood amidst his kin, his stance commanding, his mind as sharp as the blade at his side.

"We shall present ourselves with honor at the games," Alisdair decreed, his voice resonating through the stone walls. "Each man must uphold the legacy of our ancestors, for the pride of McClain is not taken lightly."

His brothers nodded solemnly, understanding the gravity woven into every word. Alisdair surveyed the faces before him, each one a testament to the unwavering spirit of their clan. Together, they would stand, a formidable force upon the fields, their unity unshaken by rivalry or the prospect of alliances hidden within the guise of competition.

"Let us retire to prepare for what lies ahead," Alisdair announced, dismissing the assembly with a firm nod.

When Alisdair strode up the stairs to the room he'd had since childhood, he was satisfied with the preparations of the soldiers for the games. They must show their strength, or the other clans would assume they had none.

He paced before the hearth, where embers still glowed from

the day's fire. The warmth did little to quell the chill of responsibility that wrapped around him like a cloak. He was expected to find a wife, but the woman he sought had a spirit who could stand beside him, unflinching in the face of adversity.

"Would that fate be so kind?" he wondered. Fiona McAfee, a name that carried the promise of such ideals, was the first woman he would approach. Yet, rumors were akin to the wind—felt but never seen, and often shifting direction. To judge her solely on hearsay was folly. He must observe her and discern her character for himself.

"Let the days to come reveal the truth of it," he resolved, the weight of expectation settling upon his broad shoulders. Alisdair knew well the game of courtship was as intricate as any battle, requiring not only strategy but intuition. If the lass possessed the essence of both warrior and diplomat, then perhaps she was the rare jewel for which he—and his heart—had been searching.

He must base his opinion of the lass on her strength and her spirit. He couldn't care if she were hideous.

THOUGH THE HOUR was late, Fiona McAfee could not sleep. Instead, she stood before the narrow window, gazing upon the moon's silvery path that illuminated the rugged highland tapestry below.

"Soon," she whispered to herself—a habit born from many nights of solace—her breath fogging the cool glass. "All will unfold as destiny decrees." The games wouldn't truly start until the following day, but the morrow was when the other clans would come and camp near their keep. They would feast on McAfee food, and they would mingle among one another—their loyalties told apart by the colors and patterns of the tartans they wore.

She traced the lines of her bow, resting against the wall—an extension of her very soul. The bow was a symbol of her strength, her grace, her unwavering determination to stand as an equal among men. The Highland Games were not merely a contest of skill. They were a boare upon which her future would be set into motion.

In the stillness of her chamber, Fiona felt the flutter of anticipation, a quiet thrill. Tomorrow, eyes would follow her every move, including those of Alisdair McClain—warrior and potential suitor. His name had reached her ears, whispers of a man whose prowess in strategy was matched only by his sense of duty.

Would he see beyond the façade of competition? Would he recognize in her a kindred spirit—one who balanced the weight of leadership with the subtleties of compassion? It was a dance she was well-versed in, the delicate interplay between what was expected and what was desired.

As she settled into her bed, wrapping herself in blankets woven with the tartan of her clan, Fiona allowed herself a rare moment of vulnerability. Her mind drifted to Alisdair once more—not as a warrior or a strategist, but as a man. What passions lay concealed behind his stoic face? Did his heart yearn for connection, as hers did, amid the duties and demands of his station?

Her questions lingered, unanswered, as she closed her eyes and surrendered to sleep's gentle embrace. But even in her dreams, she anticipated what was to come, painting scenes of laughter and competition, of pride and perhaps… of romance.

＊

CHAPTER TWO

A MID THE CLATTER of the castle kitchen, where scullery maids busily scrubbed pots and the air was rich with the aroma of roasting meat and freshly baked bread, Fiona sought the counsel of one wiser than most. Her gaze swept past the bustling activity, settling on the familiar form of her mentor nestled in a quiet corner. The cook for the castle, who held the additional distinction of being her grandmother.

The old woman stood in front of the stove, stirring a huge pot of rabbit stew. "Are ye looking forward to the games, lass?"

Fiona watched her grandmother for a moment, noting how the flickering light of the hearth danced across the wise lines etched into her face. There was timeless knowledge within her, a depth of understanding that came not from books, but from life itself.

The weight of Fiona's troubles lessened ever so slightly in her grandmother's presence. Here was one who knew the burdens of duty, the sacrifices required by those born into a lineage where the needs of the many often eclipsed personal yearnings. Yet, even as the political tides surged and pulled at Fiona's sense of self, she found solace in this place, where love for family interwove with the responsibilities vested upon her by birthright.

Fiona closed the distance between them. With a gentle grace, she enfolded the diminutive figure of her grandmother in an embrace, the solidity of the old woman surprising with as small as she was. "Granny," Fiona began, "I find myself confused about the games. I am in need of your guidance." Having lived her entire life without a mother, she often went to Granny when she needed something.

Granny continued to stir the stew and peered up at Fiona, the lines around her eyes crinkling as a smile spread across her face. She laid a tender hand on Fiona's arm, a touch that held the strength of generations. "Come, lass. Sit down," Granny beckoned, gesturing toward a wooden chair pulled close to the hearth.

With a nod of gratitude, Fiona settled onto the offered seat, the sturdy wood creaking beneath her weight. Her gaze lingered on the cookfire's glow, the flames casting a golden hue upon the stone walls of the kitchen.

Granny deliberately turned back to the bubbling pot. She tore a generous piece of a crusty loaf of bread and handed it to Fiona. "Eat, child. A full belly steadies the heart when the mind is troubled."

Fiona accepted the bread and bit into it, the simple act grounding her as she prepared to unravel the threads of her quandary before the woman who had borne witness to her life since its very inception.

"Now, tell me what's troubling you, child."

Fiona took a deep breath. "As you know, the games will start tomorrow. I will compete along with my sisters against the men of other clans. My father says that he is watching the games closely this time, trying to find a man worthy of being both laird of the clan and my husband."

Granny's gaze softened as she considered Fiona's words. A knowing twinkle danced in her eyes as she met Fiona's troubled gaze, and she spoke with a voice as soothing as a lullaby.

"Lass, the path ahead may be shrouded in uncertainty, but remember this—your heart knows truths that even the wisest minds may overlook," Granny reassured her. She reached out and gently held Fiona's hand. Fiona's heart grew as warm as the hearth fire beside them.

"Fiona, you are more than a prize to be won in a contest of strength and skill. Your worth lies not in the outcome of these games but in the steadfastness of your spirit and the depth of your love. Do not let the expectations of others dim the light that burns within you," Granny continued, her words carrying the weight of experience and wisdom that had weathered many decades.

Clarity washed over Fiona. The weight of expectation, the looming specter of political machinations that threatened to overshadow the joy of the games, began to recede like morning mist under the sun's gentle caress.

With a newfound resolve shining in her eyes, Fiona met her grandmother's gaze. "Thank ye, Granny," she whispered. "I will not let the expectations of others dim my light. I will compete with all my heart, but I shall follow where my heart leads regarding matters of love."

Granny beamed at Fiona, her eyes alight with pride and affection. "That's my girl," she murmured, a note of approval filling her voice. "In the days of my youth, my heart was as wild as the land, untamed by duty or promise."

Fiona leaned forward. Her grandmother was the best storyteller around, and if she was going to tell a story, Fiona would listen intently.

"Ye ken, there was a time when I stood where ye stand now, Fiona," Granny continued. Her gaze settled upon Fiona with an intensity that bore the weight of experience. "Love came to me in glances that spoke to my heart. It was a force that could not be denied, yet it conflicted with duty, and no matter what I chose, there would be a measure of sacrifice."

Fiona's eyes, the color of the stormy sea, shimmered with a fusion of emotions. Curiosity flickered within her, while determination etched itself into the lines of her face.

"Following one's heart," Granny's voice dipped, "is a journey fraught with peril and exaltation in equal measure. It is the silent whisper of the loch, calling the soul that dares to listen."

Granny's voice carried a haunting quality as she delved into the depths of her own past, drawing Fiona into a world where duty and desire intertwined. Her eyes glistened with memories that spanned many years.

"When I was but a lass," Granny began, "I stood at the edge of a precipice, torn between two hearts that beat as one yet belonged to different realms. One was a warrior, fierce in battle and tender in whispers by moonlight. The other was a son of noble blood, bound by oaths forged in steel and sealed with the wax of ancient pacts."

Fiona leaned in closer, her breath caught in the tapestry Granny spun with each word. The fire crackled beside them, casting flickering shadows that danced upon the walls like specters of the past.

"I loved them both," Granny murmured, her voice laden with the weight of reminiscence. "One offered me the wild expanse of the moors, where he pledged his sword to protect and cherish me. The other beckoned with the promise of lands and titles, a life of comfort and prestige. Duty whispered in one ear, while desire sang in the other."

Fiona's eyes widened, reflecting the flames that cast a warm glow upon her face. She hung on every word, her grandmother's tale weaving a spell around her, stirring echoes of uncertainty and longing within her own soul.

"I stood upon the precipice," Granny continued, her gaze distant yet piercing as she relived those moments from a lifetime ago. "My heart was torn by the tug-of-war between love and obligation. The warrior offered passion that set my soul ablaze, while the nobleman offered a future paved with golden promises."

And yet, amid the turmoil of emotions that threatened to engulf her, Granny spoke of a decision that would shape the course of her destiny. "In the quiet depths of night, I sought solace in the ancient oaks that whispered tales of those who came before. Their branches intertwined like lovers bound by fate, their roots delving deep into the heart of the earth, grounding me in a reality where love and duty collided like titans at war."

Fiona's breath caught in her throat as she saw the strength and vulnerability in her grandmother's gaze.

"I made my choice." Granny's voice was as steady as the mountain that loomed in the distance, unyielding yet ever watchful.

Fiona listened intently, her breath held in anticipation of Granny's next words. The fire crackled softly in the hearth, casting dancing shadows on the walls of the cozy cottage. The scent of lavender and sage hung in the air, soothing her restless heart as she awaited the continuation of Granny's tale.

"I was but a young lass, much like you, Fiona," Granny continued. "And I found myself torn between two paths, each leading me to a different destiny. One was paved with the stones of duty and honor, where my hand was promised to a man of wealth and power, a union meant to forge alliances and secure our clan's future."

Granny paused, her gaze distant as she delved into memories long buried but not forgotten. Fiona could see the flicker of sadness cross the woman's face. "In the end, I followed the destiny set out for me by others, but I still wonder what would have been had I followed my heart and married my warrior."

"No!" Fiona cried. She must sound like an overly romantic child, but she couldn't imagine leaving the man she loved for the one her father chose for her.

"Ye must ken, lass, the weight of a name, the burden of blood," Granny spoke, her hands still for a moment. "It is no' just yer own heart ye carry, but the hopes of all who share yer crest."

The air thickened with the truth of those words. Fiona furrowed her brow, the warrior within wrestling with the specter of obligation that loomed large in her thoughts. "But how does one measure the worth of their desires against the call of duty?" she asked.

"Ah, Fiona, 'tis the question that has echoed through the halls of time." Granny's gaze held the flickering candlelight. "Yer heart is yer compass, yet ye must be careful to honor yer destiny. I don't look back and wish I'd made a different choice. If I had, I wouldn't have had ye nor yer mother."

The silence that followed was not empty but laden with contemplation. Fiona absorbed her wisdom.

"Granny, when the clan's needs press heavy against me own wishes, where do I find the strength to honor both?"

"Within, child. Within." The old woman's eyes met Fiona's, clear and deep. "Ye are of my blood, and strength runs fierce in our veins. Ye'll ken the right of it when the moment comes. Trust in that and let nae man sow doubt in yer mind."

"But how do I know?"

Granny's gaze held a flicker of mirth. "Ye must ken that the heart has its own voice, Fiona," she spoke with gentle firmness. "It's a wild thing, not easily tamed by logic or duty. Ye'll do well to listen when it whispers, for it speaks truths that the mind may try to silence."

Fiona kneaded the bread absentmindedly. The scent of yeast and warmth from the hearth mingled, comforting yet stirring a restlessness within her. Her grandmother's words fanned the embers of possibility, breathing life into the smoldering sparks of her deepest hopes.

"Be open to the winds of change, my child," Granny continued, reaching across the worn wooden table to cover Fiona's. "Remember, the most enduring love is oft found in the glens and shadows where ye least expect it. It's there, hidden among the stones of ancient ruins, where dreams entwine with destiny."

Courage surged in Fiona's chest. Granny's assurance was a beacon, guiding her through the fog of uncertainty that had settled upon her spirit. "I am grateful for your guidance, Granny. Your words bear the weight of truth, and purpose anew stirs within me heart."

The room seemed to hold its breath, the crackling of the fire the only sound as Granny nodded, her expression a tapestry of pride and affection. "There is a fierce light in ye, Fiona McAfee," she whispered, yet her words carried the strength of stone. "Let it shine and let naught dim its brilliance."

"Aye, Granny," Fiona replied softly.

"Remember this, my child." Granny's whisper echoed through the hallowed kitchen. "Ye are the blood of the McAfee, born of courage and compassion. Dinna let the world make ye forget who ye are, and never forsake yer principles for the fleeting promises of power or passion."

In her grandmother's wisdom, there was no room for doubt, only the unwavering certainty of one who had walked the path of life with honor and had emerged tempered like steel in the forge of experience.

"Thank ye, Granny," Fiona replied reverently, rising from the wooden chair.

As she stood, Fiona felt as if the entire lineage of the McAfees' was focused on her, waiting for her to make the right decision—a lineage that whispered of battles won not only with sword and shield but also with cunning and conviction.

"Ye have given me more than guidance this day," Fiona said. "Ye have reminded me of the strength that lies in staying true to myself, no matter how the tempest rages."

Fiona stepped across the flagstone floor, the hem of her tartan skirt whispering against the cold rock with each measured step. Her grandmother's teachings clung to her mind. Each word settled deep within her, a comforting weight that grounded her despite the tempest of uncertainty that loomed beyond the castle walls.

Fiona put her hands on her grandmother's shoulders from behind and gave Granny's weathered cheek a kiss, a tribute to the woman whose spirit lingered in the warmth of the embers. "Ye have armed me well for what is to come," Fiona murmured. At that moment, love and duty intertwined within her.

FIONA MCAFEE STEPPED out from the shelter of her father's keep, admiring the bustling encampment where tents rose like a field of vibrant wildflowers. Each standard fluttered in the gentle breeze, signaling the presence of allied families and honored guests.

Clad in her plaid, which announced to all that she was a member of Clan McAfee and one of their hosts, she regarded the weight of her bow and quiver, a familiar comfort upon her back. Fiona moved with purposeful grace. Her stride was one borne of many years pacing the cobbled paths that wound like serpents through her ancestral lands. It was here that the McAfee legacy had thrived.

As she navigated the throng of kinsmen and visitors, Fiona gazed upon three figures adorned in the distinctive plaid of Clan McClain. There were many others in the plaid as well, but these three were probably the leaders. The middle of them stood as if he had been chiseled from the highland stone itself—broad-shouldered, imposing, yet undeniably human in his bearing. His hair was dark, but his eyes… his eyes were of the purest blue loch she had ever seen.

A sudden stir within Fiona's breast gave rise to the unbidden desire to approach, to engage the McClain son in discourse, perchance to glean insight into the mind that had orchestrated victories that were sung of in hushed tones beside hearth fires. Yet, as quickly as the impulse surfaced, it was quashed by the remembrance of her grandmother's counsel, words steeped in the wisdom of generations: "Remember, child, the fate of our clan rests not on the whims of the heart, but on the strength of our lineage."

With nary a glance nor gesture to betray her turmoil, she pressed onward, past the men of McClain, silently acknowledging the sacrifice that came with being the laird's eldest daughter. For it was not the allure of comeliness in a man that could sway her from her path, but the steadfast duty to her bloodline, the unwavering commitment to be the proud daughter her father—and all the McAfees—expected her to be.

Fiona joined her sisters at the far end of the field, where the targets had been erected for practice. She took her stance with an assured grace, nocking an arrow to her bowstring as she had done countless times before. With each measured breath, she loosed her arrows. The satisfying thrum of the bowstring and the swift flight of feathers cut through the cool air.

Beside her, Ailis stood poised, the glint of her blade catching the weak rays of the sun. She threw the knife with deadly precision, punctuating the silence with a thud as it found its mark in the target. Her concentration unwavering, Ailis embodied lethal elegance.

To Fiona's right, Moira practiced with her sword, the blade an extension of her own fierce determination. The youngest McAfee's movements were a whirlwind of strength and agility, her vibrant energy a stark contrast to the steadfast focus Fiona and Ailis maintained.

As she retrieved her arrows for another round, Fiona sensed someone gazing upon her. It bore into her back, a tangible pressure that appraised her every move. She knew without checking the source of this scrutiny. The intensity was all too familiar, reminiscent of the sight of Alisdair in his McClain plaid. Yet she resisted the urge to seek out the onlooker, her mind anchored by the heavy mantle of duty that draped her shoulders.

"Let them watch," Fiona whispered to herself. She must embody the proud daughter her father expected, a paragon of the McAfee clan's storied heritage. Her form was impeccable, her shots true. The clatter of arrows piercing wood a testament to her skill and discipline.

There was no room for distraction, not when the eyes of clansmen and rivals alike judged not only her prowess but her family's.

$$\text{\textbf{—————•—— ⚜ ——•—————}}$$

CHAPTER THREE

F IONA NOCKED AN arrow to her bow with practiced ease. A hush had befallen the onlookers, their breaths caught in anticipation. With the precision of a seasoned warrior, she drew back the string, anchoring it firmly against her cheek. The world narrowed to the target. The silence stretched, taut as the bowstring in her grasp. Then, release. The arrow flew true, slicing through the chilly air and embedding itself squarely in the bullseye.

The crowd erupted into cheers, yet amidst the cacophony, one figure remained silent, his gaze locked upon the archer with an intensity that bordered reverence. Alisdair McClain observed the flight of Fiona's arrow with a warrior's focus, noting not just the outcome but the elegance of her form, the unwavering determination set upon her striking features. Admiration flooded him, mingling with a curiosity that went beyond the mere appreciation of her prowess.

Alisdair stood slightly apart from the crowd. His piercing blue eyes, so often assessing strategies and opponents, now studied Fiona as though she were a fascinating enigma to unravel. The formal tenor of the gathering did little to mask the deep captivation that took hold of him. The very air around Fiona vibrated with her strength and spirit.

A tether pulled at Alisdair's senses, urging him closer to the source of his intrigue. He observed, almost wistfully, the way her long blond hair, bound in a practical braid, had a few rebellious strands that danced with the morning breeze.

There was an undeniable pull, a gravitation toward a woman who held her own with such fierce independence. For Alisdair, whose life was a constant balance between duty and personal desire, Fiona represented an alluring challenge. She was a force, a flame, and he could not help but wonder what warmth or burn might come from drawing too near.

And it didn't help that she wasn't a troll at all, but a truly beautiful woman—one who made him want to move closer and get better acquainted with her.

Her next shot was equally as impressive. Alisdair smiled despite the gravity of his usual demeanor. He was witnessing excellence, and it stirred something within him—a yearning to understand the mind that guided the hand so steady and sure.

In the lull that followed, as Fiona prepared for another arrow, the whispers of political machinations and the weighty expectations placed upon his shoulders momentarily lightened. Watching her, Alisdair found himself longing for a reprieve from the constant talks of alliances and power—a reprieve he scarcely knew he craved until that very moment.

Alisdair wasted no time before approaching Laird Duncan McAfee. "Laird McAfee," Alisdair began, "I've watched your daughter, Fiona, with great admiration. I'm very impressed by her ability with a bow and arrow." He paused. "I seek not just her hand for the unity it might bring between our clans, but to understand the mind behind such strength. To cherish her, if she would have me."

Laird Duncan's gaze, sharp and discerning, assessed Alisdair's earnest expression. "You speak of desires beyond duty, young McClain," Duncan replied. His words were measured, betraying none of the turmoil that surely roiled beneath the surface. "Such matters are not decided lightly."

"No, they are not," Alisdair agreed. "But I would like to approach her with the thought of marriage between us."

The laird nodded slowly, the subtle lift of his brow granting silent acknowledgment of Alisdair's plea before turning his attention back to the archery range where his daughter still stood with her sisters. "I have promised Fiona she will have a say in whomever I choose as her husband. Ye may get acquainted with her, but understand that no decision will be made today."

Fiona overheard the last fragments of their exchange as she was about to take another shot, her arrow poised unflinchingly on the string. Her heart beat with the rhythm of rebellion against the notion of being bartered like some prize steed, though just the day before, she'd agreed with her grandmother that she must remember her place when it came to marriage. After a swift release, her arrow sliced through the air, hitting its mark with a resounding thud. Yet her smoldering indignation overshadowed her satisfaction at the bullseye.

Clenching her fists at her sides, she prickled with anger. Her rage made its way up her arms. Her blue eyes, mirrors of the turbulent sky above, flashed fiercely. She gritted her teeth against the injustice. She had been given more freedom than most women, and she wanted to keep that freedom. It didn't matter that the man discussing her hand with her father was the very man she'd get to know.

"Used as a pawn in a game where I control neither board nor pieces," she muttered, rebelling against the tradition and expectation that threatened to drown her aspirations.

Fiona McAfee would not be maneuvered so easily. She would meet this challenge as she did all others—with a keen eye and a steady hand, ready to assert her place not as a mere piece to be moved at whim.

With the echo of her arrow's impact still ringing in the glen, Fiona's ire coalesced into a force as formidable as her archery. She strode across the field, each step a defiant drumbeat against the earth. Her eyes blazed. The crowd parted for her as if she were the blade of a claymore cutting through the air—a warrior on a battlefield of her own making. She had expected more from Alisdair from the mere glimpse she'd caught of him, but she knew that much was her own fault. She hadn't gotten acquainted with him, and had assumed he would see her and desire more than a political alliance.

Alisdair, who had been conversing with a group of his clansmen, turned to see her walking toward him. His gaze met Fiona's. There was no mistaking the fervor that propelled her. He straightened himself, his stance mirroring the readiness of one versed in the art of war. Yet it was not a physical confrontation that awaited him.

"Alisdair McClain," Fiona began resonantly and commandingly, arresting the attention of all who stood near. "Ye think to propose a union with me as though I'm naught but land to be claimed or a title to be secured?" She reached out and poked him in the middle of his chest, unsurprised at his thick muscles.

Alisdair's brow furrowed, taken aback by the intensity of her challenge. "Fiona, your valor is known far and wide—"

"Ah, my valor," she scoffed, her sarcasm sharp as a dirk. "A convenient trait, I suppose, when it suits the ambitions of men."

He held her gaze, recognizing the fierce intellect behind her words. "I sought only to express my admiration for you, not to reduce ye to a mere—"

"Admiration?" Fiona tilted her head. "Is that what ye call it? Forgive me, I mistook it for an attempt to secure an alliance through marriage without so much as asking for me consent." She put her hands on her hips and glared up at him.

The corners of Alisdair's mouth twitched, betraying his appreciation for her despite the gravity of the discourse. "I've underestimated the depth of your spirit, Fiona. Let it not be said that Alisdair McClain does not recognize the worth of a true partner."

"Then regard me as such," Fiona demanded, her tone softening ever so slightly, inviting a truce. "Not as a pawn, nor a prize, but as an equal. If ye truly wish to know me, do so on my terms."

"And what might those be?"

"Firstly," she began, a mischievous glint appearing amidst the storm in her eyes, "ye'll cease these covert discussions with my father about our future and speak to me directly. After all, 'tis I who would be standing beside ye, and sleeping beside ye, should such a future come to pass."

"Fairly spoken," Alisdair conceded, a smile gracing his lips. "And I must say I do like the idea of sleeping beside ye."

"Secondly," Fiona continued, emboldened by his acquiescence, and willing to ignore his racy comment, "any courtship shall be genuine. No pretenses of duty or power—just Fiona and Alisdair, learning the measure of each other."

"Agreed," he replied earnestly. "I would have it no other way."

"And third," she concluded, her voice carrying the weight of her final condition, "should either of us find the match unsuitable, we part ways with honor, free from obligation or expectation."

"An honorable release, should it come to that," Alisdair affirmed, extending his hand.

"Then we are agreed," Fiona stated, accepting his hand with a firm shake, her expression almost trusting.

"Aye, we are," he replied.

She still glared at him, but it wasn't as intense as when she'd first approached.

"Forgive me, Fiona," he faltered. "I did not mean to... I've not considered your thoughts on this matter as I should have."

"Ye'll need more than gentle words and soft glances to mend this, McClain." Her voice was steady despite the tempest raging within her. Fiona was unyielding, a fortress unto herself, and she would not allow her defenses to be breached by remorse alone.

"Ye ken nothing of what I want or who I am," she continued. "If ye truly seek to know me, then ye must understand—I am no prize to be bartered."

Alisdair, recognizing the truth in her declaration, nodded slowly, the weight of his misjudgment on his shoulders. He'd approached her father as he would any father. He should have spoken to her first, for she was not like any other woman. She was a warrior in her own right.

"Then let us begin anew," he offered tentatively, aware that the path to her heart would be fraught with trials of its own. "On your terms, Fiona. Teach me to see you… not as a McAfee or a means to an alliance, but simply as yourself."

Alisdair's gaze met Fiona's, his blue eyes a mirror to her own. "Fiona," he began, the timbre of his voice betraying a rare tremor of uncertainty, "I have been a warrior all my life, trained to wield sword and strategy over words. But this moment calls for honesty, not arms."

He paused, searching her face for signs of softening, for a crack in her armor. "I admire ye, not just for your skill with the bow or your command on the battlefield, but for the fire within you that refuses to be quenched. You've captivated me in ways no other has, and the thought of joining our clans… it is more than politics to me."

"Ye speak of admiration, Alisdair McClain," Fiona replied, her voice less steely than before, "yet ye understand little of who I truly am. What is it that ye desire? Is it the woman standing before ye, or the alliance she represents? Or is it the idea of having a warrior defend ye as ye sleep?"

"'Tis you," he replied, each word deliberate, as if he were laying down his weapons at her feet. "Aye, I cannot deny that an alliance would benefit us both, but 'tis not my sole desire. I wish to understand the lass who can outshoot any man, who speaks her mind without fear, and whose laughter is a melody that I've come to yearn for, even from afar."

"Ye yearn for my laughter?" she asked, amusement in her tone.

"Aye." Alisdair smiled hopefully. "Your laughter, your spirit, your heart. All of you, Fiona McAfee."

And though she did not voice it, Fiona acknowledged that perhaps there was more to Alisdair McClain than she had believed. But if he desired a marriage between them, she must observe what was there.

FIONA'S LAUGHTER MINGLED with the rustle of leaves, a sound as unexpected as it was delightful. Alisdair stood before her, mock indignation on his face, having just recounted an exaggerated tale of a misadventure involving a stray goat and his brother Lachlan.

"Ye expect me to believe that a wee beastie outwitted all three of the McClain brothers who are here?" Fiona teased, her blue eyes sparkling with mirth. "I suppose next ye'll be telling me the goat now sits at yer council meetings."

"She does," Alisdair played along, his broad shoulders shaking with suppressed laughter. "The creature has proven itself quite the tactician. Perhaps I should seek its counsel on how to win the affections of a certain lass."

"Och, if ye require the wisdom of goats, then ye may be in dire straits indeed," she snorted, her blond braid swaying as she tilted her head, regarding him with amusement.

As their laughter subsided, they found themselves standing mere inches apart, the air charged with a newfound intimacy.

"Ye've a way with words, Alisdair McClain," Fiona murmured, her voice carrying a new warmth.

"Only when inspired by the right company," he replied, his gaze fixed on her lips.

Her breath hitched slightly, as if the gravity between them pulled her closer still. And then, as natural as the wind that caressed the highland heather, Alisdair lowered his head and brushed his lips against hers—a kiss as tentative as it was tender— a first bloom of passion.

Drawing back, Fiona met his gaze, silently conversing with him. Her heart pounded like the drums of war, yet for a moment, all talk of alliances and duties faded into the background.

"Alisdair, I—" Fiona stammered. "I'm not certain ye should be kissing me yet."

He nodded, his expression serious. "Ye canna make that a

condition of courtship. It would be the death of me!"

"Ye are truly a silly man, Alisdair. I would like to get to know ye. Truly know ye," Fiona declared. It was a gesture of truce, a sign of her willingness to explore the depths of this unforeseen connection.

"Agreed," Alisdair responded.

Fiona and Alisdair reluctantly released each other's hands as they walked within sight of the games and the keep. The lingering touch was a silent pledge.

"Ye ken," Fiona began, her voice low and steady, the words rolling off her tongue, "take this path we are to tread is fraught with bramble and thistle."

Alisdair's gaze held hers. "Aye, but every path has its perils. We shall face them together, Fiona McAfee. I swear it upon my honor."

"Tomorrow," Alisdair continued, "we present a united front to our clans. I need my men to understand that we are both in favor of this partnership… if it is to truly happen."

"Yet," Fiona replied, "let them not mistake our union for submission. I am my own, Alisdair McClain, and you'd do well to remember that."

His chuckle resonated in the cool evening air yet spoke volumes of his admiration for her spirit. "Dinna fash, lass. It's your fire that warms my thoughts."

"Come the morn, we must finish the games," Fiona murmured.

"Then let us finish them, and I will best all who come my way," Alisdair agreed, seeking her hand.

FIONA MCAFEE FOUND Alisdair McClain with ease. He was a head taller than most of the men there, though his brothers matched him in height. Fiona liked that because she was taller than most men, and many were intimidated by her. The clamor of clashing steel and triumphant cries blended into a jubilant cacophony as kinsmen vied for glory. Yet, as Fiona watched, it was not the games that caught her attention but the man who appeared so strong and commanding, not to mention handsome.

Alisdair lifted the caber with a power that spoke of countless battles fought and won. His form was precise, every muscle coiled and released in a dance as old as the clans themselves. Fiona felt a surge of pride as he tossed the massive log end over end, earning cheers from onlookers. Their eyes met across the field, and for a fleeting moment, the clamor dulled, the world narrowing to the silent exchange between them.

As the day progressed, Alisdair presented Fiona with a wreath of wildflowers with richly-colored petals. He shared tales of his victories, each word laced with respect for his adversaries. They walked side by, their steps in sync as if they had walked this path together many times.

Their laughter mingled with the melodies of pipes and drums, an unspoken acknowledgment of a growing bond, yet unclaimed.

Fiona retreated to the sanctuary of her family's tent. There, she found solace in the company of her sisters Ailis and Moira.

"His actions speak of honor," Fiona confessed, the formal tone of her voice hiding the turmoil within. "Yet, he seeks our father's blessing before me own. It is a gesture of tradition, I know, but..."

Ailis regarded Fiona with a knowing glance, her silence an invitation for further confessions.

"I find myself adrift," Fiona continued, "caught between admiration and ire. For how can I yield my heart to one who must first ask leave of another?"

"Perchance he aims to show respect, not only to our father but to you, through his deference," Moira offered gently, her adventurous spirit understanding the complexities of love and duty.

"True," Fiona conceded. "Yet, should he wish to stand beside me, he must prove himself worthy not to our sire, but to me—the woman he would claim."

Her sisters exchanged glances, both moved by Fiona's resolve. The weight of her words hung heavy in the air.

"Then let him be tested," Ailis declared, her voice steady as the earth itself. "For if his intentions are pure, he shall rise to meet your challenge and win not just your hand, but your heart."

Fiona nodded, her blue eyes reflecting the flickering flames, a silent vow etched within their depths. Alisdair McClain would have to demonstrate his worth, not as a suitor sanctioned by the hands of her father, but as a man who could stand equal to Fiona McAfee, in spirit, in strength, and in love.

ALISDAIR'S BOOTS CRUNCHED over the early morning frost, a mist rising from the mossy earth as he trudged deeper into the forest. His breath fogged in the chill air, scanning the woodland for the hues of wildflowers that he knew would captivate Fiona's heart. Each step was guided by an unwavering purpose: to find a token of nature's beauty that mirrored his own affection. Fiona wasn't exactly pleased with how he had handled talking to her father before speaking with her. He had to do something that would improve his standing in her eyes. He delicately parted ferns and bracken in search of the perfect blossoms.

His brow furrowed with concentration, a subtle indicator of his determination. It was not enough to gather any flowers. They had to be the prettiest, just as he sought to convey the depth of his sentiment. As he walked, the beauty of the area should have had him in awe, but he barely noticed, intent on his silent quest. Time lost its meaning as the sun climbed higher, filtering shafts of light through the dense canopy above.

Just as the hour neared its end, Alisdair spotted them—a

cluster of wildflowers nestled at the base of an ancient oak, their petals a vivid dance of colors that seemed to sing in harmony with the morning. Carefully, he knelt, his large frame surprisingly graceful, and plucked each stem with a reverence reserved for sacred rituals.

After assembling the bouquet, he made his way back toward the keep. He waited for Fiona to emerge from the keep with the patience of a hunter, hidden in the shadow of the stone walls.

Fiona stepped outside, her blond hair catching the sun in a brilliant cascade. She moved with the grace that characterized both her spirit and her body. The moment her foot crossed the threshold, Alisdair stepped forward, emerging like a specter born from the very earth.

"Mo chridhe," he began, his voice a soft rumble as he extended the bouquet towards her. "For ye, the bonniest blooms I could find." He lowered his head slightly to show he honored her.

Her intelligent eyes widened in surprise, brightening like the dawn itself. Fiona reached out, her fingers brushing against his as she took the wildflowers from his grasp. Her touch sent a shiver up his spine, more powerful than any clash of steel.

"Alisdair, they're beautiful," she whispered, her lips curving into a smile that crinkled the corners of her eyes and echoed the warmth of her heart. She brought the bouquet to her nose, inhaling the sweet fragrance. "Ye've a fine eye for beauty."

"Only because it surrounds me," he replied, a hint of color rising to his cheeks despite the coolness of the morning.

Gratefully, Fiona clutched the bouquet close, a symbol of the burgeoning affection that grew between them, as wild and untamed as the Highland heather. In this simple exchange, the complexities of clan politics and expectations lay momentarily forgotten, replaced by the sincerity of a gesture and the silent language of shared glances.

CHAPTER FOUR

FIONA, HER BLOND hair bound in its customary braid, stood poised at the archery range with the determination of a seasoned warrior etched into her stance. The whispering wind carried the faint sound of bagpipes from afar.

An assembly of kilted men had gathered, their eyes fixed upon Fiona as she drew her bow with graceful strength. One by one, the arrows flew, each finding their mark with unerring precision. Murmurs of admiration rustled through the crowd like leaves in a gentle breeze. Not a man present could match her skill—none save for Alisdair McClain, whose broad-shouldered silhouette stood aloof, watching her intently with his piercing blue eyes but declining to engage in the contest.

"Alisdair McClain," Fiona called, her voice carrying across the field after the final arrow hit its target. "Will ye not test your aim against mine?"

He shook his head, a ghost of a smile gracing his face. "I'd no' be wantin' to shame a lass in front of her kin," he replied teasingly yet respectfully.

"Ye underestimate me," Fiona retorted, the corners of her mouth twitching upward. She understood well the impropriety of challenging a man she was courting, but the competitive fire within her blazed too fiercely to be tamed by convention.

"Perhaps later, just the two of us?" she proposed, her blue eyes locking with his.

Alisdair nodded, a silent agreement passing between them.

The crowd dispersed, their anticipation for this private competition hanging in the air like the mist over the loch.

As the clamor of the games continued, Ailis McAfee took her place at the knife throwing line, her gray eyes filled with a serene confidence. The spectators watched as the blades, one after another, sang through the air and struck true. Even Fiona and their younger sister, who knew their own attempts would fall short, could not help but admire Ailis's effortless prowess.

"Ye've outdone us all, sister." Fiona wrapped Ailis in an embrace that spoke volumes of their bond—a fortress of familial love that no rivalry could breach.

"Ye did wonderful, Ailis," their sister chimed in, her hug equal parts proud and affectionate.

Ailis acknowledged their praise. Yet behind her gentle demeanor lay the steel of a warrior, just like her sisters. People who didn't understand Ailis would assume she was not as strong or driven as her sisters, and they would be wrong. Ailis had a gentle heart and demeanor, but she was a warrior through and through.

The field of combat lay strewn with the pride of fallen warriors, a testament to the ferocity of the Highland Games. Within this arena, Moira McAfee, youngest of her kin, faced her challengers with a spirited defiance that belied her petite frame. The men towered over her; their muscles honed by the relentless tutelage of war and labor, yet in her emerald gaze, a fire blazed.

As she stepped into the circle of hand-to-hand combat, her stance was low and ready, her fiery red tresses tied back to reveal the keen focus etched upon her visage. The crowd's murmur rose to a crescendo, a symphony of anticipation for the spectacle that was to unfold.

"Remember yer training, lass," someone whispered from the assembly—her father, perhaps, or maybe it was but the wind that carried words of encouragement to her ears.

The first opponent approached, a mountain of a man with knuckles like stones and eyes cold as the deepest loch. They circled each other, two predators assessing the threat before them. The clash was swift, the dance of combat a blur to those who watched with bated breath. Moira's agility was her ally. She ducked and weaved, her fists finding home upon her adversary's flesh.

Yet, despite her valiance, the sheer strength of the men proved overwhelming. One by one, they bested her, not through skill but by force that would topple oaks. When the dust settled and scores were tallied, Moira emerged within the top five. She held her head high even though victory had eluded her grasp.

A murmured respect hummed through the crowd as she exited the fray, her limbs weary but spirit unyielded. There was no time for reprieve, however, as the sword fighting competition beckoned—an arena where finesse might triumph over brute strength.

Now armed with her blade, a lithe extension of her own fierce heart, Moira entered the competition again. The weapon was modest in size compared to the broadswords of her opponents, yet it sang a deadly tune in her hands. With each bout, she parried and thrusted, her movements a fluid poetry that spoke of countless hours honed in secret glades and moonlit clearings.

One by one, the men fell before her, their larger swords cumbersome against the alacrity of her own. The final opponent lay disarmed at her feet. A hush enveloped the throng of spectators. Moira McAfee stood amidst the silent battlefield, the victor at last.

Raising her hands above her head, blade gleaming in the waning sunlight, she claimed her triumph not with a roar, but with a smile that outshone the gilded rays of the day's end. A cheer erupted, rolling like thunder across the glens and valleys—a cheer for the maiden who had defied the expectations of her station, for the sister whose valor matched that of any Highland warrior.

At that moment, as the echo of her name rang forth from the lips of clansmen and kin alike, Moira knew the taste of victory was sweet indeed.

ALISDAIR HESITATED AT the edge of the clearing, resting his hand on the worn leather grip of his bow—a silent testament to countless hours of practice. He watched Fiona McAfee with a mixture of wariness and admiration. Her confidence was as unyielding as the ancient oaks that stood sentinel around them.

"Yer awfully quiet, Alisdair." Fiona's voice cut through the hushed murmur of the gathered crowd, each member awaiting his response. "Has the thought of facing me in this contest dampened yer spirits?"

"Hardly," he replied with a smile. "I was merely pondering whether 'tis fair for me to compete against someone who may not be my equal."

"Then perhaps ye should start praying, for I intend to show ye exactly how an equal bests her opponent." The twinkle in Fiona's eye contradicted her sharp words.

"Pray? Nay, 'tis ye who might seek divine favor before this day ends," Alisdair retorted, stepping into the clearing, his hesitation gone as if carried away by the breeze that rustled through the leaves above. He lingered on Fiona, noting the way she nocked an arrow with such effortless grace. Clearly, she was no ordinary adversary. She stirred something within him—a deep respect for her prowess, coupled with an attraction he could neither deny nor ignore. Not that he wanted to. No, what he really wanted was for the wedding to be over, so they could get on with the wedding night.

"Let the gods witness our contest then," Fiona declared, lifting her chin in defiance. Her stance was poised, her eyes locked on the distant target as she drew back the string. "And may the best archer win."

"He will," Alisdair murmured, watching as her arrow soared into the air, striking the straw bullseye with a satisfying thud. He stepped up beside her, their arms brushing momentarily—a fleeting touch that sent a jolt of awareness through them both.

Fiona took her stance. A hush fell over the gathered crowd as she nocked an arrow to her bowstring with practiced ease. Fiona's eyes, as piercing blue as the loch, twinkled with mischief as she faced Alisdair.

"Are ye certain ye wish to best me in this contest, Alisdair?" Fiona playfully challenged. "Or do ye fear that a lass may outshoot ye before yer own kin?"

Alisdair, broad-shouldered and resolute, offered a smirk that did not quite reach his eyes, which remained fixed on the target ahead. "I've never been one to shy away from a worthy adversary," he replied, his cadence steady and sure. "And I'll admit, 'tis a rare pleasure to be bested by a lass as skilled as yerself—should that unlikely event come to pass."

Fiona howled, a sound as clear and bold as the call of a battle horn, though her hands remained steady as she drew the bow. The surrounding McAfee and McClain clansmen watched with bated breath, sensing the undercurrent of flirtation beneath their banter.

As Fiona released her arrow, the tension among the onlookers tightened like a drawn bowstring. The arrow sailed through the air, striking the center of the target with unerring precision. A collective murmur rippled through the crowd, in awe of Fiona's skill.

Alisdair stepped forward with the fluid grace of a seasoned warrior. With a determination that matched Fiona's, he drew back his own bow, the muscles in his arms flexing beneath his tunic. His arrow flew true, landing mere inches from Fiona's.

"Ye shoot well," Fiona conceded with a nod.

"Yet not well enough," Alisdair countered, a glint of respect in his gaze. "The day is still young, Fiona. Let us see if fortune favors ye again."

Back and forth they went, releasing arrows that sang through the air and found their marks with deadly accuracy. During each shot, the crowd held their collective breath, caught up in the mounting tension between the two archers. Fiona's fingers caressed the fletching of her arrows as if conferring silent blessings upon them, her lips curving into a daring smile each time she met Alisdair's challenging stare.

"Yer turn, McClain." Her tone was light, but her gaze was challenging.

"Watch closely, McAfee," he replied, drawing his own bow with practiced ease. His arrow flew, piercing the target close to hers, yet the precision of her shot was not lost on him.

"Ye've the eye of a hawk," Alisdair admitted, grudging respect coloring his voice. "But this competition is far from over."

"Would ye have it any other way?" Fiona asked, her lips curving in a smile that hinted at shared secrets and unspoken promises.

"Never," he answered. For a moment, the world beyond their duel ceased to exist.

The final arrows would determine the victor of the day. Fiona, her blond braid swaying with each step, approached the mark, her blue eyes filled with the fire of competition. She notched her arrow, the feathers brushing against her cheek as she drew the string to her ear.

"Make it a good one, lass," Alisdair called, his tone rich with anticipation and a touch of something else—something that lingered in the space between jest and earnest.

Fiona sighed slowly, releasing the arrow as if relinquishing a part of her soul. It sliced through the cool air, a silent messenger of her prowess. The crowd held their breath as the shaft struck true, hitting the center of the target with unerring accuracy. A cheer erupted from those assembled.

"Ye shoot as if Artemis herself has blessed yer bow," Alisdair praised. "I concede to none but the worthiest of opponents."

"Perhaps 'tis not Artemis, but rather my determination that guides my hand," Fiona replied.

Alisdair's gaze lingered on her, admiration etched in every line of his visage. "Determination, ye say? It appears I have underestimated the depth of yours."

"An oversight ye shall not soon forget, I trust," she teased, her smile as sharp and true as her arrows.

As the light waned, so too did the festivities, leaving Fiona and Alisdair standing at the fringe of the clearing. Their companions had drifted away, giving them a semblance of privacy in the vastness of the highlands. The tension between them crackled like the first sparks of a fire, igniting possibilities neither dared to voice.

"Today, ye have bested me," Alisdair began. "But tomorrow is yet unwritten."

"Indeed, tomorrow is another day," Fiona agreed. "And with it comes the promise of new challenges."

"Challenges I look forward to facing," he added, taking a step closer, close enough that she could see the flecks of gold in his eyes. "With you, Fiona McAfee."

Their gazes locked, and for an infinite moment, the world paused on the edge of possibility. The air crackled with an unspoken tension, a silent understanding passing between them.

Alisdair's hand lifted, brushing against Fiona's cheek in a gesture both tentative and deliberate. His promising caress was like a silent question hanging in the air. Fiona's breath caught in her throat, her heart thundering against her chest as she met his gaze.

In that moment, time slowed to a languid crawl. Each beat of their hearts echoed in the stillness of the night. Without words, without preamble, Alisdair's lips descended toward hers with a hesitant grace. The kiss was a gentle exploration, a meeting of hearts as much as lips—a whisper of tenderness that stirred something deep within Fiona's soul. Her eyes fluttered closed as she melted into the kiss, savoring his lips against hers.

A tidal wave of desire and longing washed over her, threatening to consume her whole. In that fleeting moment, she cast all doubts and uncertainties aside, leaving only the undeniable pull she felt toward Alisdair. His scent enveloped her, a heady mix of pine and leather, grounding her in the reality of their shared intimacy.

As the kiss deepened, Fiona shivered Her veins blazed with an intensity she had never known. It was as if all the stars in the sky had aligned just for this singular moment, this juncture where their worlds collided in a symphony of passion and yearning.

Her toes curled in response to the sheer magnitude of sensations coursing through her, each brush of his lips against hers a revelation in itself. In that embrace, Fiona's mind raced with a whirlwind of thoughts and emotions. The taste of him lingered on her lips, a heady blend of desire and unspoken promises.

Could it be that in Alisdair's arms lay the answer to her unvoiced prayers, the missing piece she had long sought? His kiss was both tender and possessive, a silent declaration of the depths of his feelings. With each heartbeat echoing in the cavern of her chest, Fiona found herself teetering on the edge of an abyss she dared not name.

As they parted, their breaths mingling in the cool evening air, Fiona could see the reflection of her own longing mirrored in Alisdair's eyes. "Until we meet again," Fiona murmured. She knew it was cowardly not to say more, but she needed to be alone to think about his kiss and how it had made her tingle before she could face him again.

"Until then," Alisdair replied, the promise hanging in the air like the last light of day.

As Fiona turned and walked back toward her kin, she could neither shake Alisdair's presence nor the anticipation that fluttered like a captured bird within her chest.

THE SHADOWED FIGURE stood at a distance, cloaked by the dimming light of dusk, his eyes fixed on the spectacle before him. Alisdair McClain, proud and victorious even in defeat, kissed Fiona as if she was already his. The unseen observer clenched his jaw, narrowing his eyes upon the pair.

"Alisdair McClain," he mused to himself, the name rolling off his tongue like a curse, "ye may be a formidable warrior, but ye are not worthy of her. Not in valor, nor in lineage."

Hidden amidst the throng of celebrants, he pondered his father's grand design—an alliance wrought through marriage, one that would bind the lands and power of the McAfees to their own. It was a vision of unity that promised strength, yet here stood Alisdair, a potential wrench in the meticulously crafted gears of political machinations.

"Perhaps it is time to prune the tree before the unwelcome branch grows too strong," he clipped. The idea of visiting Alisdair's chambers under the cloak of night, a dirk in hand, brought a cruel smile to his lips. He could almost hear the hushed gasp of surprise, envision the fleeting moment of realization before the finality of silence.

Distracted by such ideas, he hardly noticed the chill of the evening air. To abduct Fiona, spirited though she might be, was another idea he entertained. Whisking her away from all she knew, he would be her savior and captor both, until she saw reason or bent to his will.

"Would it be by stealth or force?" he pondered, weighing each possibility like a merchant assessing his wares. "A diversion during the hunt, perhaps? Or the appearance of an enemy raid?"

Beneath the revelry around him, the seeds of discord were sown, watered by his dark intentions.

"Whatever it takes," he vowed silently, the conviction resonating deep within his core. "Fiona McAfee shall be mine, and Alisdair McClain will be naught but a memory."

Not far from this tender tableau, Alisdair's brothers, Lachlan and Brodie, leaned against the sturdy trunk of an ancient oak, their conversation a private murmur amid the celebratory clamor.

"Look at them," Lachlan remarked, a grin spreading across his youthful features. "Could it be that our Alisdair has finally met his match?"

"Perhaps," Brodie replied, his gaze thoughtful as he watched the pair. "And if the stars align, we might be speaking of alliances not just of land, but of hearts as well."

"Marriage?" Lachlan's voice lifted with intrigue. "To think that Fiona McAfee could be the one to allow him to lead as he wants. He can't have our clan, that lairdship must go to Boyd, but the McAfee Clan… that one is open to whomever marries the eldest daughter of Duncan McAfee…"

"Such a union would befit both clans," Ewan mused. "But time will tell if love's aim proves as true as Fiona's arrows."

Unseen by the brothers, shrouded in shadow, the man lingered, his presence an unseen blemish upon the serene landscape. As he absorbed their words, his jaw clenched tight, the muscles working beneath the surface like serpents coiling in the depths. A marriage, they said. An alliance of hearts and lands. But to him, such musings were nothing but obstacles in the path to his desires.

"An alliance," he hissed. "A foolish dream that shall never come to pass."

His eyes, cold and calculating, followed the McClains as they continued their discussion, unaware of the malevolent intentions that brewed in the darkness. He committed their words to memory. The embrace that onlookers had regarded as a beginning was, to him, a prelude to an end—an end that he would orchestrate with cunning and precision.

"Alisdair McClain," he vowed silently, his gaze locked on the object of his ire, "you shall not have her. I swear it upon my honor, upon my very life."

With the stealth of a shadow, he slipped away, his form

blending with the encroaching night, leaving behind only the echo of unspoken malice and the certainty of a confrontation yet to come.

FIONA SAT BEFORE a looking glass, fingers deftly weaving strands of blond hair into an intricate braid. Her sisters attended to their own preparations. Their visages, reflected in the polished surface, bore the serene focus of warriors girding themselves for a different kind of battle—a dance in the great hall that loomed but an hour hence.

"Tell me, sister," Ailis, with her chestnut locks, implored with an impish grin, "have ye shared a kiss with Alisdair yet?" Her eyes held a mirthful glint, eager for tales of romance.

A fleeting blush stained Fiona's cheeks, a sovereign's confession. "Aye," she admitted, her voice a soft whisper betraying the intimacy of the act.

Proud Moira, with fiery tresses as untamed as her spirit, scoffed at the revelation. "A man whom you could best with a bow has claimed your lips? Preposterous!" She bristled at the notion, pausing her handiwork.

"Yet there is a tenderness in his strength," Fiona countered, defending the moment shared with Alisdair. "A gentleness underneath the warrior's facade." She spoke not just to convince Moira, but perhaps to reassure herself of the truth in her heart— the balance between the might of arms and the vulnerability of affection.

Ailis, ever the dreamer, returned to her own fanciful musings. "The dance," she sighed, her gaze lifting toward the heavens as though she could already hear the strings and flutes playing. "Mayhap this night shall bring the one fated to stand by *my* side."

"Strong and loving," Ailis declared, her voice a crescendo of longing. "A man whose heart knows both the steel of resolve and the warmth of kindness." Her star-filled eyes bespoke the depth of her desire, a yearning for a union that would endure through trials and triumph.

Moira McAfee stood before the looking glass, her fiery mane tamed into an elegant braid, a stark contrast to the wildness that lived within her. She caught Fiona's blue gaze in the reflection and held it steady, the flicker of rebellion burning bright in her green eyes.

"Mark my words, sisters," Moira declared. "I shall never be shackled by wedlock nor swaddled by babes. I am mistress of my fate, sovereign over my heart's domain." Her voice carried the strength of steel. "To live as a spinster is a destiny I embrace, for freedom is the very air that fills my lungs."

The weight of her declaration hung heavily in the chamber like a cloak of defiance. Fiona pondered Moira's avowal, understanding the fierce independence that fueled her sister's spirit. Ailis, however, watched Moira with a softened gaze, her dreams of love and marriage worlds apart from the younger girl's oath of solitude.

As the time for the dance approached, the sisters gathered their skirts and prepared to descend to the great hall. Fiona, a vision of strength with her golden locks, took the lead. Ailis followed, her brunette waves reflecting the candlelight, hope embroidered in every step she took. And then came Moira, the embodiment of fire and fervor, her red tresses a bold banner of her indomitable will.

Together they stepped down the grand staircase, each footfall echoing through the stone corridor. Their presence commanded the attention of all gathered below. Whispers spread like ripples in a still pond as the famed daughters of the McAfee clan made their entrance.

These women, known throughout the lands for their prowess in battle, now revealed an allure that transcended the legends of their physical feats. The crowd parted as the sisters moved with regal grace toward the heart of the festivities.

$$\text{❖}$$

CHAPTER FIVE

THE GREAT HALL of McAfee Keep was aglow with the flicker of torchlight, casting shadows upon stone walls that had borne witness to countless feasts. Yet tonight's celebration eclipsed them all in splendor and significance, for it marked the triumphs of Laird Duncan McAfee's daughters—the valiant lasses who had bested many a man in feats of strength and skill.

Duncan himself presided over the festivities, guffawing through the rafters as he clapped warriors on their backs and raised his cup in salute to the heroines of the hour. His heart swelled with pride at the sight of Fiona, Ailis, and Moira, each garbed in finery, tartan plaids interwoven with threads mirroring the colors of the Highland sky at dusk.

"Let us eat, drink, and revel in the honor ye have brought to our name!" the laird proclaimed, his voice rich with the timbre of a leader who had seen his legacy assured in the mettle of his offspring.

"Father is overjoyed," Ailis whispered to Fiona, the corners of her eyes crinkling in contentment. "Look how he beams."

"Indeed, his joy is a bountiful feast in itself," Fiona replied, her gaze traveling across the room where clansmen and maids twirled in a dance as old as the hills themselves. The rhythm of the music, steady and sure as the heartbeat of the earth, echoed the very pulse of her blood. And there, amidst laughter and song, she and her sisters were the embodiment of the McAfee spirit— undaunted and indomitable.

"Would that we could extend the challenge on the morrow once more," Moira sighed, her green eyes alight with the fire that had driven her sword arm to victory.

"Aye," Fiona agreed, her lips curving in a wistful smile. "But tonight, we celebrate what has been won, and honor the sacrifices made to achieve such ends."

As the night went on, Fiona was drawn into the dance, her movements a testament to the grace and poise befitting her station. Yet beneath layers of silk and lace beat the heart of a warrior maiden, ever restless, ever striving for the next horizon.

And though duty bound her to the path laid before her, Fiona knew that the tension between the desires of her soul and the responsibilities of her birthright would be a lifelong companion. For now, however, she would embrace the merriment of the moment, honoring the love and sacrifices of her father, even as the embers of competition smoldered, awaiting the breath of challenge to ignite them anew.

Through the throng of swaying bodies and the swirl of tartan, Alisdair moved with a purpose that parted the crowd. His gaze, as sharp as the blade at his side, found Fiona, her blue eyes reflecting the flickering torchlight that illuminated the grand hall.

Fiona stood among the revelers. As Alisdair approached, she smiled, looking forward to a bit more time with the man.

"May I have the honor?" Alisdair cut in, his hand extended toward her.

With a nod, she placed her fingertips into his waiting palm, a silent acknowledgment of the dance's necessity. His lips brushed over her fingers, sending an unspoken promise spiraling through the air.

The music beckoned them to join, a lively tune that made Fiona want to move with it. They stepped onto the floor, their movements initially hesitant. Laughter bubbled up from Fiona's chest as they stumbled over one another's feet, the practiced steps of the dance lost in the spontaneity of the moment.

"We are better suited to the battlefield than this dance," Alisdair remarked, smirking playfully.

"We are! There's no time to learn to dance when you're busy learning to be a warrior," Fiona agreed. "But 'tis a battlefield of a different kind—one where missteps lead to bruised pride rather than bruised shins."

Around them, the dance continued, but in their shared missteps, they found a rhythm all their own. They laughed at themselves easily and found yet another thing they had in common.

"Would ye like to escape the noise? Perchance a stroll by the loch?" Alisdair raised his voice above the clamor.

The thrum of the crowd pressed upon Fiona, who longed instead for the crisp highland air and the gentle lap of water against the shore. "Aye, that would be most welcome," she replied.

Together, they extricated themselves from the crush of bodies, passing beneath the arched doorway where torchlight danced upon stone walls. The night enveloped them in its cool embrace as they emerged from the confines of the grand hall. As soon as they were outside, Fiona sighed, more at ease than she had since the games had started.

Their footsteps whispered across the grass, away from the castle's glow and toward the tranquil expanse of the loch. The moon cast its reflection upon the water's surface, a pathway of light beckoning them.

"Tell me of yer latest adventure," Alisdair urged, his curiosity kindling the embers of conversation between them. A faint smile spread across his face. He was eager to listen to tales of daring and bravery from the fierce warrior at his side.

"'Twas but a fortnight ago," Fiona began, painting vivid images of shadowed forests and mountain peaks that scraped the heavens. She recounted the quest to retrieve a lost lamb from the treacherous cliffs, her voice embodying both the thrill of the challenge and the tender care for the creature. "The young shepherd who was supposed to be watching him had fallen asleep, and he knew his father would be angry, so I came to the rescue."

"Ye amaze me, Fiona McAfee," Alisdair declared. "You are a fierce warrior woman with a soft side, who won't let a boy be punished for falling asleep on the job."

"Pray tell," Fiona urged with measured curiosity, turning her gaze upon Alisdair. "What tales of valor might you share from your past?"

Alisdair's piercing blue eyes met hers, and a faint smile graced his lips as if the memory itself amused him. "There is one thing you might enjoy hearing about. A night under the cloak of darkness, where I found myself outnumbered amidst the tumult of clashing steel."

"Outnumbered?" Fiona asked, her interest piqued.

"Aye," he answered, nodding solemnly. "The enemy had encircled us, their intentions clear as the cold glint of moonlight upon their blades. Yet, 'twas not a time for fear but for strategy. With naught but the whispering wind as my confidant, I devised a cunning plan. We formed a phalanx, narrow as the eye of a needle, and charged."

"Such bravery," she murmured, envisioning the harrowing scene.

"Bravery born of necessity, Fiona." Alisdair's tone was modest, yet she could detect the pride swelling beneath his words. "We broke through their ranks, scattering them to the winds like chaff, securing victory against daunting odds."

"That tells me a great deal of your leadership, Alisdair." Fiona's admiration was genuine, her heart stirred by his gallantry.

"Yet I am certain your own exploits hold equal measure of daring," Alisdair intoned, casting a respectful glance toward Fiona McAfee, who walked alongside him.

"Ah," Fiona interjected, a playful twinkle lighting her intelligent blue eyes. "My tales are of a different sort, though they lack not for adventure." She paused, gathering the threads of her recollections. "I recall a day of summer past when my sisters and I endeavored to reclaim our father's prized steed, spirited away by mischievous brigands."

"Oh?" Alisdair prompted.

Fiona nodded. "With naught but guile and the cover of dusk, we tracked the rogues to their hideaway. Ailis, with her sharp wit, devised a ruse most clever, whilst Moira and I crept silently as shadows to the enclosure where the steed was bound."

"And were you successful in this clandestine venture?" Alisdair asked, his tone laced with the excitement of shared secrets.

"Triumphantly so," Fiona replied, her chest swelling with quiet pride. "We liberated the steed and led it back to the safety of our keep, all without raising the alarm or drawing the blade."

"Such resourcefulness speaks highly of your courage and bond." Alisdair noted the fierce loyalty that bound the McAfee sisters as tightly as any knight's honor.

Alisdair McClain, the robust first son of the McClain clan, collected his thoughts for yet another tale.

"Allow me to recount the time I found myself amidst the wilds of the northern moors," Alisdair began. "A white boar, majestic and elusive, had been spotted—a creature said to herald great change."

Fiona noted the gleam in Alisdair's eye, a reflection of the thrill that came with the chase, mingling with a sense of duty to his people. For capturing such a beast was not merely a test of skill. It was an omen eagerly sought by his clan.

"Days we spent, tracking the ghostly hart across the treacherous terrain," he continued. "Each evening brought forth the lament of our fruitless pursuit, yet dawn renewed our resolve."

"And did ye capture this steed?" Fiona inquired.

"Capture? Nay, my lady." Alisdair smiled wistfully. "The boar led us to a stranded traveler, injured and near death. Our quarry escaped, but the life we saved… Perhaps that was the change foretold."

"Aye, a noble sacrifice for a worthy cause," Fiona remarked, the theme of duty shaping her understanding of his story.

"I have a tale that shall surely lighten yer spirit," Fiona announced, her blue eyes dancing with mischief. "'Twas the eve of All Hallows', when Moira, Ailis, and I chanced upon a scheme most daring."

"Under cover of night, we donned the guise of specters, draping ourselves in sheets pilfered from the laundress," Fiona recounted, her voice tinged with the warmth of fond remembrance. "We set out to haunt the unwary—or so was our intent."

"Go on," Alisdair urged, a smile threatening to take over his face.

"Alas, our spectral debut was not to be," Fiona jested. "We had not reckoned with the castle hounds, who, upon scenting familiar ghosts, proceeded to frolic and cavort with such fervor that our ghostly raiments were soon in disarray."

"Yer own hounds foiled ye?" Alisdair asked, trying to hide his laughter.

"Aye, they did," Fiona admitted, joining Alisdair in a rare moment of shared mirth. "By the time we returned to the keep, our gowns were awry, our dignity besmirched, and the hounds... The hounds were convinced they had bested the spirits themselves."

"It sounds like fun was had by all. Isn't that what matters?" he asked, grinning at her.

Alisdair and Fiona continued their walk. Fiona's breath came in steady rhythms, her warrior's poise unyielding even in leisure, but her eyes gleamed with a mischievous light.

"Alisdair," she chirped, her voice dancing on the wind, "I challenge ye to a race to the willow!" She started running before he had time to think on what she'd said.

Alisdair took off after her, chuckling as he chased her toward the tree.

Their sprint was a thunderous rhythm across the earth, a symphony of heartbeats and hurried breaths that echoed through the stillness of the night. Laughter spilled from their lips, pure and unrestrained, as they dashed, racing toward victory and freedom alike.

Fiona's lungs burned with exertion, her muscles tensed like the string of a bow, yet she surged forward with relentless determination. Her braid had come undone, allowing her blond hair to stream behind her.

As the willow drew near, Fiona dared to glance over her shoulder. Alisdair was at her heels, the embodiment of strength and agility, yet his smile spoke not of conquest but of delight in the moment itself. With one final burst of speed, she reached the tree's sanctuary, a triumphant laugh escaping her as she declared, "Victory is mine!"

Breathless and exhilarated, Alisdair caught up to her, his hands braced against the ancient trunk. "Aye, ye have won the race, but the night is young, and the prize yet undecided."

Their eyes locked, and the world held its breath. A current of desire threaded through the space between them, pulling them closer. They stepped into the shelter of the willow's drooping boughs.

Alisdair lifted Fiona's hand to his lips, pressing a kiss upon her fingertips with the reverence reserved for sacred oaths. His caress ignited a flame within her, casting shadows of doubt and duty to the corners of her mind. Slowly, deliberately, their faces drew near until their lips met in a kiss that shook her to her very core.

Passion burgeoned, fervent and fierce, as their hearts raced not from the exertion of the run but from the proximity of their bodies.

As they parted, the world resumed its spin. Reality beckoned with the weight of responsibility. But the kiss remained, a testament to the truth that lay within their entwined hearts—a truth that would sustain them through the trials yet to come.

Resuming their leisurely stroll along the tranquil shores of the loch, Fiona and Alisdair found themselves caught in a gentle rhythm, their hands occasionally brushing as they walked side by side. The hum of the distant revelry faded, replaced by the soft whisper of the wind and the occasional call of a night bird.

"Your kin are an enigmatic lot," Fiona remarked with a lilt of amusement in her voice, breaking the serenity that had enveloped them. "The tales that drift through the Highlands—oh, they paint quite the picture. It is said the youngest son is destined for greatness, not the eldest. Curious, isn't it?"

"It is," Alisdair replied, his deep chuckle mingling with the rustling leaves. "And there's more. Whispers claim we're all witches, concocting spells under the moonlight."

"Mm, and the lairds?" Fiona prodded, her eyes twinkling with mirth. "Can they truly heal with but a single touch, or command the weather as easily as they lead their men?"

"Ah, if only," he responded, feigning a wistful sigh. "It would make the harsh Highland winters far more bearable. But alas, we are mere mortals, bound by the same laws of nature as any other." He couldn't tell her the whole truth of his family, but he could chuckle with her at the tales that were spread.

Their laughter echoed softly, dissolving into the cool air until only the sound of their synchronized steps remained. As the frivolity subsided, a thread of earnestness weaved its way into their conversation.

"Alisdair, I have dreams… dreams of more than just a political marriage," Fiona confessed, her gaze fixed on the shimmering reflection of the moon upon the loch's surface. "I seek a love that is more than duty and obligation—a union forged from affection, respect, and shared ambition.

"Such a love is rare, especially for those of us born to lead," she continued. "But I cannot accept anything less—not when my heart knows what it yearns for."

In the stillness that followed, Fiona wondered if she had revealed too much, if her boldness might be mistaken for imprudence. Yet when she gazed upon Alisdair's face, she found no judgment, only the dawning recognition of a kindred spirit.

"Your candor honors me, Fiona," Alisdair replied sincerely. "I share your pursuit of a bond that transcends mere alliance. A love born not out of necessity but of genuine desire. I thought I would be happy with a political marriage, but getting better acquainted with ye has taught me differently. I crave passion."

As they walked on, he continued, "Ye speak of love as though it were a companion on the battlefield, one that ye would fight beside, not merely accept as an ally."

"'Tis true," Fiona replied. "Love ought to be an ally chosen for its valor, not just for the colors it bears."

Her earnestness resonated with him, stirring camaraderie that went beyond the hope of a political alliance.

"Then let us hope," Alisdair declared, "that our hearts' banners may one day fly as one."

Fiona's lips curved into a smile, and a slow laugh escaped her. "Ye sound like yer writing bad poetry!"

He responded in kind. "Do ladies not want poetry?"

"I canna tell ye what other ladies want, but I myself enjoy good poetry. Just not the bad. And that, Alisdair, was bad."

They found a stone bench near the loch and they both approached it without a word. Silence fell comfortably between them, not as a void but as a vessel carrying unspoken thoughts and shared understanding.

"Did ye ever dream of something other than war and leadership?" Fiona's question pierced the hush around them, tentative yet laden with curiosity.

Alisdair turned to her, his blue eyes reflecting the twilight. "As a bairn, I fancied myself an explorer," he confessed, a rare smile tugging at the corner of his mouth. "I'd set off into the wilds, imagining lands no McClain had ever trod."

"An explorer," Fiona repeated softly, the idea stirring a wistful yearning within her own breast. She chuckled, envisioning a young Alisdair. "And I—the lass who would rather shoot an arrow than stitch a sampler. We were not the children our mothers envisioned."

His voice was thoughtful, tempered by the weight of his position. "But perhaps 'tis for the best. Our dreams shape us more than any expectation."

Fiona nodded, finding solace in his words. Her gaze drifted across the darkening waters, pondering the unknown future and the role she would play in it. "I fear…" she began, then hesitated, a vulnerability creeping into her normally steadfast tone. "I fear the loss of myself in a loveless marriage, arranged for naught but political gain. Most men wouldn't allow me to keep my bow and arrows. In fact, they would expect me to tend to the castle and do little else."

Alisdair's hand found hers, a gesture both comforting and emboldening. "Fiona McAfee," he began with resolve, "I vow to fight for your happiness with the same fervor I would defend my own land. The heart wants what it wants, and should it yearn for freedom or for love, it shan't be denied."

In that moment, the seeds of hope took root within Fiona. Here was a man who understood the tug-of-war between heart and duty. Perhaps he was just the man she needed.

"Thank ye, Alisdair," Fiona whispered, her eyes glistening with unshed tears. "For seeing me—not just as a McAfee, but as Fiona."

They spent a few moments just sitting together, gazing up at the stars overhead.

"Ye ken the stars?" she asked softly. Their hands remained entwined.

"Aye," Alisdair replied. "My da taught me their names when I was but a lad. Said they'd guide me home should I ever lose my way."

A small, tender smile played on Fiona's lips. "Mayhap they'll guide us both," she murmured. The idea was comforting, as was the steady pressure of Alisdair's fingers laced with hers.

"Shall we return?" Alisdair's query broke the tranquil spell, his tone laced with reluctance. The dance, with its whirl of colors and flurry of motions, awaited their presence, a stark contrast to the serenity they found by the loch.

Fiona nodded, her resolve fortified by the newfound understanding that shimmered between them. "Aye, let us go back," she agreed. With a shared glance that held a world of unspoken thoughts, they turned toward the torchlit hall where their clans mingled and merriment reigned.

MALCOLM SINCLAIR, HIDDEN in the alcove's embrace, watched Fiona and Alisdair slip away from the boisterous feast. His keen eyes, so like a hawk's, followed their retreat with a predator's silent calculation. They meandered through the throng of kinsmen and allies, their laughter lost amidst the din of merriment. Unseen, Malcolm trailed them, his steps measured and soundless.

Outside, the moon hung heavy above, its pale glow shimmering across the loch's placid surface. A cool breeze whispered through the heather, carrying with it the scent of pine and the distant echo of bagpipes melding with the night. Malcolm's gaze never wavered from the figures strolling by the water's edge.

Every stride taken was laden with the gravity of his station, each thought a chess piece moved upon the board of his ambition. The weight of his father's expectations pressed upon him like the yoke of an invisible mantle: to secure the future of Clan Sinclair, to prove himself worthy of the legacy left to him—a future where Fiona McAfee might stand by his side, not as a choice of her heart but as a conquest of his will.

Malcolm pondered the myriad paths before him, his mind a tempest of schemes and stratagems. To challenge Alisdair, to best him in combat would be a deed of valor, yet such an act could ignite a feud that would consume both clans in flames of war. No, bloodshed would serve no purpose here—not when subtler means might secure the prize.

Kidnapping—the word itself was a serpent that slithered through his mind, venomous and alluring. To spirit Fiona away, to hold her within the stronghold of Clan Sinclair until she yielded to his claim… It was a gambit fraught with peril, yet one that might yield untold rewards.

For a moment, Malcolm luxuriously imagined her fierce spirit tempered into something softer within the confines of his keep, her piercing blue eyes reflecting not defiance but a begrudging respect for the man who dared to capture her. Yet even this idea was tainted by the specter of consequence, the knowledge that every action bore its own shadow of retribution.

He drew back into the shadows, his heart a battlefield of desire and duty. There, under the watchful eye of the moon, Malcolm Sinclair, heir to the legacy of his clan, made his choice. He would have Fiona McAfee, not through the honor of courtship, but through the audacity of abduction. And though the heavens might scorn him for it, he would risk the ire of gods and men alike to make her his wife.

THE REVELRY OF the dance hall swirled around Fiona as she and Alisdair came to a gradual halt, their steps slowing in the throng of merrymakers. For a fleeting moment, her warrior's heart now kept time with the gentle rhythm of violins and flutes.

"Ye have my gratitude for this evening." Her voice was steady and imbued with the formality that the setting demanded. The words were simple, yet they carried the weight of unspoken promises and secret confessions.

Alisdair's gaze held hers, intense and unwavering. "The pleasure was mine, Fiona," he replied, his tone equally measured, rich with the cadence of sincerity. "This night shall remain etched in my memory."

Their fingers lingered together for a heartbeat longer than propriety dictated.

She could sense the eyes upon them, the subtle shifts in the air as whispers and speculations weaved through the crowd like wayward breezes. Yet within the shelter of Alisdair's presence, such concerns were distant, muted by the resounding echo of shared laughter and the soft lapping of loch waters against the shore.

"Then we part here," Fiona stated. The regal poise she wore as a mantle never faltered, even as something akin to reluctance tugged at the edges of her resolve. She withdrew her hand from his, a symbolic gesture that marked the end of an interlude outside of time.

"Aye, for now." Alisdair's smile was a quiet beacon in the sea of faces. "But not forever."

With a nod, Fiona turned away. Yet her heart fluttered against its bony cage, buoyed by the whisper of possibilities that had taken root, nourished by stolen moments and hopeful glances.

As she rejoined the dance, Fiona carried with her the silent vow that bloomed in the hidden corners of her heart.

As she danced with her own clansmen and others from around the Highlands, her thoughts were still filled with Alisdair. He was a good man, and she wanted to be his bride. But she was going to make him wait and ask her, not her father. She was the mistress of her own destiny, whether either man wanted it that way or not.

Fiona twirled through a sea of tartans. Lairds in their finery and soldiers in their regalia, men of strength and valor, all succumbed to the allure of the McAfee's eldest daughter. They approached with brawny arms extended, seeking the honor of a dance, their expressions aglow with admiration for the maiden whose reputation as a fierce warrior contrasted the elegance she now displayed with her blond hair flowing around her.

As the music swelled, Fiona found herself momentarily lifted from the weight of expectation resting upon her shoulders. With each partner, she surrendered to the dance, allowing herself to be guided through the steps.

But the respite was fleeting, for soon Malcolm Sinclair, heir of

Clan Sinclair, approached, his stride confident—a predator assured of his quarry. His sharp features were set into a mask of entitlement, and as he offered his hand, there was a possessiveness in his grip that sent a shiver through Fiona's spine, one not born of the chill Highland air.

She'd known all three sons of Laird Sinclair since childhood, and they all were like snakes to her—vile and full of poison. She had no desire to dance with the man, but she couldn't embarrass her father by refusing him. Laird Sinclair was her father's closest friend.

"Fiona," Malcolm intoned with a voice that sought to envelop her in its depth. "The pleasure of this dance is mine, I trust."

"Malcolm," Fiona replied, betraying none of the unease that stirred within her. She placed her hand in his, the gesture one of courtesy rather than desire, and they joined in the dance.

Malcolm led with an assuredness that bordered on arrogance, his movements precise and calculated. He steered her not just across the floor but seemingly toward a future he had already envisioned—one where she played a role scripted by his ambition and his father's will.

Fiona danced, her mind whirling not with the music but with thoughts of duty and sacrifice. To refuse Malcolm openly would risk offense, yet to acquiesce to his silent claim would be to forsake her own dreams.

"Your beauty outshines even the tales told of it," Malcolm gushed, attempting to weave words of flattery into their exchange.

"Beauty is but a fleeting thing," Fiona countered. "It is the strength of one's character that endures."

"True," Malcolm conceded, a flash of something unreadable crossing his gaze. "And our clans could benefit greatly from an alliance that combines both beauty and strength."

"I suppose they would. But I am not interested in an alliance of that sort," she replied flatly.

As the melody drew to a close and the dance neared its end,

Fiona took a breath and prepared to step back into the role carved out for her by birthright. She was the McAfee's heir, and with that came responsibilities that often clashed with the yearnings of her heart.

"Thank you for the dance, Malcolm." She curtsied with a poise that masked her turmoil. "I am certain your father awaits your presence."

With a final nod, Fiona withdrew, leaving Malcolm Sinclair to ponder the enigma of the woman he'd just danced with.

The dance floor's lively energy waned as the evening pressed on, yet Fiona found herself once again swept into the spirited whirl of the ceilidh. The music, a rich tapestry of fiddle and drum, beckoned all to partake in the traditional Highland fling. Lachlan McClain, with his ever-present mischievous grin, approached her, extending a hand that promised mirth rather than courtship.

"Would ye honor me with this dance, Fiona?" Lachlan's voice carried over the din, his eyes twinkling with brotherly affection.

As she accepted, Fiona was aware of the curious glances cast their way. As they danced, Lachlan's jests and quips continually made her laugh, and she was grateful for the reprieve from the boring men she'd been dancing with for the past hour.

"Ye've stepped on my toes only twice this eve," Lachlan teased with a roguish smile. "Is it mercy, or are ye losing your touch?"

"Perchance ye are simply more nimble than the rest," Fiona countered, her smile betraying a flash of amusement.

Brodie McClain, quieter in nature, joined them, seamlessly taking his brother's place as the dance demanded. His movements were precise, his gaze thoughtful as he guided Fiona through the intricate steps.

"Ye dance beautifully, Fiona," Brodie intoned, his voice steady and calm. "Free and unyielding."

"Your words are kind, Brodie," she replied. However, a twinge of confusion knitted her brow, for she was unaccustomed to such treatment from warriors of their stature.

As the final notes of the piper's song faded, Fiona and her sisters exchanged knowing glances. They retired from the grand hall with a weariness that clung to their bones.

As her sisters' breaths deepened into the rhythm of sleep, Fiona remained wakeful, ensnared by visions of Alisdair—his strong hands, the intensity in his gaze, and the unspoken promise that lingered between them.

Lying upon her bed, she traced the patterns of the tapestry draped above her, her thoughts adrift. Fiona grappled with the mantle of duty that rested upon her shoulders. With Alisdair, could she have both? A great passion and duty fulfilled?

CHAPTER SIX

I N THE DIM light of the McAfee clan's formal study, Fiona stood before her father, the heavy oak door softly thudding behind her. The room exuded the power and history of their lineage, every tapestry and artifact mementos of duty and sacrifice. Laird Duncan McAfee was seated in a grand chair that commanded attention.

"Father," Fiona began. "I have given much thought to the matter of Alisdair McClain."

Duncan's eyes, sharp as the dirk he kept at his side, studied Fiona's face. "Ye ken my concerns, Fiona. I have been approached by Arran Sinclair with a match between you and Malcolm."

"Nay. I will not marry that man," she replied, the corners of her mouth tightening ever so slightly. "He makes me uneasy, and I dinna trust him."

"I merely ask ye get ta know him better."

"Nay, Father. There is something about him that turns my insides to stone. I danced with him, as I felt it was my duty to do so, but he sickened me. Not like Alisdair."

"A merger between our clan and the Sinclairs would mean a much larger area of land that we would control. It would be a good arrangement."

"Nay. Nay. Nay."

Duncan sighed. "And ye suppose Alisdair McClain is the man ye should marry?"

"I am not certain yet, but I feel it is possible. But as ye have taught me, my mind must guide me, not haste. Alisdair is a man of honor, and I find myself drawn to the depth of his character. I wish to discern if his heart aligns with the values we hold dear, if his ambitions will bolster our kin or place them at risk."

Duncan leaned back in his chair, the creak of leather soft in the silence that followed. His fingers drummed a thoughtful rhythm upon the arm of his chair.

"Ye are headstrong, like yer mother was," he finally spoke, a hint of pride coloring his words. "But this decision bears the weight of our future. Can ye assure me that in seeking yer own path, ye will not lose sight of the needs of our clan?"

"Father, it is because I am yer daughter that ye need not fear." Fiona's stance remained unwavering. "I seek only to understand the true measure of the man who may stand by my side. Give me time, and I shall discern whether Alisdair McClain can be both a political ally and a companion worthy of my hand."

"And if ye decide he is not, will ye at least consider Malcolm Sinclair?"

"Nay, I will not. He is not a man who I could ever lie with. He makes me want to vomit."

The laird regarded Fiona, the lines of his face softening as he recognized the same resolve that had steered their clan through countless trials. "Then take the time ye need, my child," he conceded, though his voice carried the weight of unspoken cautions. "But dinna let yer heart lead ye astray from the duties that bind us."

"Thank ye, Father." Fiona's lips curved into a grateful smile. With a bow of her head, she turned to leave.

LAIRD DUNCAN MCAFEE paced the stone floor, his tartan sash swaying with each measured step. Alisdair stood by the window. "And tell me why ye think ye are the man to marry me eldest daughter? Me Fiona?"

Alisdair turned from the window, his gaze meeting Laird Duncan's with a steady intensity. "Laird McAfee, I stand before ye not as a man seeking easy favor, but as one who recognizes the gravity of the alliance I seek to make. Fiona is a woman of incomparable strength and grace, a warrior."

He paused, choosing his words with care, aware of the weight they carried in this crucial moment. "I offer naught but sincerity in my intentions toward Fiona. As the eldest son of the laird of Clan McClain, I have shouldered the burdens of command and fought to protect our kin with every fiber of my being. But in Fiona, I see a partner whose courage matches my own, whose unwavering loyalty to her family echoes the values that guide my own actions."

Drawing closer to Duncan's grand chair that commanded attention, Alisdair's presence filled the room with a quiet authority. "I understand the concerns that weigh on yer heart, Laird McAfee. But I would ask ye to consider this—our union would not only bind our clans in alliance but in spirit as well. With Fiona at me side, I see a future where our peoples thrive, where our strengths complement each other in ways that will strengthen the very core of our lands."

His blue eyes held a glint of determination as he continued, "I do not seek to claim Fiona out of duty or convenience. Nay, Laird, I stand before ye today to declare that it is out of genuine admiration for all that she is. Her spirit kindles a fire in me that burns brighter than any battlefield victory."

Alisdair's voice resonated with sincerity, each word carefully chosen to convey the depth of his feelings. "I pledge to ye now, Laird Duncan McAfee, that I will honor and cherish Fiona as my equal and my partner in all things.

"Ye ken well the whispers that surround the McClain clan," Duncan began. "Ye are thought to be a cunning lot, and I fear yer intentions might not be as honorable as yer courtship implies."

Alisdair held Duncan's gaze, his piercing blue eyes unwavering as he spoke with conviction. "Laird McAfee, I understand the doubts that linger in your mind, but I swear by the blood of my ancestors and the honor of my clan that my intentions toward Fiona are pure. I seek nothing but her happiness and well-being, for her heart is a treasure that I would guard with my life." Alisdair made sure to stare straight at the laird as he finished speaking, so the man would acknowledge the truth that he spoke.

Duncan McAfee, his expression unreadable, watched Alisdair carefully. The words rang with sincerity, resonating within the stone walls of the great hall where they stood. After a moment of contemplative silence, the laird finally spoke, his voice gruff yet measured.

"Alisdair McClain, I hear the earnestness in yer words and see the conviction in yer eyes," Duncan began more softly. "I will trust Fiona's judgment and the purity of yer intentions. But know this, laddie, there is another suitor whose claim to Fiona's hand I hold in high regard. Malcolm Sinclair, a man of wealth and standing, has expressed his interest in allying through marriage with the McAfee clan. His lands are vast, his warriors fierce, and his loyalty unwavering." Duncan paused, his eyes searching Alisdair's face for any hint of reaction.

Alisdair remained composed, though inwardly a storm raged within him. Despite his resolve, a flicker of concern danced in his eyes as he met Duncan's gaze.

"Laird McAfee," Alisdair began steadily, "I am aware of Malcolm Sinclair's suit for Fiona's hand. While I hold respect for his accomplishments and the strength of his clan, I must say that I have feelings for your daughter. Can Sinclair say the same?"

Duncan stared at Alisdair for a moment before admitting, "I do not know."

"Give me time to win her heart. Please."

Duncan finally nodded.

Fiona stood firm as the silence swelled within the stone-clad chamber of her father's study. "Father," she began, her voice carrying the strength of her convictions, "I ken well the duties that bind me to our clan. My loyalty to our name is unwavering." She paused, her hands clasping before her in a gesture of sincerity. "But I must also heed the call of my own heart in matters of love and life."

Duncan's gaze did not waver from his daughter's, though the lines on his weathered face deepened with concern. His voice, when it broke the charged stillness, held the gravity of his station. "Fiona, my child, ye are braver than most men I have known and sharper than the tips of your arrows. Your accomplishments speak of your strength and wisdom." He rose from his seat, moving closer to her, his tall frame casting a long shadow across the room.

"Yet even the strongest fortress may fall to treachery," he continued, his words echoing with a father's fear. "The McClains are shrouded in whispers of deceit and ambition. They say Fearghas McClain, Alisdair's father, seeks alliances not for honor, but for power that could upset the delicate balance among the clans."

Fiona listened, her braid shifting over her shoulder as she inclined her head to acknowledge his point. She felt the pull of her heartstrings, taut with the desire to explore what might bloom between her and Alisdair, yet she could not dismiss her father's foreboding.

"Ye speak of rumors, Father," Fiona countered gently. "Rumors are naught but shadows—insubstantial and often born of malice or fear. Should we not seek the light of truth ourselves?"

Laird Duncan McAfee's gaze softened then, pride mingling with the worry in his eyes. "Aye, Fiona. It is your right to seek out such truth. Be careful, lest you find yourself ensnared in a McClain's trap."

She heard the unspoken love behind his caution, understanding the depth of his fears. "I will tread carefully, Father," she promised, her resolve as steadfast as the ancient stones that formed the walls around them. "For the good of our people, and for my own heart's sake."

She started to leave, but paused, turning back to face the laird. "Father, I cannot depart without expressing the depth of my gratitude. Your counsel is very important to me, and I promise to weigh every word of it before I make a decision."

"Your words honor me, Fiona." His deep voice resonated through the room like a distant rumble of thunder over the highland moors. "Your independence, though it may fray my nerves, makes me a very proud father."

"Your love and support are what I need to guide me through this time," Fiona replied, her blue eyes holding his in a moment of silent acknowledgment.

"Go now," Laird Duncan urged, warmth seeping into his demeanor. "And remember, whatever path you choose, you do not walk it alone. My love goes with ye, as does the pride of the McAfee name."

Fiona stepped out into the brisk air. Her gaze swept over the grounds where the Highland Games had unfolded in days prior, the remnants of competition and camaraderie reduced to trampled grass and a sparse assembly of lingering tents. Yet among this desolation of festivity, the McClain tent remained, its robust canvas flapping softly against the whisper of the wind.

She moved across the field. As Fiona drew near, the sound of familiar voices reached her ears. Alisdair was engaged in earnest conversation with his brother, gesturing animatedly as he spoke, his broad shoulders squared.

Lachlan responded with equal vigor, his smile infectious even from a distance. But it was Alisdair who captivated her attention. The way his presence commanded the space around him, the sharp wit that flashed in his piercing blue eyes, the subtle gentleness that underscored his strength.

"Ah, Fiona," Alisdair called, catching sight of her. A ripple of surprise crossed his features, quickly replaced by a welcoming expression. "I've been graced by your father's generosity—he has permitted me to extend my stay within your clan's stronghold."

The words stirred a mixture of elation and apprehension for Fiona. It was a concession she had not anticipated, a gift of time that might allow her to unravel the enigma that was Alisdair. She considered his countenance carefully, searching for any hint of the rumors that her father feared, yet finding only the open visage of a man who wished to get better acquainted with her.

"Your presence honors us, Alisdair," Fiona replied, allowing the formality of manners to cloak the fluttering of her thoughts. The prospect of his extended company promised both risk and reward, a challenge to her judgment and an opportunity to explore the depths of her desires.

"Shall we walk?" he suggested, extending an invitation with a slight tilt of his head toward the rolling expanse of the McAfee lands.

"Certainly," she consented steadily as she stepped forward to join him.

"Would ye do me the honor of joining me on a hunt?" he inquired, his piercing blue gaze softening with an earnestness that beckoned to Fiona's adventurous spirit.

"Nothing would please me more," Fiona responded with a quickened heartbeat. Grasping the opportunity to witness his prowess beyond the battlefield and to test her own skills beside him, she excused herself with a graceful nod and hastened back toward the stronghold.

She knew for a certainty that Malcolm Sinclair would never ask her to hunt with him. He was the type of man who thought a woman should be seen and not heard. Nay, what she needed was a man like Alisdair, who accepted her for who she was.

Fiona navigated the familiar corridors with swift, determined strides. Her eyes sparkled with anticipation as she reached her chamber, retrieving her cherished bow and quiver of arrows.

The weight of the bow in her grasp felt like an extension of her very. With her hunting gear secured, she rushed through the castle.

Her path led her to the warm heart of the stronghold—the kitchen. There, in the middle of preparations for the evening meal, stood her grandmother, a pillar of wisdom and comfort in Fiona's life.

"Granny," Fiona began, "I believe I have found him—a man who is both a capable ally for our clan and a kindred spirit for my heart."

Her grandmother paused, eyes locking with Fiona's with an intensity that spoke volumes of her love and concern. Without a word, Fiona wrapped her arms around the diminutive figure, feeling the warmth and strength that had guided her since childhood. She planted a tender kiss atop the silver crown of hair.

"Be wary, child, but be true to yourself," her grandmother uttered softly.

The door to the kitchen swung closed with a gentle thud. Granny's eyes remained fixed on its sturdy oak panels, as if through sheer will she could still glimpse the granddaughter who had just departed.

Granny's hands, gnarled like the ancient branches of the rowan tree outside her window, clutched at the edge of the worn wooden table.

As the lass hastened toward an uncertain future, the familiar tides of trepidation rose within Granny's chest.

"Choices," she murmured to herself. Aye, the decisions Fiona faced were as rugged and daunting as the Highlands themselves. Would she find a path through the heather-laden fields that allowed her both the joy of love and the strength of alliance? Or would she, like so many before her, lose herself in duty and sacrifice?

A gentle clinking of metal drew Granny's gaze to the hearth, where a pot hung simmering over the low flames. She watched as the bubbles rose and popped, a slow and steady rhythm that matched the beating of her own heart. In the dance of firelight and shadow, she saw reflected the trials of her own youth—the choices made, the love cherished, and the sacrifices endured.

"Guide her, ancestors," Granny whispered. "Shield her heart from folly, but let it not be hardened by the chill of politics."

It was in such moments of solitude that Granny afforded herself the luxury of worry, for in the presence of others, she was the matriarch—the keeper of stories and wisdom. But here, in the quiet aftermath of Fiona's departure, she permitted the fears of a grandmother to swell within her bosom.

FIONA STRODE PURPOSEFULLY alongside Alisdair. Oblivious to her grandmother's fretful musings ensconced within the stone walls of their ancestral home, she ventured into the woods.

"Your father would have preferred your sisters' company on such a venture," Alisdair remarked, his voice a deep timbre that vibrated through the trees themselves.

"Aye," Fiona agreed, her eyes flickering with unspoken thoughts. "But 'tis not my sisters I wish to steal away with." She cast a sidelong glance at him, her blue eyes sparking with daring, revealing a glint of the desire that lay hidden beneath layers of duty.

They made their way to a clearing known only to those who bore the secrets of the land. The chill of the morning mist clung to Fiona's skin, but it was the anticipation of what was to come that sent shivers down her spine. A hush settled over the clearing as if even the wildlife held its breath for the moment about to unfold.

"Alisdair," Fiona murmured. He stepped toward her, a silent understanding passing between them.

His hand found hers, strong and warm against the cool air, and he drew her closer. Their lips met, and the world faded into insignificance. Fiona lost herself in the embrace, her warrior's guard falling away to reveal the woman whose heart yearned fiercely.

As the kiss ended, they stood forehead to forehead, breath mingling. For now, in this secluded enclave, duty and sacrifice were distant echoes, drowned out by the beating of two hearts entwined in the timeless dance of longing and affection.

"Come." Fiona's voice was steady despite the turmoil that raged within. "Let us begin our hunt."

And with the taste of Alisdair's kiss still lingering upon her lips, she led the way deeper into the woods, an arrow notched and ready, the huntress once more in command.

CHAPTER SEVEN

I N THE FOREST, Fiona and Alisdair stood motionless, eyes fixed upon their respective prey.

"Ready?" Alisdair's voice was barely above a whisper, his gaze never wavering from the large boar that had wandered into the clearing.

Fiona nodded curtly. Her fingers flexed on the bowstring, her breath steady as she eyed the doe grazing near the brook. "Ready."

"Then... now," he replied. Two arrows flew swift and true. Thuds sounded almost in unison as each arrow found its mark, the animals collapsing upon the forest floor.

With the hunt concluded, the tension dissolved into mirthful chuckles and an ease borne of success. They approached their quarry, Alisdair reaching the boar first and laying a hand on its antlers with a respectful nod.

"An impressive shot, Fiona," Alisdair complimented, glancing over to where she examined the doe.

"Yours matched it well enough," Fiona replied, a spark of pride lighting her eyes. She brushed a loose strand of hair behind her ear, the braid having come loose during the hunt.

The laughter came easily as they set about preparing the animals for transport. Alisdair moved to hoist both creatures onto his shoulders, but Fiona stepped forward with a raised hand.

"Think you're the only one with shoulders broad enough to bear the weight?" she teased, her blue eyes glinting with good-natured defiance. "Who do ye think carries my game back to the keep when ye are not here?"

"Never would I underestimate a McAfee," Alisdair countered.

Fiona hefted the deer with a practiced ease. Its lifeless form draped over her shoulders like a macabre shawl. Beside her, Alisdair matched her stride for stride, a boar slung across his back as if it were naught but a sack of grain.

"Ye know," Fiona began, her voice laced with a mirth that belied the weight she bore, "I'm thinking we might need to fashion ye a kilt from this beast. 'Tis a fine plaid pattern in its bristles."

Alisdair guffawed. "Aye, and should I start practicing my oinks, or would that be taking the commitment too far?"

"Only if I can call ye 'Laird Boarish' at the feast tonight," she retorted.

"Then ye best be ready to curtsy to your swine laird," Alisdair shot back with playful defiance.

"Curtsy?" Fiona feigned shock, nearly stumbling in her exaggerated dismay. "The day I curtsy to a man, even one of your esteemed rank, pigs will surely fly."

"Then let us hope this boar takes flight, for I long to see such a day." Alisdair lingered on Fiona with an admiration that reached beyond their jests.

Their laughter mingled in the air, floating toward the keep where duty awaited them, a fleeting respite before the mantle of responsibility settled upon their shoulders once more.

The rest of the journey back to the keep was punctuated with shared jokes and tales. As they traversed the wooded terrain, Fiona's laughter rang out, clear and bright, mingling with Alisdair's deeper chuckles.

Though the weight of the deer was heavy, Fiona refused to show any sign of strain, her back straight and her steps purposeful. Alisdair matched her pace, his own burden equally shared.

"You know, you didn't have to prove a point quite so literally," Alisdair remarked, a hint of amusement in his voice as he glanced at Fiona struggling under the weight.

Fiona glared at him. "I can handle it just fine. I don't need you questioning my strength, McClain."

Alisdair raised an eyebrow, a small smile playing at the corner of his lips. "No one doubts your strength, Fiona. But there's no harm in accepting help now and then."

"I'm not some fragile maiden who needs rescuing," Fiona retorted.

Alisdair fell into step beside her, his gaze softening. "I understand that underneath that warrior facade, there lies a woman of remarkable strength and unwavering determination. But even the mightiest oak tree can bend without breaking, Fiona."

She paused for a moment, considering his words as they continued their trek through the dense forest. The cool air whispered through the trees, carrying the scent of pine and damp earth. Fiona's mind drifted back to a time long ago, a memory that still stung with the ache of her own stubbornness.

"There was a time," Fiona began slowly, "when my stubbornness nearly cost me more than I could bear."

Alisdair listened intently, sensing the weight of her words. Fiona's steps became measured, each one carrying the burden of her past.

"It was during a particularly harsh winter," Fiona continued, her eyes fixed on the path ahead. "Food was scarce, and our clan was struggling to survive. I was determined to prove that I could hunt for my family and provide for them, refusing any assistance or guidance. My pride blinded me to the wisdom of our elders and the experience of our hunters."

Alisdair kept a respectful silence, his gaze unwavering as he let Fiona unravel the tale of her past.

"I set out alone, chasing after a herd of deer," Fiona quavered. "I was so consumed by my need to succeed that I ignored the signs of an approaching storm. By the time I had caught up to the deer, the blizzard had descended upon us like a wrathful spirit."

Her words painted a vivid picture of snowflakes swirling

around her, obscuring her vision and numbing her limbs.

"I was lost in a white void, unable to find my way back home. My stubbornness had led me into a trap of my own making," Fiona confessed, a tremor in her voice.

Alisdair's expression softened with understanding, his blue eyes filled with empathy as he grasped the depth of Fiona's story. The weight of her past stubbornness hung heavily between them, the unspoken regrets and lessons learned echoing through the silent forest. As they walked, the undergrowth thickened around them, creating a natural barrier that mirrored the emotional walls Fiona had built around herself.

The shadows lengthened as the sun dipped lower in the sky, casting a golden hue over the path ahead. Fiona's steps grew slower, each movement laden with the memories she carried. Alisdair walked beside her, a steady presence in the shifting currents of her emotions.

"And did ye find yer way back?" Alisdair prompted gently, his voice a comforting anchor in the sea of Fiona's recollections.

Fiona nodded, her gaze distant yet focused. "I stumbled through the storm, battered by icy winds and weary to my bones. Just when I thought all hope was lost, a figure emerged from the blizzard—a hunter from our clan who had been tracking my footsteps. He guided me back to safety, his quiet strength a stark contrast to my reckless determination."

As she spoke, Fiona's eyes shimmered with unshed tears, the vulnerability of that moment still raw in her heart. Alisdair remained silent, letting her words weave a tapestry of resilience and regret.

"That day, I learned the hardest lesson of all," Fiona choked. "Strength is not just in shouldering burdens alone but also in knowing when to lean on others for support. My stubbornness nearly cost me everything, but it also taught me the value of humility and trust."

Alisdair reached out, his hand lightly brushing her arm as if offering silent solidarity. Fiona met his gaze, gratitude shining in her eyes for his understanding without judgment. In that shared moment of vulnerability and connection, a newfound acceptance replaced the weight of her past mistakes.

"Ye truly are as stubborn as the legends claim," Alisdair remarked as they neared the stronghold's gates, the walls rising stoically against the backdrop of the Highlands.

"Stubbornness? Nay, 'tis merely a fair division of labor," Fiona retorted, a grin playing at the corners of her mouth. "Wouldn't want ye thinking us McAfees shirk our duties, after all."

"Perish the thought," he responded, his voice filled with amusement.

As the pair entered the keep, the sound of their merriment echoed off the stone walls, heralding the return of the hunters and the promise of a feast. But beneath the surface of their jests, there lingered respect and mutual understanding.

THE GREAT HALL of the McAfee keep reverberated with the low hum of evening preparations as Fiona approached her father, the laird seated at the head of the long oak table. His stern visage softened upon her approach, his piercing gaze inquiring silently.

"Father," Fiona began steadily, "may I extend an invitation to Alisdair and his brothers for supper this eve? His company would be most welcome. And it was he who slayed the boar that we will be feasting on."

Laird Duncan regarded his daughter, the lines on his face etching years of wisdom and authority. After a measured pause, he nodded. "Aye, Fiona. Invite the McClain lads. 'Tis good to keep strong ties with other clans. And if they end up enemies, 'tis good to know as much as we can about them."

"Of course, Father." Fiona's lips curled upward ever so slightly as she turned to dispatch the invitation, her braid swaying with each purposeful stride.

As TWILIGHT DESCENDED upon the keep, the McClain brothers made their entrance, the heavy wooden door closing behind them with a resounding thud. Alisdair's led the way, followed by Lachlan's easy gait and Brodie's quiet step.

"Welcome," Fiona greeted, extending a hand first to Alisdair, whose firm grip spoke volumes of battles past and present. Her eyes then flitted to Lachlan, who offered a roguish smile and a wink that brought a momentary warmth to her cheeks.

Moira, with a glint of mischief that had Brodie smiling, sidled up beside him, engaging him in a conversation that entertained both. Ailis found herself drawn into the grinning Lachlan, their exchange subdued but sincere.

Fiona observed the pairings unfold, a silent acknowledgment passing between her and Alisdair. There was an ease in their proximity, a shared understanding. Neither wanted to be political pawns, but instead, they were truly getting to know the real person.

Laughter and soft chatter filled the space as the group congregated near the hearth, the flickering firelight casting a warm glow over the assembly. The weight of legacy and loyalty pressed upon them all, yet, for a fleeting moment, the prospect of unity and friendship held sway.

Fiona, acutely aware of the scrutiny from her father, maintained a composed facade. In the presence of the McClain brothers, the future was not merely a question of her desires but a matter of strategic alliances.

Fiona watched as Ailis, her usually reserved sister, was caught in a cascade of giggles, her cheeks flushed with genuine amusement as she spoke with Lachan McClain.

"Yer pleased," Alisdair remarked, his voice low and tinged with curiosity as he stepped to Fiona's side. "What stirs such mirth in yer heart?"

Turning toward him, Fiona inclined her head toward their siblings. "It is a rare gift, to see Ailis so at ease with one she barely knows," she confessed. "She is usually quite shy when she finds herself one-on-one with a man."

Alisdair followed her gaze. "Aye, Lachlan can charm even the most guarded person." Pride laced his tone.

Laird McAfee watched the three McClain brothers with an appraising eye. With each observation, he weighed their worth, both for their character and for the potential they held as allies— or threats.

The weight of his scrutiny was almost tangible. Fiona sensed it acutely. It was a stark reminder of the role she would one day inherit, the mantle of leadership that would fall upon her shoulders. Her father's gaze met hers across the room.

In the solemnity of the moment, Fiona regarded Alisdair once more. He stood across from her now. She pondered the curious twist of fate that had brought them together this night, a meeting orchestrated by political necessity but warmed by the flickering hope of something deeper.

As the fire crackled and the shadows lengthened, Fiona imagined, just for a moment, a future where her desires aligned with the obligations of her birthright. It was a dangerous indulgence, yet as she watched Alisdair converse with her father, she could not help but wonder if the heart might sometimes find its own path amid duty.

The dining hall echoed with the clinking of goblets and the whisper of tartans sliding over wooden benches as the family settled for supper. Laird Duncan surveyed his guests with a measured gaze that spoke of a mind attuned to the subtleties of clan politics.

"Tell me," he began, "the tales that weave through our country speak of peculiar customs within the McClain bloodline. Why does your youngest inherit, when tradition bestows such honor upon the firstborn?"

Alisdair McClain met the laird's inquiry calmly. "Aye, 'tis

unconventional," he conceded, "but tradition within our clan holds that the seventh son possesses an insight… a fortuity that is not common among men."

"Seven sons in every generation," Fiona murmured, adrift on the currents of legacy and lore. She watched as Alisdair's broad shoulders eased under the weight of his words.

"Strange happenings, too, are spoken of," Laird Duncan pressed on, his eyes narrowing slightly. "Is there truth to these whispers that dance on the wind?"

Lachlan's charming smile did not falter, though his answer was carefully crafted. "Stories grow in the telling, Laird. The peculiar becomes strange, the unexplained turns into legend."

Across from Fiona, Alisdair's gaze found hers, holding it with an intensity that bridged the space between them. It was as if he sought solace in her clear blue eyes, a reprieve from the scrutiny of her father's questions. When Duncan turned to him next, he carried a note of curiosity tinged with respect in his voice.

"Ye bear no bitterness, Alisdair? To be the eldest and yet watch as your younger brother inherits what by rights could be yours?"

There was a pause as Alisdair contemplated his response. "In truth, there is a part of me that yearns for the right to lead my clan," he admitted. "But resentment finds little foothold when one understands the necessity of fate's design."

"And what ability does your brother possess that marks him as leader?" Laird Duncan prodded further, not unkindly.

Lachlan interjected before the silence grew too ponderous. "I guess you could call it luck." He tilted his head with a nonchalant grace that contradicted the gravity of the conversation.

"Fortune favors the bold," Fiona remarked. She considered the ties that bound duty to desire, the delicate dance of destiny that ensnared both the laird's daughter and the warrior across from her. In Alisdair's steady gaze, she discerned the reflection of her inner conflict. Longing versus obligation. She must choose somehow.

As the meal progressed, the discussion ebbed and flowed around notions of leadership, inheritance, and the intangible qualities that made a clan endure. Fiona listened, her senses attuned not just to the words but to the unspoken language of glances and gestures that wove through the dialogue.

Duty, sacrifice, and the ever-present tension between personal desires and political responsibilities hung over the table like a canopy. And beneath it all, Fiona perceived the stirrings of something perilous and potent—an emotion that threatened to unravel the very fabric of her resolve.

The remnants of supper lingered in the air as the company migrated to the small parlor, a chamber where the McAfee clan had often whiled away evenings with laughter and spirited conversations.

"Let us play a guessing game," proposed Fiona, cutting through the polite hum of post-dinner chatter. Alisdair inclined his head in agreement, the shadows playing across his strong features as he moved to stand beside his brothers. "We sisters against the three brothers. Father will give a word. One person must act out what the word is for their teammates."

Laird Duncan settled into an ornate chair. He spied the McClain brothers, pondering whether the whispers of oddity that trailed behind them held any truth. And there, in the crucible of this innocent game, he sought to discern the mettle of Alisdair— the man who might one day claim his daughter's hand.

The game commenced with a flourish of pantomime and fervent guessing. The sisters faced off against the McClain brothers, whose camaraderie in battle translated seamlessly into this domestic arena. From Duncan's point of view, it was a well-choreographed dance, each movement, each pause pregnant with meaning.

Fiona stepped forward, commanding the room's attention. With her hands, she mimed an archer drawing a bow, her movements deliberate and fluid. "Robin Hood!" exclaimed Brodie, his voice a triumphant crescendo among the murmurings of approval.

Next, Lachlan took a turn, his frame exuding a playful ease that contradicted the sharpness of his intellect. He enacted the forging of a sword, his arms hammering the air with invisible steel. "Excalibur!" Ailis called, her laughter mingling with the fire's crackle.

Alisdair stood, a figure of stoic elegance, and began a silent portrayal of taming a wild stallion. Fiona guessed correctly, her smile a reflection of admiration and something deeper, something yet unspoken. Their eyes met across the divide of siblings and kin, an unvoiced conversation passing between them.

Through the progression of the game, Laird Duncan watched, not just the performance but the interplay of glances, the subtle shifts of body language. The way Fiona's eyes sparkled with delight at Alisdair's correct guesses, the manner in which Moira leaned in closer to Brodie when he struggled to convey his wordless clues.

As the merriment unfolded, the laird's gaze hardened, considering the implications of these alliances forming under his roof. Were the McClain brothers as peculiar as the rumors suggested? Or did their reputation merely mask a deeper cunning, a strategic prowess that could prove advantageous—or perilous—to the McAfee lineage?

THE HOUR HAD grown late, and the parlor's warmth began to wane. Laird Duncan rose from his seat. "'Tis time we all sought our beds," he declared, casting a paternal glance at his daughters and their guests.

Fiona, her blue eyes still shining with the mirth of the evening's entertainment, nodded obediently. She led the way alongside her sisters, escorting the McClain brothers to the heavy oak door that marked the threshold between the keep's stone walls and the cool embrace of the Scottish night.

As they approached the door, Ailis murmured a soft excuse, her gaze briefly flitting toward Lachlan before she retreated with Moira, whose own eyes were lit with an unspoken secret shared with Brodie. The sudden departure left Fiona and Alisdair standing in a pocket of silence, the atmosphere thick with unvoiced sentiments.

Alisdair turned to Fiona. His blue eyes held hers. "Fiona," he rumbled, "I dinna wish to part with just a simple farewell."

His words hung between them, a delicate invitation. Fiona's breath caught in her throat, her usually confident demeanor faltering under the weight of his gaze. Her heart urged her closer.

And then, they kissed—a fleeting brush of lips that spoke of promise and restraint. It was a chaste kiss by any measure, yet it ignited a fire within Fiona, a yearning for something deeper than anything she had ever known.

As Alisdair's brothers called him, breaking the spell with their abrupt departure, Fiona wished for his lips upon hers. They parted with whispered goodnights, leaving a trail of unspoken desires lingering in the air.

Fiona made her way back to her chamber, her mind racing. In the solitude of her room, she paced before the hearth, where embers glowed like dying stars. How was it that Alisdair McClain, a man who wielded his authority with such casual ease, had managed to stir such unfamiliar emotions within her?

No other man had ever drawn her gaze twice, but Alisdair— with his sharp wit and commanding presence—had somehow breached the fortress of her heart.

Duty and desire warred within her, a tempest matched only by the howling winds outside. Fiona, fierce warrior of clan McAfee, lay adrift in a sea of emotion.

It was not merely kisses she desired from Alisdair McClain, she realized, but the possibility of a future entwined with his—a future that might demand sacrifice but promised the sweetness of a love yet to be fully discovered.

With these ideas swirling in her head, Fiona surrendered to the embrace of her bed, the linen sheets cool against her heated skin. As sleep claimed her, the echoes of Alisdair's kiss lingered, a tender caress upon her soul.

MALCOLM SINCLAIR STOOD before his father, the lines of worry etched into his rugged face a testament to the weight of his burden. He shifted uneasily in the dimly lit chamber as the flickering shadows cast by the fire danced across the walls.

"Father," he began, "I have observed Fiona McAfee. Her eyes, they shine with favor, but not toward our kin. 'Tis Alisdair McClain who has captured her fancy."

Arran Sinclair, seated upon his carved wooden chair, regarded his son with an unwavering gaze that had seen many winters and the strife they brought. "And what thoughts crossed thy mind upon this discovery?" he asked, his tone measured yet expectant.

"Dark thoughts, Father. I contemplated riding forth to challenge Alisdair—in the heat of my ire, even to slay him." Malcolm clenched his hands, whitening his knuckles. "But such an act would ignite a feud between our clans, a war we cannot afford."

"Aye," Arran nodded solemnly. "Yer consideration of the clan's welfare is commendable. What do you propose instead?"

With resolve hardening in his piercing blue eyes, Malcolm straightened to his full imposing height. "I shall take matters into my own hands. I plan to kidnap Fiona and bring her to our keep. There, she will remain until she consents to unite our houses through marriage."

"Ye must tread carefully, Malcolm. Such a deed could still provoke the wrath of the McClains if discovered." Arran's expression was stern, his advice borne of years of leadership and the delicate balance of alliances. "Dress in a tartan that belongs to no clan. Disguise yer intent, and above all," he paused, the gravity of his words like a stone in the silence, "ye must not bring Fiona back here to our keep. Take her elsewhere, to a place where none can trace her to us."

Malcolm nodded, understanding the consequences should his actions lead back to their door. The mere thought of dishonoring his clan galled him, yet the prospect of securing their future through this union drove him forward.

"Wherever I take her, she will be treated with the respect due a lady of her standing," Malcolm vowed, his ambition to strengthen his clan evident in his resolute stance.

"See that it is so," Arran replied, a note of finality in his voice. "Remember, son, the fate of our house rests upon yer shoulders. A heavy burden, indeed, but one I trust ye are capable of bearing."

Malcolm bowed, the weight of his father's trust anchoring him to his duty. With his path set, he turned to leave, the echoes of his footsteps a steady rhythm against the stone floor. He would never be bested by a McClain. He would not allow it!

✦

CHAPTER EIGHT

ALISDAIR STOOD BEFORE Laird Duncan, his broad shoulders back and chin held high. The fire's crackle filled the hall as he presented his counsel, the flames casting dancing shadows upon the stone walls.

"Laird," Alisdair began, "I believe it would be most beneficial for Lady Fiona to acquaint herself with the lands and kin of Clan McClain. It is not just her presence I seek, but that of all three McAfee sisters, accompanied by a retinue of seven guards to ensure their safety. I would be happy to provide the guards, or ye may provide them if that pleases ye. I think a visit to our clan would help to put to rest the worries ye both have about Clan McClain."

Laird Duncan regarded Alisdair from his grand seat at the head of the long table. His eyes met Alisdair's with an unwavering gaze that weighed the merit of his proposal.

"Your request is heard, Alisdair," the laird replied after a pause that stretched as far as the moors themselves. "The journey shall be as you say. Prepare for departure on the morrow. I will send seven men to guard my daughters. And they will travel with ye and yer brothers for the extra protection ye may provide."

FIONA AND HER sisters gathered in the chambers above, the air ripe with anticipation.

"Five nights in McClain territory, can ye imagine?" Moira exclaimed, her eyes bright as the stars that would guide their way. She deftly folded garments into a traveling chest, her movements betraying none of the nerves she felt. "Father's never even let us leave McAfee land before. I think he's ready to let ye marry Alisdair, Fiona."

"I think so as well," Ailis added. "We shall learn much, and we'll have new stories to tell."

Fiona watched over the preparations. She could not deny the stirring of adventure within her own heart. "Let us not forget the honor in this invitation. We represent Clan McAfee. Our conduct must reflect the dignity of our father's name."

Her sisters nodded, understanding the unspoken weight of responsibility that rested upon their shoulders, as heavy as the tartan cloaks they would don against the chill of the journey ahead.

"Of course, Fiona," Ailis assured her, "we shall carry ourselves with grace."

"Grace, and a wee bit of mischief," Moira added, her playful wink sparking laughter among them.

With their belongings readied and hearts brimming with the promise of the unknown, the sisters retired for the night, their dreams filled with the impending journey.

FIONA AND HER sisters traveled the half day's distance to Clan McClain with Alisdair and his brothers. As soon as they saw the castle in the distance, Fiona couldn't help but stare. The stone walls rose before them like silent sentinels guarding the secrets within. Alisdair McClain, flanked by his brothers Lachlan and Brodie, moved to ride beside the sisters.

"Welcome to our home," Alisdair sang as they stopped their

horses before the keep, men coming to take care of their horses for them. Alisdair dismounted and helped Fiona down from her horse. She did not mention the ache she felt from riding for so long, but it was there nonetheless.

"Thank ye for havin' us," Fiona replied, her tone matching his for authority, yet laced with an undercurrent of curiosity. Her eyes surveyed the stronghold, seeking to understand the people who thrived in its shadow.

After hearing tales of the McClains for so many years, she couldn't wait to see what the people of the clan were truly like.

With a courteous nod, Alisdair turned, leading the party through the arched entrance. Within the bailey, the air was filled with the muted sounds of life: the clanging of a smithy at work, the laughter of children playing, and the distant lowing of cattle.

"First, let me introduce ye to my parents," Alisdair enthused while his brothers helped her sisters, waiting to guide them into the great hall where two figures rose from their chairs to greet their guests. His father, Laird Fearghas, stood tall, his once blond hair now mostly white. Beside him stood his wife, Lady Caitlin, her graceful beauty untouched by time, her hair still long and blond. They were the living embodiment of the clan's esteemed heritage.

"'Tis an honor to meet the daughters of Clan McAfee," Laird Fearghas boomed. His sharp gaze, softened by a welcoming smile, took measure of the sisters.

"Ye grace us with yer presence," Lady Caitlin added.

"Thank ye, Laird, Lady," Fiona replied, dipping her head in respect.

"Come now, let us acquaint ye with the rest of our kin," Alisdair continued, leading them deeper into the heart of the castle. With each introduction, Fiona felt the threads of history weave around her, binding her ever closer to the McClains' storied past—a past that was both alien and strangely familiar.

As the McClain clan bustled about, Fiona stood slightly apart, her eyes keen and discerning as she observed their interactions.

There was Alisdair, sharing a quiet word with his mother. Her laughter filled the hall as she patted his arm with a tender familiarity that spoke of motherly affection.

Her sisters, Ailis and Moira, appeared entranced by the lively exchanges around them, yet Fiona's gaze lingered with an edge of skepticism.

"Ye must be famished after yer journey." Caitlin gently broke into Fiona's observations. "Would ye honor us by breaking bread at our table?"

"Of course, Lady," Fiona replied measuredly, betraying none of her inner turmoil. "We would be most grateful."

Caitlin's smile deepened, a knowing glint in her eye as if she perceived the careful dance of diplomacy playing out before her. With a graceful gesture, she led them to the grand dining hall where the table was laden with an abundance of food, showing both the clan's prosperity and generosity.

Taking her place among the McClains, Fiona's senses were greeted with the rich aromas of roasted meats and freshly baked bread. The chatter of voices melded into a tapestry of sound, each thread a vibrant part of the whole. Yet, beneath the surface pleasantries, Fiona remained vigilant—watchful for any sign that might reveal the true nature of the McClains.

Despite the opulence before her, she could not ignore the steady thrum of caution pulsing through her veins. She glanced sideways at Alisdair, who gave her an imperceptible nod, a silent reassurance that all was well.

"Ye must tell us of your training, Lady Fiona," urged Lady Caitlin, her eyes filled with genuine interest. "I've heard tales of your prowess with a bow and arrow."

"Aye," Laird Fearghas chimed in. "Our Alisdair speaks highly of your skills and valor."

"Such flattery," Fiona replied with a smile. "Our training was simple. Our father longed for sons, and he instead received three daughters, so he trained us in arms, as if we were sons. I excel with a bow and arrow, Ailis with knives, and Moira with her sword."

"And are you happy ye can defend yerselves?" Lady Caitlin asked admiringly.

Moira answered for herself and her sisters. "We are."

"It takes discipline and dedication to become as good as the three of you are reputed to be," Fearghas declared, raising his goblet in a silent toast.

"Ah, but what of merriment and mischief?" interjected Lachlan, sliding into the conversation with a sly grin. "Surely there is room for joy along with duty?"

"Joy is found in the fulfillment of duty," Fiona replied, challenging him with her steady gaze.

"Spoken like a true warrior." Lachlan chuckled. "But even warriors need respite from the clanging of swords. Tell me, do ye ever indulge in pursuits less… martial?"

"Occasionally," Fiona conceded, the corner of her mouth twitching upward. "When time permits, I find solace in the quiet of the glens."

"Ah, a kindred spirit!" Lachlan exclaimed. "The wilderness whispers secrets to those willing to listen. Perhaps I could show ye some hidden gems on our lands."

Alisdair shook his head. "I think not."

Fiona regarded Alisdair for a moment. "I can answer for myself."

"Ye speak of the wilderness as if it were a confidant," observed Lachlan, leaning forward slightly, acting as if Alisdair hadn't spoken. "Is it the silence or the echoes of nature that ye cherish?"

"Both," Fiona admitted, her guard lowering just a fraction as she met his probing gaze. "There is wisdom in the stillness."

"Ye are full of surprises, Lady Fiona," Lachlan remarked, his tone warm with admiration. "I had not anticipated such depth beneath the warrior's facade."

"Nor I the philosopher beneath the charmer's veneer," she retorted, the words slipping out before she could catch them.

After that, Fiona McAfee quietly observed the McClain family's revelry. Her keen gaze rarely wavered from the man who had brought her to these foreign yet inviting lands.

It was then that a subtle shift caught her attention—a softening in Alisdair's posture as his younger brother Boyd approached him. A lean figure with eyes as piercing as winter frost, Boyd moved with a deliberate grace. He whispered something into Alisdair's ear, perhaps a private jest, since the corners of Alisdair's mouth twitched upward in a rare display of unguarded mirth. He rested his hand on Boyd's shoulder, a silent testament to their fraternal bond.

"This is my youngest brother, Boyd, who will someday be laird of Clan McClain."

Fiona felt a pang of something unexpected—a yearning for such intimacy within her own clan. She watched as Alisdair ruffled Boyd's blond hair, an affectionate gesture that spoke of their closeness. In this fleeting interaction, Fiona glimpsed the tender core beneath Alisdair's exterior. Her admiration for the McClains deepened.

The moment was broken by the commanding timbre of Fearghas McClain, patriarch of the clan, as he rose to address those gathered. With a presence as sturdy as the castle walls, Laird Fearghas embodied the very essence of leadership.

"Kin and honored guests," he boomed, "let us not forget the journey our ancestors took to forge this stronghold. 'Twas during England's turmoil that they traveled north, seeking solace in these highland crags."

Every ear bent to listen. Fiona found herself ensnared by the tales of valor and sacrifice. Fearghas recounted stories of the clan's past with reverence, each word etched with the weight of honor and duty. He gestured grandly, painting pictures of battles fought for the sanctity of their land and people.

"Through blood and fire, we've carved our legacy," he declared, his gaze sweeping across the faces of his sons. "And so shall we preserve it—not just for ourselves, but for the generations to come. For without honor, what are we but whispers on the wind?"

Fiona listened, rapt, as the history of the McClains unfolded before her. It was more than the recitation of events—it was the sharing of a sacred trust, a declaration of identity. She was drawn in by the gravity of their tale, understanding at last the bedrock upon which the McClains built their lives.

"Ye carry yerself with the strength of a chieftain, Fiona McAfee," Caitlin began softly yet resonantly within the stone walls. "Tell me, what is it like for ye, knowing that ye and yer husband will one day be leading yer kin?"

The question stirred Fiona, and she opened up to the matriarch of the McClain clan. "It is an honor, though not one without its trials." Fiona paused, choosing her words with care. "As women, our leadership is oft under more scrutiny than that of our male counterparts."

"Aye." Caitlin nodded, understanding lighting her eyes. "We must be twice as wise and thrice as brave to earn half the respect."

"Aye," Fiona agreed with a wry smile. "But I wouldnae trade my duties for the world. 'Tis a sacred trust."

"Ye speak truth," Caitlin affirmed, her smile reflecting pride. "Our clans may thrive or falter on our counsel. 'Tis a heavy burden, but also a great privilege."

As they spoke, Alisdair appeared, his presence commanding even in silence. "Might I steal Fiona away for a tour of the castle?" he asked, his gaze seeking his mother's.

"With pleasure," Caitlin replied, giving Fiona a knowing glance before excusing herself.

Alisdair extended his arm to Fiona, and she placed her hand atop it, feeling the solid strength beneath her fingers. They traversed the corridors, his footsteps sure and measured. He guided her through the great hall, past the dining chamber, and into the heart of the McClain stronghold.

"Here we have the armory." Alisdair pushed open a heavy

wooden door. Inside, rows of gleaming weapons stood sentinel, each piece a testament to the clan's readiness to defend their lands. "Every blade here has tasted battle," he remarked with pride.

"Ye honor your ancestors with such diligence," Fiona observed, her gaze lingering on a sword with a hilt wrought in the shape of an eagle.

"Aye," Alisdair replied, moving closer. "This was that of one of my great-grandfather's. He wielded it during the skirmishes when we first came to these lands, fleeing unrest in England."

"The weight of history lies heavy upon these blades," Fiona whispered, tracing the intricate metalwork.

Their tour continued, each room unveiling more of the clan's legacy.

Finally, they were in a quiet corner of the castle, away from the watchful eyes of kin and clan, peeking out a window over the land.

"Ye've shown me much this eve," Fiona began steadily as she gazed out upon the view, "and yet I find myself adrift in thoughts most troubling."

Alisdair turned toward her, his expression earnest, the lines of duty etched upon his brow. "Speak freely, Fiona. What casts shadows upon yer heart?"

Her blue eyes met his, a tempest of doubt and longing swirling within their depths. "I came to yer lands wary of intentions hidden 'neath pleasantries and grandeur. I feared that alliances sought through marriage were naught but political machinations."

"Such fears are not without merit," he conceded, his stance solemn, the fading light casting his face in relief. "But hear me now, Fiona McAfee, my intentions toward ye are as clear as the skies above our heads. I seek not just alliance, but companionship, understanding... perhaps even love, should it deign to take root." He shook his head. "For me this is a political alliance, aye, but more than that... It's one of the heart."

Fiona's breath caught at the sincerity lacing his words, her warrior's guard beginning to fray at the edges. "And what of duty?" she asked, the question heavy on her tongue. "How does one weigh the heart's yearnings against the needs of the clan?"

"'Tis a balance most delicate," Alisdair replied, moving closer, his presence both commanding and comforting. "One I believe we can navigate together, should ye be willing."

Fiona pondered his words, the stoic facade she presented to the world softening as she considered the man before her. Could it be that her initial skepticism was misplaced? That among the tapestries of duty and honor, a thread of genuine affection had woven itself into the narrative?

"Perhaps…" Fiona murmured, "perhaps there is room for trust to grow where suspicion once took root."

"Nothing would honor me more." Alisdair reached out gently for her hand, his touch a promise of solidarity.

Fiona's doubts lessened. The path forward was fraught with uncertainty, but the possibility of unity—of shared burdens and intertwined destinies—began to paint a future she had not dared to envision.

"Then let us walk this path together and see where it may lead." His unwavering gaze fortified her resolve.

Hand in hand, Fiona and Alisdair stepped through the arched doorway, returning to the grand hall where the McClain family gathered. The warmth of the hearth greeted them, a stark contrast to the cool twilight that had begun to envelop the castle grounds. As they entered, the murmurs of conversation ceased, all eyes turning toward the pair. Alisdair's brothers Lachlan and Brodie exchanged knowing glances.

All eyes were upon Fiona, and she expected that. She hoped to marry the eldest son of Clan McClain. He'd made his feelings about the alliance abundantly clear. She was there to see if she would do well as a member of their family.

As Malcolm Sinclair surveyed the ragged silhouette of the abandoned stronghold, his steely blue eyes betrayed no hint of doubt. The ruins stood defiantly near Clan McClain's borders—a strategic vantage point for the task at hand. He had handpicked his father's most able men, those whose loyalty to the Sinclair name was as unwavering as the ancient stones before them.

"Ye'll don these." Malcolm's commands echoed against the walls as he distributed McAfee tartans to all the men assembled. "We'll not be marked as Sinclairs."

A murmur of assent rippled through the men, though it carried undercurrents of uncertainty. One among them, a burly warrior with furrowed brow, could contain his concern no longer. "But Laird McAfee stands as friend to our laird. Why go against such bonds?"

"Quiet your tongue," Malcolm snapped, his sharp glare cutting through the lingering protest. "Duty calls us to act, and we shall obey without question." His tone left no room for further debate, the weight of his father's legacy pressing down upon him like the heavy Scottish fog.

Returning to the heart of the matter, he meticulously outlined the plan, each detail a testament to his cunning mind. "We take Fiona—not as foes, but as strategists securing an advantage for our clan." His words hung in the cold air, imbued with the gravity of their mission.

The men gathered closer, their faces a mix of grim resolve and flickering doubt, as Malcolm delineated every step of the abduction. And though none could see it, the smallest crack appeared in the fortress of Malcolm's composure—the slightest tremor of the burden he bore, the duty that demanded sacrifice and blurred the lines between honor and necessity.

✦

CHAPTER NINE

FIONA MCAFEE FOUND herself in the middle of the bustle of the Clan McClain's morning rituals. She stood against the stone parapet, her gaze following the disciplined movements of the kilted warriors below. Their swords clanged in a harmonious rhythm, each strike demonstrating their dedication and prowess.

Her sisters, beguiled by the wild beauty of the expansive estate, ventured further afield under Lady McClain's gentle guidance, leaving Fiona to her observations. The air was crisp, carrying the distant laughter of Ailis and Moira as they disappeared into the forest, their spirits unburdened by the importance of the decision weighing so heavily on Fiona's mind.

As she watched, Alisdair commanded the training yard with an authority that resonated from his very core. His muscular frame moved with precision, his sword a mere extension of his will. Beside him, his brother Lachlan mirrored his actions, though his strikes lacked the gravity of Alisdair's.

As she watched, she could picture Alisdair in the McAfee plaid, leading her father's men. She knew her father grew weary of always leading, and he was ready for a man he found worthy to take his place. She only hoped her father would find Alisdair as worthy as she did. To her, Alisdair was the answer to the McAfees' prayers.

He was a strong man, who was destined for leadership. He also made Fiona think of things that she never would have thought of before. She longed to see his bare skin, to caress him in ways that shouldn't happen before marriage.

With a quiet sigh, she turned away from the scene. Her heart was torn between the desire to believe in the honor before her eyes and the caution that her father's words had instilled since childhood.

Later, Fiona found herself standing at the edge of the training field, her gaze lingering on the castle's rugged stone facade. The clang of steel had long since ceased, leaving a stillness that hung heavy in the air. Alisdair approached from the direction of the barracks, his stride purposeful yet unhurried.

"Fair evening to ye, Fiona," he greeted. "Ye seem rather pensive."

"Good evening, Alisdair," Fiona replied. "The day has been… enlightening."

"It has?" Alisdair's blue eyes searched hers. "I would value your insight on our methods. It is not often we have the honor of hosting a warrior of another clan."

"Your men are skilled," she conceded. Yet, she held back the swell of doubts that accompanied her praise. "And they obey your every command quickly without questioning. Ye are a good leader."

"I have been trained well," Alisdair replied. "My men are loyal to me. But bonds of loyalty extend beyond blood, do they not? They are forged in trust and common cause."

"That is true," Fiona answered. Her mind raced, pondering the layers of meaning behind his words and wondering if he sensed the guarded nature of her own. Did he realize she was thinking of him as a potential husband? A potential laird for her clan? Of course, that decision wasn't hers alone, but with what she'd seen so far, she had an inkling her father would approve.

"Perhaps you would join me for a walk?" Alisdair suggested, gesturing toward the castle grounds. "The gardens are best enjoyed at this hour."

Fiona hesitated, aware that the stroll could lead them into dialogue for which she was not yet prepared. Still, the offer was genuine, and the chance to speak away from prying ears was enticing. "I would be pleased to," she finally answered, betraying none of the turmoil that churned within.

Together, they walked in the direction of the gardens, the graveled path crunching beneath their boots. Fiona remained acutely aware of Alisdair's presence beside her, the breadth of his shoulders casting a protective shadow in the dying light. They passed a bed of flowering heather, its purple blooms a stark contrast against the greenery.

"Tell me, Fiona," Alisdair began, "what you want from the future. Are you searching for a man who will lead beside you or someone who will bend to your will and allow you to make all the decisions for your clan?"

She contemplated his question. "I don't want merely a political alliance. I want a man who feels for me and I for him," Fiona explained carefully, "but whomever I marry must be willing to lead along with me, and not just take the rule of my clan from me. I must marry a man who respects me enough to give me a voice and listen to it."

"That makes sense." Alisdair gazed upon the horizon where the first stars began to twinkle. "Many women would not want to be involved in leading their clan. They would want their husbands to do so. Or they would want all the control, and not leave any to their husbands. Hearing you want to share helps me understand so much more about you."

Their conversation flowed, touching upon matters of clan, kinship, and the delicate balance of power that dictated their lives. Fiona felt the pull of admiration for Alisdair's wisdom, yet she could not shake her need for caution where he was concerned.

The rumors of Clan McClain were so odd, and though she'd seen nothing that would make her feel they were true with her own eyes, she still wondered where they had come from.

"Tell me, Alisdair," Fiona began steadily despite the fluttering of uncertainty within her chest, "what dreams does a man like ye have? Beyond the call of clan and sword, what visions do ye cherish in the quiet of night?"

Alisdair's gaze met hers, blue eyes reflecting the solemnity of her inquiry. "My dreams are for my people, the strength of our bonds, and the prosperity of our lands," he replied. "And yet, there is also the dream of companionship, one who understands the weight of leadership."

She weighed his response, searching the depths of those earnest eyes for a flicker of deceit. But there was nothing but sincerity. This vexed her, for she understood the complexity of alliances built on the fragile foundation of sentiment.

THE FOLLOWING MORNING, Fiona was walking with her sisters through the same area, and as Ailis talked on and on about how much she would love to be mistress of a place such as Clan McClain, she knew that Boyd, the youngest son of the current laird, would be much too young for her to marry.

It was then that murmurs drifted toward them.

"Brother, the McAfee lass is comely, aye, but think ye not of the power such a union would bring?" The voice belonged to Lachlan.

"Power is but one consideration, Lachlan," Alisdair replied. "An alliance must be rooted in more than advantage. Respect and understanding are the bedrock upon which true partnerships are built."

"Respect and understanding," Fiona murmured. What about the love she sought? Did he think nothing of that? She felt her doubts reinforced by their words, this candid exchange revealing layers of motive that left her heart longing for more. If that's all she was to get from a marriage, why not marry Malcolm Sinclair? Well, other than the reason that he made her skin want to crawl off her body and jump into the loch to cleanse itself.

Moira glanced at Fiona, obviously wondering how her sister

felt about what they had heard, but when Ailis shook her head slightly, Moira remained silent.

Later, Fiona walked with Alisdair again, around the loch this time, and he gestured to a stone bench, covered with moss. "Come," Alisdair murmured, extending his arm toward the bench. "Let us rest awhile and speak of lighter matters."

But Fiona remained standing, her gaze locked onto the horizon where the last light of day surrendered to the encroaching night. A decision loomed before her, as imposing as the McClain stronghold that towered in the distance.

"Another time, perhaps," she replied. "For now, I find peace in the solitude of my reflections."

Fiona wandered through the gardens, her thoughts a tempest as turbulent as the skies above the rolling Highlands. The stone path beneath her feet led to the sanctuary of her family's quarters within the McClain keep.

Upon entering the chamber she shared with her sisters, Fiona found Ailis seated by the hearth. The flickering flames cast a warm glow upon her gentle features, and the soft hum that escaped her lips ceased as she lifted her gaze to meet Fiona's troubled eyes.

"Ye appear as though the weight o' the world rests on yer shoulders, sister." Ailis patted the space beside her on the plush bench.

Fiona joined her, exhaling deeply, her braid falling over her shoulder like a cascade of burnished copper. "Aye," she admitted, her voice barely above a whisper. "I ken not what course to chart."

Ailis reached out, her touch as comforting as her smile was tender. "Let not fear guide ye, Fiona. Trust in the wisdom of yer own heart. Our father's words are forged from caution, but 'tis yer life to live."

The elder McAfee pondered her sister's counsel, her brow furrowing. "But what if my heart leads me astray? What if my desires blind me to the perils that lie in wait?"

"Then ye'll face those perils with courage, as ye always have," Ailis assured her.

As they spoke, the door creaked open. Moira bounded into the room, her presence a burst of energy that dispelled the shadows of doubt. "Why such somber faces?" she asked, tilting her head with playful curiosity.

"'Tis the matter of alliances and intentions that weighs heavily upon our sister," Ailis explained, glancing at Fiona.

Moira approached, her lithe form settling across from them. "Ah, the dance of courtship and politics!" she exclaimed. "But remember, Fiona, 'twas not just talk of clans and kinship that lit up yer eyes when ye spoke o' Alisdair. Recall the laughter and the shared secrets, the moments of true connection."

"True," Fiona conceded, a small smile tugging at the corners of her mouth. "There were moments untainted by the machinations of power."

"Then cling to those," Moira urged, gesturing emphatically. "Let those moments be yer compass, for they speak of something far deeper than mere alliances."

Fiona regarded her sisters, their unwavering support helping her. In the quiet confidence of Ailis and the fiery optimism of Moira, she found a semblance of peace amidst the turmoil.

"Thank ye, both," Fiona murmured, her heart swelling with gratitude for the bond they shared. "I shall take heed of yer words and let the morrow reveal its own truths."

THE MISTY AIR of the McClain castle grounds was heavy with anticipation as Fiona McAfee faced Alisdair McClain in the training yard. Clad in leathers that hugged her athletic form, she wielded her sister's sword with solemnity, knowing this bout was more than a mere display of martial prowess.

"Are ye prepared to test the mettle of a McAfee, Alisdair?"

Fiona's voice carried across the courtyard, her tone laced with the gravity of her intentions.

"Only if ye are ready to witness the strength of a McClain," Alisdair replied, his own weapon at the ready.

As their swords met with a resounding clang, a dance of steel and strategy unfolded. Each strike, each parry, was a question posed, a measure taken—not just of skill, but of sincerity and dedication. Fiona sought to uncover the depth of Alisdair's commitment to her safety and that of her kin. She needed to discover if his heart was as steadfast as his blade.

With every advance and retreat, Fiona found herself drawn closer to the man before her, his presence commanding yet enigmatic. The intensity of the moment bound them, warrior to warrior, spirit to spirit.

Their eyes locked, meeting in an unspoken understanding. In the space between breaths, in the middle of the symphony of clashing swords, they acknowledged something profound— something that transcended the politics of marriage and alliance. It was a recognition of mutual respect, a hint of burgeoning desire that neither could fully dismiss.

Alisdair pressed forward, the force of his attack driving Fiona back step by step. She countered with equal fervor, her mind alight with the ferocity of the spar, yet troubled by the stirrings within her chest. The sword was not her favored weapon. She knew she could not outfight him, though the way he treated her when she was defeated would tell her what kind of man he truly was.

"Ye fight with honor, Fiona," Alisdair praised, even as he advanced.

"And ye, Alisdair, possess a loyalty that cannot be feigned," Fiona conceded, her words carrying the weight of her conflicted emotions.

Their blades met once more, the clash ringing out. As they paused, the charged atmosphere lingered around them, an invisible shroud that cloaked the true nature of their connection.

THE ECHOES OF steel against steel still rang in her ears, a testament to their earlier clash, but it was the unspoken duel between heart and mind that held Fiona captive now. Alisdair's prowess had been unmistakable. Yet beyond the admiration stirred by his skill lay a maze of trepidation, each pathway leading to a different facet of uncertainty.

Could she entrust her heart to a man whose life was consumed by clan allegiances and strategic maneuvers? The very essence of their encounter on the sparring field had revealed a mutual respect, a shared language of blades and honor. But respect was the foundation upon which alliances were built, not necessarily love. And love was a luxury often sacrificed upon the altar of duty.

Her fingers trailed along the cold, rough edges of the battlement, a poignant reminder of the permanence of stone and the nature of human affections. An alliance with the McClains promised strength and unity for her people, yet the specter of political machinations loomed large, casting long shadows over the sincerity of any tender words exchanged.

"Can a heart divided by loyalty ever truly be mine?" Fiona murmured into the encroaching night.

As darkness enveloped the land, wrapping the castle in its silent embrace, Fiona remained atop the battlements, a solitary figure wrestling with the dichotomy of desire and responsibility.

If she was not worried about love, then marriage to Malcolm Sinclair made more sense, as their lands were together, and they could make a larger clan out of them. But if her heart were to be considered... well then only Alisdair would do. For she had fallen in love, and she wanted nothing to do with it.

She decided then and there that what she needed to do was talk to Alisdair McClain and ask if he had true feelings for her or if he was simply wanting a political alliance, for she would not be a pawn in anyone's games.

✦

CHAPTER TEN

FIONA CROSSED THE threshold of the grand hall, scanning the tapestried walls for the lady of the house. Whispered conversations hushed at her arrival, the weight of her reputation preceding her—a warrior with a mind as sharp as the blade at her side.

"Lady McClain," Fiona began commandingly.

"Ah, Fiona McAfee, what brings you to our hearth?" Caitlin inquired, her smile genuine, her gaze perceptive.

"Rumors are as rife as air," Fiona began, her blue eyes locking onto Caitlin's. "It is said that the McClains seek to weave alliances with other highland clans to upset the balance of allies. They speak of ambitions to lead all the highlands."

Caitlin's laugh, light and untroubled, echoed through the hall. "I've heard no such tales within these walls," she replied, her eyes sparkling with mirth. "But should you desire certainty, you must lay your questions at the feet of my husband. Fearghas can dispel the shadows of doubt better than I."

With a respectful nod, Fiona took her leave, her braid swaying with each determined step toward the laird's study.

The heavy oak door groaned softly as Fiona entered Laird Fearghas McClain's sanctum, the scent of peat and parchment greeting her. He stood by the window, his broad silhouette framed against the rolling highland vista.

"Ah, Fiona," Fearghas greeted, turning from the view of his lands. "To what do I owe the pleasure?"

"Word has spread like wildfire through my clan," Fiona answered, her stance firm. "They speak of your desire to unite the highland clans beneath the McClain banner, to be sovereign over all."

Fearghas guffawed, the notion clearly as ludicrous to him as a clear day in the midst of the rainy season. "Lead all the highlands? Nay, I have no thirst for such a burden—too bitter with responsibility. My heart lies with my kin, my duty to care for the McClain clan alone."

Fiona absorbed his words, watching him closely. In his eyes, she sought the truth, and in his laughter, she searched for deception. Yet, there was an ease about him that could not be feigned, a sincerity that spoke of a leader content with the mantle he already bore.

"Thank ye, Laird Fearghas," Fiona replied, her voice softer now but still resonant with the authority of her lineage. "Your words have brought peace where whispers sowed discord."

"Then let it be known," Fearghas declared, "that the McClains stand by the McAfees, allies in honor and truth."

With a final, respectful inclination of her head, Fiona retreated from the laird's company.

Fiona strode from the great hall of the McClain keep, her mind awhirl with the echoes of her recent conversations. The cold Highland air caressed her cheeks, whipping strands of blond hair from the confines of her braid. She paused, allowing the brisk breeze to clear the fog of uncertainty that had clouded her thoughts.

As she gazed upon the sprawling vista of lochs and glens, sunlight dappled through the clouds, casting a soft glow over the rugged landscape. In this moment of solitude, Fiona turned inward, reflecting upon the assurance provided by Lady Caitlin and Laird Fearghas. Their laughter, devoid of malice or ambition, resonated within her, dispersing the shadows cast by the rumors like mist before the morning sun.

"Idle whispers," Fiona murmured to herself. A smile tugged

at the corners of her lips as she considered the absurdity of the tales that had so troubled her clan. Her father's concerns, though born of a protective heart, were now rooted in naught but the fertile soil of unfounded fear.

Her duty to one day lead the McAfees was paramount. Yet here, amid the rolling hills of her homeland, Fiona indulged herself by envisioning a future where her personal desires aligned with the responsibilities that awaited her.

"Mayhap there is room yet for the heart in matters of the clan," Fiona whispered, the notion taking root within her like the ancient pines that clung to the rocky crags.

With a deep breath, she squared her shoulders, the determination that marked her lineage shining bright in her piercing blue eyes.

Resolved, she turned back toward the keep, ready to share her newfound conviction with her father. For in the end, it was the bonds of honor that held the Highlands together, stronger than any whispered conspiracy or fleeting shadow of doubt.

FIONA WALKED ALONGSIDE Alisdair. The day's training was over, yet her mind wrestled with a more pressing battle—a tangle of emotions and duty that no amount of swordplay could unravel.

"Alisdair," she began steadily despite the fluttering in her chest, "I must ask you plainly. Is what lies between us naught but a strategic maneuver? Or do you hold a genuine affection for me?" Fiona's piercing blue eyes sought his, searching for the glint of truth that might dwell there.

The warrior beside her paused midstride, gazing upon the loch that mirrored the twilight sky. A silence stretched between them, not uncomfortable, but laden with the weight of a future yet to be decided. At last, Alisdair faced her, his eyes reflecting a solemn intensity.

"Truth be told," he confessed, "when first we met, my thoughts were consumed by potential alliances and their added strength. But as the days have worn on, I've come to know ye, Fiona. Ye are fierce and valiant, a woman of both wit and compassion."

A breath escaped him, as if releasing the guards around his heart. "That affection which began as embers has been kindled into a flame that I believe will grow into love. It is ye I desire for my bride, not just for the unity of our clans, but for the companionship of our souls." His declaration hung in the air, a testament to the merging of political foresight and personal longing.

Fiona stood motionless, the gentle lapping of the loch's waters whispering against the shore. She gazed into Alisdair's eyes, searching for the veiled truth within their depths. The warmth of his words still lingered in the cool evening air, and Fiona felt the steady rhythm of her heart quicken, daring to beat not just for her clan, but for herself as well.

"Alisdair," she began, her voice imbued with a softness seldom permitted to surface, "I've wrestled with the demands of my birthright and the whispers of my own heart. I believe your intentions to be true, as is the affection you profess." Her fingers grazed the hilt of her sword—an anchor to her warrior's spirit. "There is a rumor about yer clan that my father heard, and he's asked me to be sure it is untrue before I agree to an alliance between our clans."

Alisdair frowned. "There are many rumors about the McClains, and they are not true."

"I am not worried about the other rumors, as I have seen for myself yer clan is as normal as any other. The way you do things is eerily similar to the way they are done in Clan McAfee. Nay, that's not the problem. This rumor states that the McClains are trying to make allies throughout the Highlands with the singular purpose of ruling all."

Alisdair stared at her in shock for a moment, before he threw his head back and guffawed. After a moment, he got control of himself and shook his head. "Nay, that is not true. We have no desire to lead more than just our clan, which is work enough."

"That is what your mother and father both told me, but I wanted to hear the words from you." She took a deep breath. "With my father's approval, I will stand by your side not only as an ally but as a woman who follows her heart. Yes, I shall be your bride."

The decision set forth a cascade of actions to unfold. With her father, the chieftain of Clan McAfee, a half-day's journey away, immediate approval was beyond reach. A trusted soldier must carry the news, traversing the rugged terrain to deliver her intent. Fiona turned to Alisdair, her face lit with the ember of determination.

"Send for Ian," she instructed, naming the fleetest of their men. "He shall bear the message to my father with haste, and we shall await his blessing upon our union."

As the sentry was dispatched into the dusky embrace of the impending night, Fiona convened with her sisters, Ailis and Moira, alongside Lady Caitlin—the matriarch whose wisdom had long guided the McClains. Together, they began the intricate task of wedding preparations.

"Ye do understand this may all be for naught," Fiona reminded them. "We still must wait on Father's approval."

Caitlin smiled. "We shall plan a wedding, and it will take place after your father gives his approval. If he does not give approval then we shall have a huge ceilidh, and invite all of our allies."

"If you're certain…" Fiona felt that they had to at least have a plan for the lack of approval from her father. If Caitlin was content to have a feast instead of the wedding, then she was happy to move forward with their plans.

Lady Caitlin's calm demeanor kept every detail under control. Under her guidance, the upcoming celebration took shape— a feast to honor the joining of two mighty clans. Lists of provisions, adornments, and guests were made, penned with the expectation of joyous revelry and the unspoken tension of political undercurrents.

A PARCHMENT, HEAVY with the weight of her father's seal, rested within the fold of her hands. The ink bore the message that would tether her heart's choice to the obligation of kin and clan. Though her father could not be present at the moment, his assurance had reached her through the words scrawled upon the page—he would bear witness to her union.

"Ye must ken the significance of this," she whispered to herself. Her sense of duty mingled with the unbidden flutter of anticipation in her chest. She had feared her father would want her to marry Malcolm Sinclair, if only for the proximity of the two clans.

Drawn away from her solitary musings by a curious sight, Fiona found Boyd McClain, the young lad. He skipped stones across the glassy surface of the water, each plip drawing a wider grin upon his youthful visage.

"Boyd," Fiona called gently, her approach measured and deliberate.

The boy turned, and upon noticing her, a light sparked in his eyes—an innocence unfettered by the encroaching responsibilities of his birthright. "Lady Fiona," he greeted. "May I call you Fiona? As ye are to be my sister soon?"

"Aye. Ye are diligent in yer pursuits." A soft smile graced her lips as she noted the butterflies dancing around the boy. Alisdair had once told her he would rather play with butterflies than learn about his duties to his clan.

"Och, 'tis naught but pleasure," Boyd replied with a shrug, his eyes following the erratic flight of the insects.

"How do ye get the butterflies to stay so close?" Fiona inquired.

"I canna tell ye that. Tis one of the secrets of the McClains," Boyd answered, casting another stone. "But there is wisdom in the flight of the butterfly. Each flutter speaks of freedom, of finding joy among the thorns."

"Aye," Fiona mused. "Yet we must not forget our role in our clans. We are bound by honor and tradition."

"Ye speak true, Fiona." Boyd stood taller, a flicker of understanding dawning in his eyes. "I shall strive to be the laird my brothers expect, even if my soul yearns for simpler pleasures."

"Ye will be grand," Fiona assured him, her hand coming to rest upon his shoulder.

AMID THE GRANDEUR of the keep, preparations for the wedding feast unfolded with meticulous care. Fiona oversaw each detail with a steady hand, ensuring that the celebration would reflect the union of not just two hearts, but of two mighty clans. Her sisters, Ailis with her gentle smile and Moira with eyes lit with mirth, were ever at her side, affirming their support as she prepared to honor Alisdair for all her days.

The great hall, usually echoing with the clamor of warriors' boasts and the clinking of tankards, had been transformed into a tapestry of splendor. Banners bearing the emblems of both McAfee and McClain hung from the rafters, their colors intermingling as a symbol of the alliance soon to be sealed. Tables were adorned with fine cloth and set with pewter and wooden platters, ready to host the array of dishes that would celebrate the feast.

Fiona surveyed the room, noting how the candlelight flickered against the polished surfaces. Her heart swelled with pride, not only at the sight before her but also at the thought of joining her life with Alisdair's. Each choice she made, from the floral arrangements to the seating chart, was imbued with the significance of their impending vows.

As the day when Duncan McAfee was due to arrive dawned, tension wove itself through the castle's usual excitement. The hours passed, yet no sign of the laird's familiar banner appeared upon the horizon. Fiona tried to quell the flutter of unease in her chest, reminding herself that delays were oft the way of travel.

It was then that a small contingent of men bearing the McAfee tartan approached the gates. Their faces were unrecognizable, which caused a brief stir among the guards, but they were soon welcomed as kin. The men spoke of unexpected hindrances that delayed the laird, their words heavy with apologies. Fiona felt a pang of disappointment. Yet, in her father's absence, her resolve to carry on with grace remained unwavering.

"Father shall be here in due time," Fiona reassured her sisters, though the sentiment was as much for her own steadying as for theirs. "He's already sent a contingent of soldiers ahead of him. I'm sure he will follow shortly."

THE AMBER HUES of twilight draped themselves across the landscape as Fiona and Alisdair strolled through the waning light. The men from Clan McAfee had been tended to—fed heartily, their tents raised in the shelter of the keep's looming shadow.

"Ye must take care this eve," Alisdair spoke, his voice filled with the subtlest undercurrent of concern. They walked side by side. "I sense a stirring on the wind, a harbinger of trials to come."

Fiona glanced at him, her eyes reflecting the indigo sky. "And is such foresight a gift of the McClains, or merely the intuition of a seasoned warrior?" Her words were laced with curiosity, seeking to pierce the veil of mystery that often shrouded her betrothed.

"If only it were so." He chuckled, dismissing the idea with an affectionate glint in his eye. "But nay, 'tis naught but the caution born of years facing unseen adversaries."

They reached the edge of the loch, standing for a moment to watch the water lap against the shore. The world around them held its breath, caught between day and night, peace and peril. Fiona felt the pulse of the earth beneath her feet, the rhythm steadying her heart as she turned toward Alisdair.

Their gazes locked, and in his eyes, she saw not just the future laird or the warrior, but the man—his desire mirrored in the depths of her soul. As natural as the rise and fall of the tides, they drew together, their lips meeting in a fervent kiss that spoke of longing and desire.

With his hands, he tenderly explored her soft curves. Fiona's breath caught as his caress ignited a fire within her, her skin tingling with each caress. She surrendered to the sensation, weaving into his cropped hair, pulling him closer.

Alisdair caught her legs and wrapped them around his waist as he lowered onto the stone bench beside the loch, her on his lap, feeling things a maiden was not meant to feel until the wedding night.

Beneath the canopy of stars, they lost themselves in the passion of their embrace. Alisdair's fingers brushed the swell of her breast, the boldness of the act sending a thrill through her veins. Their kisses grew more fervent, the heat of their bodies merging as one.

"I wish we were already married," she whispered against his lips. "Then we would not have to stop."

"The wedding is tomorrow. Do we have to stop?" he asked, ready to pull away if that's what she wanted.

Yet, even as the flames of desire threatened to consume them, Fiona held onto the threads of duty that bound her. With a gentle firmness, she guided his hand away, their foreheads resting together as they both fought to catch their breaths. "We must stop. Tomorrow," she whispered, the word a promise wrapped in sacrifice. "When I am yours before the clans and the heavens."

Alisdair pressed his lips to her forehead, his acceptance silent but resolute. In that moment, they stood united—not just by the passion that flared between them but by the shared understanding of what tomorrow would bring: a union of hearts, clans, and futures intertwined.

As they parted ways for the evening, retreating to their separate quarters within the stone walls of the keep, they sensed something impending in the air.

MALCOLM SINCLAIR STOOD in the shadow of the ancient pines that bordered the McClain village, his gaze fixed upon the bustling courtyard below. The afternoon sun cast a warm glow over the stone walls, but its cheer did little to ease the cold knot of displeasure tightening in his chest. From this clandestine perch, he observed with a simmering indignation as Alisdair dared to draw Fiona closer to his side.

The sight of Alisdair's broad hand, calloused and sure, as it swept around Fiona's waist and pulled her astride him, ignited a silent fury within Malcolm. His jaw clenched, muscles tensed beneath the fine fabric of his doublet. It was all he could do to suppress the primal scream clawing at his throat, a demand for Alisdair to unhand the woman who was destined to be his own bride.

"Compose yourself," he murmured, conscious of his position and the need for discretion. The words were barely audible. Fiona, ever so practical and direct, would have laughed at the notion of him skulking like a common outlaw, yet here he was, driven to such measures by circumstance and his own unchecked desire.

The desire to stride forward, to assert his claim before the entire clan was palpable, yet Malcolm knew that self-restraint was paramount. To reveal himself to those loyal to the McClains, would prove foolhardy. Recognition would come swiftly, followed by questions he was not prepared to answer—not yet. He was as much a fixture of the Highlands as the clans themselves. His stature was known far and wide. His presence would not go unnoticed, nor unchallenged.

Malcolm shifted slightly, the leather of his boots silent against the pine needles carpeting the forest floor. His eyes never left the pair, his mind racing with thoughts of duty and the sacrifices demanded by birthright. The weight of his father's legacy pressed heavily upon his shoulders, an inheritance of expectation and the unspoken demand to eclipse the greatness of generations past.

"Patience," he whispered to himself, the word a mantra meant to quell the tempest of emotions within. What Malcolm Sinclair desired, he would obtain through cunning and strategy, not brute force. For now, he would watch and wait, the very picture of nobility, even as the fires of ambition and longing burned fiercely in the heart of a man who understood all too well the tension between personal desires and political responsibilities.

Malcolm withdrew into the shadow of an ancient oak, his gaze never leaving the pair that frolicked in the clearing. From afar he observed them, the way Alisdair's hands were so familiar upon Fiona's waist, how she threw back her head and laughed with a carefree mirth that spoke of deep affection. The sight twisted in Malcolm's chest like a dirk, every moment they were together a blow to his pride.

"Naught but a momentary jest," Malcolm assured himself. He clutched the hilt of his sword—a sword that had seen the downfall of many—a visible symbol of the power he wielded and the lengths to which he would go to claim his birthright.

"Fortune favors the patient," he intoned, the solemn vow resonating within his heart. Soon the games would end, and destiny would unfurl as meticulously planned. His mind danced with thoughts of tomorrow, the intricate machinations he'd set in motion, poised to ensnare Fiona in a web from which there was no escape.

A smirk tugged at the corners of his lips, a rare display of triumph that he allowed himself in the solitude of his watchful exile. How sweet it would be, the moment when dawn's light revealed not a union blessed by kin and clan, but the shattering of expectations, the ultimate checkmate in a game played by kings and pawns alike.

"Imagine, Alisdair," Malcolm whispered, reveling in the unsaid words, "to stand before your people, your heart ripe with joy, only to find your bride spirited away by the very hand of fate—or rather, by my hand."

The thought warmed him, a flicker of satisfaction against the cool Highland breeze.

Malcolm knew the price of greatness. It was etched in the annals of his forebears, a saga of sacrifice and relentless ambition. Fiona, with her warrior's stance and eyes filled with intelligence, would be his wife. And through her, he would ascend, not merely to fulfill his own aspirations but to elevate his name and secure his place in the tapestry of history.

"By this time on the morrow," he vowed, "all will be changed." Malcolm turned his back on the scene, the contours of his plan as clear as the path he now walked alone.

WHEN FIONA REACHED the room she shared with her sisters, she found them sitting on their beds, talking about the wedding. For a moment, she stared out the window, and then she joined them.

Ailis studied Fiona for a moment. "Ye appear flushed. Are ye well?"

Fiona smiled. "I'm flushed from kissing Alisdair. The man knows how to make me want things a maiden shouldn't want."

"Tell us more," Moira gushed. "I will never marry, so I must understand how he makes you feel."

Fiona settled onto the edge of Ailis's bed, her cheeks still aglow with the remnants of passion. She leaned in conspiratorially, as if sharing a well-guarded secret.

"His kisses are like wildfire on my skin, searing yet gentle, igniting a desire that courses through me like a tempest," Fiona began, her eyes alight with an inner flame. "When he lets his hands roam, he unravels every knot of restraint within me, leaving me bare and unguarded before him."

Ailis's eyes widened at her sister's fervent words, while Moira leaned forward eagerly, her expression hungry for every detail.

"And his caress..." Fiona paused, savoring the memory. "It's both a promise and a plea, a silent oath spoken through caresses that leave me breathless and yearning for more."

Moira let out an exaggerated sigh, falling back onto her bed dramatically. "It sounds as if the two of you were ready to claim each other then and there," Moira teased, her eyes twinkling mischievously. "I can only imagine how passionate your wedding night will be, sister."

Fiona chuckled, a rosy hue still tinting her cheeks. "Oh, Moira, you have a vivid imagination. We must abide by tradition until tomorrow's ceremony."

Ailis, ever the voice of reason, interjected gently, "It is a delicate balance we tread between desire and duty. Tomorrow marks the beginning of a new chapter for you and Alisdair."

As they talked late into the night about love, duty, and the uncertain future that lay before them, Fiona found solace in her sisters' presence. Despite the trials that awaited her as the future Laird's wife, she knew that with Ailis and Moira by her side, she could weather any storm.

Fiona knew that her sisters' unwavering support would be her anchor in the tumultuous sea of change ahead. As they wove dreams and whispered secrets in the late hours of the night, the bond between the McAfee sisters grew stronger.

In the quiet depths of that chamber, where the flickering candlelight cast dancing shadows on the stone walls, Fiona found herself at peace. The weight of her impending union with Alisdair still lingered, but in the safety of her sisters' company, she could set aside the burdens of duty for just a moment.

As the night deepened and sleep began to tug at their eyelids, Ailis rose from her bed and approached Fiona with a tender smile. "Rest now, dearest sister," she murmured, brushing a stray lock of hair from Fiona's forehead. "Tomorrow will bring Father and the wedding. I canna believe it's happening!"

❦

CHAPTER ELEVEN

BEFORE HER SISTERS were awake the following morning, Fiona crept from the quiet of their room and through the keep. She took her bow and arrow with her, needing to focus on something other than her impending nuptials. Father had not yet arrived, and she had no idea where he could be. He'd promised to be there in time for the wedding, and the wedding was only a few hours away.

She went to the forested area near the loch, her bow and arrow at the ready. Perhaps she could do some hunting and share it with some of the village, as she did when she was home in McAfee land. She liked to help the orphans and widows, and this was the best way she'd found to do it. Mayhap the McClains would enjoy the same type of help.

She loosed an arrow and shot a rabbit, walking over to collect it. As she was best to pick up her bounty, she stopped for a moment, listening. She put her hand on her hip where she kept her dagger. She wasn't nearly as good with knives as Ailis, but she was good enough to protect herself. When it wasn't there, she reached over her shoulder to the quiver. Someone caught her hand as she moved to take an arrow from it.

The stillness of the forest was shattered by the sudden charge of men. Soon Fiona was surrounded by men in McAfee plaids, but she knew they couldn't be her father's men, for his men were trained to protect her and her sisters to the point of laying down their lives for them.

The one who had grabbed her hand, who appeared to be the leader, declared, "Yer father has commanded you come with us."

Fiona struggled against his hands, knowing full well that none of her father's men would put hands on her without her permission.

Betrayal seized her heart as she recognized the deceit in the garments of her assailants—men she didn't recognize disguised in the familiar patterns of her own clan.

"Seize her," came the steely command from amongst the intruders, and the men followed his orders exactly.

She was dragged away from the forest and toward the border of McClain land. She hesitated to scream, for that was a woman's defense, calling for others to help her. Yet after a short time, she knew it was what she must do.

"Unhand me, ye cowards!" Fiona cried out. Her long braid whipped about her as she struggled against the sinewy arms that bound her. Yet, even as fear clawed at her insides, Fiona's thoughts raced not to her plight but to the safety of her sisters. She hoped they would not follow and be taken captive as well.

Her captors were relentless, their grips tightening as they dragged her away from the McClain ancestral lands. Despite her warrior's training, the sheer number overwhelmed her. The shock of the ambush, so deftly executed, left her reeling—their deception a bitter taste upon her tongue.

"Ye may take me, but ye'll never break the spirit of the McAfees," Fiona declared, her voice a mixture of defiance and dread.

As her feet stumbled over the uneven terrain, forced onward by her captors, Fiona's mind raced with the possibilities, each more foreboding than the last.

In that anguished moment, caught between the duty to her kin and the stark reality of her capture, Fiona vowed that no matter the cost, she would not yield to fear, nor would she allow her personal desires to sway her from the path of sacrifice required by her noble station.

She screamed… one loud piercing cry, and she knew that Alisdair heard it… for he must.

"Quiet, lass," grumbled one of the guards.

Another of the men took a piece of cloth and stuffed it into her mouth so she couldn't cry out again.

MOIRA WOKE AND realized it was Fiona's wedding day. She searched around for the sister in question, but she was nowhere to be seen. Moira frowned, realizing it was late in the day for them to not be readying themselves for the wedding that would take place at noon.

She shook Ailis awake. "Where has Fiona gone?"

Ailis frowned, rubbing her eyes and trying to focus. "Fiona? She must be with Lady Caitlin or mayhap she went for a walk."

Moira rushed from the room, finding the lady in question. "Fiona, she's not in her bed. Do ye know where she could be?"

Lady Caitlin shook her head slowly. "Nay, I haven't seen her this morn." Within moments, she had her sons out watching for Fiona, though she had yet to spot Alisdair.

Caitlin sent one of the servants to tell Alisdair Fiona was missing, though she had probably gone for a morning walk. But Alisdair knew better. He'd sensed the impending danger the night before, and his hunch was much stronger now.

Alisdair stood amid his brothers and loyal warriors, his face a mask of controlled fury. The very air stilled as he stepped forward. With an imperious gesture, he summoned his kin to gather close.

"Brothers," Alisdair began, "a grievous wrong has been done this day. Fiona McAfee, daughter of our ally, and my affianced bride has been taken from our lands. She's not merely hiding or wandering. I sense it."

Lachlan exchanged glances with Brodie, each brother's resolve mirroring the others. Brodie, ever the silent sentinel, nodded minutely, his every sense attuned to the unfolding strategy.

"We shall not suffer such affronts to go unanswered," Alisdair declared. "We will marshal our forces and reclaim what has been unjustly seized."

The warriors, bound by fealty and honor, murmured their agreement, the sound like the rustling of leaves before a storm. Alisdair cast his gaze upon the rugged expanse of highland terrain that lay beyond their gates.

"Her captor must believe the land cloaks him in secrecy," Lachlan posited, his voice carrying the confidence of one well-versed in the art of deception. "But it is our ally as much as it is his."

"More our ally," Alisdair added, "for these are our lands." His mind was already tracing paths through dense thickets and hidden trails. "Brodie, your eyes have always seen what others overlook. I trust you'll guide us through the terrain."

"Under cover of nightfall, we shall move unseen," Brodie agreed.

"We cannot wait until night," Alisdair declared. "We must go now." He spotted his youngest brother, who stood watching everything with wide eyes. "Boyd, you must ask your *friends*."

Boyd immediately understood what his brother was saying and nodded. "Aye." With that, the boy ran back to the safety of the keep.

"The McAfees who arrived yesterday… their tents are gone," Lachlan observed. "Could they have taken her back to her father?"

"Nay, her father has agreed to our marriage. We must make haste," Alisdair called. "We shall split our force—Lachlan, take a handful of men and scout the eastern ridge. Brodie and I will lead the main force through the Glen of Shadows."

"Let us then prepare our arms and our spirits for the task ahead," Lachlan proclaimed, a rallying cry that roused the hearts of all who heard it. The men dispersed, each to his given duty, their steps sure and silent.

THE RUSTLE OF leaves beneath her feet was the only sound that pierced the heavy silence as Fiona strained against the ropes that bit into her wrists. Her captors, men of Clan Sinclair adorned in the unmistakable McAfee plaids, had not anticipated her warrior's resolve nor the cunning that sparked like flint in her mind.

"Ye think ye can hold me with mere twine?" she muttered to herself. Fiona worked a small stone between her fingers, abrading the rope stealthily.

As soon as they were beyond the border of McClain land, a man stepped out of the shadows, his eyes meeting Fiona's. His towering frame loomed at the edge of the fray, his eyes a cold reflection of the calculating mind behind them. Fiona's piercing blue gaze met his but for a moment.

Her eyes, wide with the terror of uncertainty, never strayed far from Malcolm, whose presence commanded the scene with silent authority. In his unyielding gaze, she saw the unspoken promise of a strategic gambit, one that sought to ensnare more than just a single lass. What plans did Malcolm Sinclair harbor that necessitated such a brazen act?

As she observed the men who had captured her, she realized they knew not that they were merely pawns in a game of political strategy, set upon the chessboard by Malcolm Sinclair himself.

'Tis only a matter of time before I turn their folly against them, thought Fiona, her gaze locked on the horizon where freedom lay beyond the craggy expanse.

As dusk settled upon the land like a cloak, Malcolm Sinclair emerged from the shadows where he'd been, his presence commanding yet weighed down by expectations unseen. Standing tall before Fiona, he surveyed her with calculating eyes.

"Fiona McAfee, your spirit is admirable, but your situation is unyielding. Accept the merger between our clans, and all this unpleasantness can be avoided."

Fiona's lips curled into a wry smile, revealing none of the inner turmoil that clashed within her—the duty to her family, the sacrifice that might be demanded, the longing for the adventures she shared with her sisters. She shook her head adamantly.

"Ye'll find that my patience has limits," Malcolm replied, his tone even, betraying neither anger nor impatience. "Consider the welfare of your clan. Is your pride worth their suffering?"

In the ensuing silence, Fiona pondered his words, her heart battling against the logic of his argument. She had always placed the needs of others above her desires. She made mumbling sounds against the cloth in her mouth, and it was removed. "If ye dare scream again, we will take your sisters next."

"Ye may try to break my spirit, Sinclair, but it is as steadfast as the highland stone," Fiona declared. She spat at his feet.

"Time will tell, Fiona," Malcolm responded, his voice a soft threat that hung in the chill air. "Time will tell."

With a nod to his men, Malcolm retreated into the night, leaving Fiona to the solitude of her thoughts and the relentless pursuit of escape. The ropes around her wrists loosened imperceptibly, the fruits of her labor slowly yielding.

ALISDAIR LED HIS kinsmen through the undulating terrain. The breeze carried the scent of heather and the distant murmur of a brook, but the beauty of the land was lost to him, his mind wholly consumed by the task at hand.

"Keep yer eyes sharp," Alisdair commanded, his deep voice resonating with authority. His broad shoulders, cloaked in the tartan of Clan McClain, moved with purpose as he navigated the rocky hillsides. His clan followed, their faces etched with determination, the weight of swords and shields a familiar burden.

They had been tracking Fiona's captors since morning, reading the signs left upon the earth—a trampled fern here, a snapped twig there. Each clue whispered secrets of passage to those who could interpret them, and none were more skilled than Brodie.

"Over here!" Lachlan exclaimed, pointing to a piece of plaid caught on a bramble. The fabric, unmistakably McAfee, bolstered their resolve. Alisdair knelt.

"Her captors are growing careless," he observed, the lines around his eyes tightening. "We're closing in."

The McClains pressed onward, the silence between them laden with unspoken vows of rescue and retribution. The air grew cooler as the evening approached, casting long shadows that danced eerily across the landscape, as if mocking their urgent quest.

Alisdair paused, signaling for quiet. He tilted his head, listening. A faint scream reached his ears, drifting from the direction of a small building not far off.

"Prepare yerselves, brothers," Alisdair addressed his kin, his voice barely above a whisper. "Our confrontation with her captors draws nigh."

Tension coiled within the group like a drawn bowstring. Alisdair studied the area, his strategic mind mapping out potential approaches, defenses, and escape routes. He was certain the trees surrounding the building were filled with their adversaries.

"Remember, we strike swift and true," Alisdair continued, his gaze flitting between his brothers. "Fiona's safety is paramount."

The McClain warriors nodded. They had faced countless battles, but this one bore the heavy cloak of personal stakes, the outcome of which would seal the fates of two clans.

As twilight descended, Alisdair led his men closer, each step measured, each breath controlled.

"Steady now," Alisdair murmured, drawing his sword with a steely rasp. The sound was a call to arms, a signal that the hour of reckoning was at hand.

HAVING SPENT MOST of the day alone within the stone walls of the fortress, Fiona had gotten her hands mostly freed, and she knew with a little more effort, she would be able to move them.

It was almost nightfall when Fiona McAfee stood tall before Malcolm Sinclair, her captor's demands echoing off the barren walls. She squared her shoulders, facing him with an unwavering gaze.

"Ye may control these walls, Sinclair," Fiona spoke, her voice a steadfast timbre in the cold room, "but ye'll ne'er control the heart and soul of Clan McAfee."

Malcolm's eyes narrowed, but his posture remained regal. "Yield now, and this can end without bloodshed. Join our clans, not through war, but through union."

"Never." Fiona's response was a whisper, yet it carried the weight of a thunderclap. She knew the stakes were greater than her fate.

The distant clamor of clashing steel suddenly pierced the silence, growing louder with each passing moment. Fiona's heart quickened. Alisdair was there with his men to rescue her. And though she'd never seen herself as a damsel in distress, she was thankful for his rescue.

A slow smile lit her face. "It sounds like my rescuers are here. Do you want to die slowly or quickly?"

Fiona's eyes gleamed with a fierce determination as she stood before Malcolm, her tone unwavering and her words laced with an undeniable threat. The weight of the situation hung heavy in the air, the tension palpable as she sought to convince him of the imminent danger looming just beyond the walls of his stronghold.

"Listen carefully, Malcolm," Fiona began, her voice low and

commanding. "Alisdair's presence outside these walls signifies the beginning of the end for you. He is a force to be reckoned with, skilled in both strategy and combat. Your reign of terror is coming to a close, and you must decide now how you wish to meet your fate."

The torchlight flickered against Malcolm's stoic expression, but a glint of uncertainty betrayed his facade of confidence. Fiona pressed on, her words cutting through the silence like a blade.

"Every passing moment brings Alisdair closer to this very spot. When he arrives, there will be no mercy from him. He will stop at nothing to see you vanquished, the remnants of your once-great clan scattered to the winds. Do not delude yourself into thinking that your vast resources and strategist skills can protect you forever, for the tide of battle is unpredictable and swift."

Malcolm's eyes bore into hers. "Fiona, you speak of doom and despair, but I have faith in my people and my ability to lead them through this storm. We are not so easily vanquished."

Fiona raised an eyebrow, her voice maintaining its steady cadence. "Ye speak with unnecessary bravado, Malcolm. It is not simply a matter of skill or numbers that will decide the outcome of this conflict. Alisdair is a cunning adversary, one who has studied and exploited the weaknesses of his enemies time and again. His tactics are subtle, his strategy calculated. He will infiltrate your strongest defenses and strike when you least expect it. Do not underestimate him, for he is not one to be trifled with."

As Fiona spoke, she could spot the worry creasing Malcolm's face. She knew that he was not ignorant of the threat posed by Alisdair, but he was stubborn and refused to accept the severity of the situation. Fiona took a deep breath, determined to drive her point home.

"Listen to me, Malcolm. This is not a game. The lives of people are at stake, and I refuse to stand idly by while you gamble with their safety. You must take action now, before it is too late. Raise the white flag. Surrender to the McClains and let them deal with you as they see fit. Save the lives of your men. Otherwise, you will *all* perish."

Malcolm's jaw clenched as Fiona's words struck a nerve deep within him. Despite the ominous warning, he couldn't help but feel a flicker of defiance ignite within his chest. His pride and determination fueled his belief in his own capabilities and the loyalty of his men.

"Fiona," Malcolm spoke, his voice filled with conviction. "I appreciate your concern, but I have led these men through countless battles, and we have emerged victorious each time. I will not cower before Alisdair or anyone else who dares to challenge us. We will prevail, mark my words."

The distant sounds of the approaching skirmish grew louder, the clash of steel against steel now echoing through the halls of the stronghold. Malcolm knew that the time for words had passed. It was time to act.

With a solemn nod to Fiona, Malcolm swiftly moved toward the door leading to the battleground, firmly grasping the hilt of his sword. As he pushed open the door and stepped onto the bloodstained cobblestones, the bitter chill of the night air bit at his face. He drew his sword from its scabbard with practiced ease, the metal glinting ominously under the silvery moonlight.

"I will do what I must to protect our people and our land," he declared. "And the woman I plan to marry. We are not so easily vanquished, Fiona. We will fight until our last breath, and we will fight with everything we have to ensure our victory."

With that, he turned away from Fiona and charged into the fray, his last few warriors following close behind. The sound of clashing swords and shouted commands filled the air as the battle raged on.

In the misty highlands outside, Alisdair surged forward, leading his kinsmen with the ferocity of a storm unleashed upon the shore. His sword gleamed under the moon's pale glow as he cut through Malcolm's men.

"Push forward!" he commanded, his voice carrying over the

din of battle. "For Fiona, for Clan McClain!"

The clash of metal rang through the night. Alisdair parried and thrusted, his movements precise, thanks to years of discipline and training. Each swing of his blade was a note in the song of their people—a melody of freedom and defiance.

Inside her makeshift prison, Fiona heard the unmistakable sound of combat. Her spirit soared with hope, yet she steeled herself against the surge of emotion. She would not be a passive damsel awaiting rescue. She had played her part in this intricate game of power and would continue to do so until her final breath.

"Ye think yer McClain warriors will breach these walls?" Malcolm asked as he walked back into the room and locked the door. His voice was laced with disdain, yet beneath the surface lay an undercurrent of concern. "They are but men, and men falter."

"Men led by love and loyalty are more formidable than any fortress," Fiona retorted.

The battle raged on, drawing ever closer to the heart of Malcolm's stronghold. With each fallen enemy, Alisdair's determination grew, his purpose clear as the stars above. He fought not just for land or legacy, but for the woman who he would marry and his future clan.

As the door to her confinement splintered under the force of McClain swords, Fiona's breath caught in her throat.

"Release her," Alisdair's command boomed through the chamber, his presence commanding attention.

With a swift motion, Fiona was free, her hands no longer bound by ropes or politics. She wanted to step forward and fight with the McClain men. Her honor was at stake! But her hands were weakened by the time they had been bound, and her shoulders throbbed from having her hands behind her back. Instead, she stepped back and made herself as small as she could against the wall as her gaze met Alisdair's. "They did not hurt me other than a few scrapes. Malcolm was trying to force my hand in marriage."

Fiona McAfee, heart thundering against her chest, stood behind the line of fierce warriors of Clan McClain. She would have preferred to have a sword in her hand as she fought beside them, but that was not possible, so she waited for the fight to be over, but she didn't cower. Nay, she would never cower before a Sinclair.

"Stand fast!" Alisdair's voice cut through the din, a beacon in the middle of the tempest of battle. Lachlan dispatched foes with a fluidity that impressed her, his presence a comfort in the relentless tide of adversaries.

As the battle waned, the thrumming in Fiona's veins echoed the rhythm of victory. With every fallen enemy, the McClains pressed on, their resolve as unyielding as the ancient mountains that bore witness to their struggle.

The moment of triumph neared, the remnants of Malcolm's men retreating before the might of the McClains. "For clan! For home!" she cried, her voice ringing clear above the clamor.

At last, as the final adversary lay vanquished at her feet, silence descended upon the battlefield like a shroud. Fiona stood among the men, her breaths coming in heavy gusts that hung visible in the crisp air.

"Ye've done us proud," Alisdair proclaimed, his gaze meeting hers with unspoken reverence. No longer did she stand as a captive, but as an equal, a warrior of indomitable will.

"Let us return home," Lachlan declared, his words carrying the weight of their collective yearning. The McClains gathered their wounded before preparing for the walk back to McClain land.

As they made their way back to the stronghold, Fiona walked with head held high, her blond hair eerie in the moonlight. As she walked, she wondered if her father had arrived. She hoped he would see that what had happened was caused by the Sinclairs, but she had a hunch he wouldn't. He would see the McClains as having done something wrong because she was taken from

McClain land. She had to convince him differently.

Under the canopy of twilight stars, the McClain stronghold loomed ahead. Fiona's pace had not waned despite the long march from the battlefield, her warrior's heart steadied by the rhythm of homecoming drums that echoed through the glen.

The clamor of celebration greeted them as they crossed the threshold—their respite from the day's grim dance of war. Yet amid the jubilation, Fiona's gaze drifted to the torchlit battlements.

"Ye need rest," Alisdair murmured, his hand briefly brushing hers with protective concern. His eyes searched hers for the toll the ordeal may have exacted upon her spirit but found only the undiminished fire of her conviction.

"Aye," Fiona conceded, though she knew sleep would be a stranger this night. Her capture, her rescue—it had all stirred the waters of change, and ripples would soon reach distant shores.

With her sisters at her sides, she headed for the chamber she had shared with them, only then thinking about how many people would have been disappointed to have traveled for a wedding that didn't take place.

"Tomorrow," Ailis murmured. "We must speak of it, sister. Of what comes next."

"Of the wedding?" Moira chimed in, ever the ember of candor in any conversation. The very mention of the union meant to merge two powerful clans hung in the air—a question, a challenge, an unyielding decree by fate itself.

"Aye," Fiona replied, her words sparing as she regarded her sisters with solemn affection. "Did Father arrive?"

"He did, and I have never seen him so angry. He said he will speak with you in the morning." Moira glanced at Fiona.

"We must convince him that the Sinclairs are to blame, and not the McClains. He has been betrayed by his closest ally, and he must realize that to continue to call Laird Sinclair friend is naught but folly."

As soon as Fiona was dressed the following morning, she went down to the great hall, where her father would be waiting to speak with her.

As soon as she entered the room, he spread his arms, and she sprinted to him, held in his arms as if she was still a bairn for just a moment.

"We must discuss what has happened." Duncan guided her from the great hall. His eyes met Fiona's, pride mingling with the gravity of consequence. As laird and father, he too understood the weight that now settled upon her shoulders.

"It was the Sinclairs, Father," Fiona insisted. "Malcolm Sinclair sent men into McClain land dressed as McAfees. I didn't recognize them, but they could have been new. I didn't know. I had too much energy yesterday morning, so I took a walk and decided to hunt a few rabbits and give them to the widows and orphans as I do at home so often."

She huffed, finding it more difficult to tell the tale than she'd realized it would be. "I shot my first rabbit, and then I felt something… like I wasn't alone. So I reached for my dagger, only to discover I'd left it in my chamber. Someone caught my hand when I reached for an arrow. They took me from McClain land, and I soon saw that their leader was Malcolm Sinclair. He took me to an abandoned fortress outside of McClain land, and there he told me he would keep me until I agreed to be his wife and merge our two clans." She left out the part where she was gagged and her hands were tied, keeping her hands behind her back so he wouldn't see the bruises from the ropes on her wrists.

"The McClains should have taken better care of ye," he growled.

"I left without telling anyone where I was. How could they have known to take care of me?"

He shook his head. "There should not have been strange men

in their village with my three precious daughters here under their care."

"Mayhap not, but I was not gone for even a day, and they brought me back. All of the men who were part of my kidnapping are now dead, their blood spilled around and inside the fortress where I was held. It is your friend, Laird Sinclair, who is at the bottom of all this!"

"That canna be true, lass. Laird Sinclair and I were friends as lads, and we are still friends to this day. We have helped them in many ways over the years, providing food for them when they had none for themselves. What reason would they have to betray us this way?"

"They want a merging of clans," she murmured. "They want McAfee and Sinclair to be as one."

Duncan shook his head. "Not possible. Malcolm must have been acting on his own."

Fiona sighed. It was just as she'd expected. Her father believed the Sinclairs were innocent and the fault lay with the McClains. She had to find a way to convince him differently.

✦

CHAPTER TWELVE

FIONA STOOD BEFORE her father in the private chamber of Laird McClain. Her braid had come loose, and a few strands framed her face.

"Father," she began, her voice steady, "I was taken not through negligence on the part of the McClains, but by the treachery of the Sinclairs."

Knowing he was thinking of ending her betrothal to Alisdair, she had come again to talk to him about what she knew was the truth after he'd had time to think.

"Ye shouldna have been taken from McClain lands," Duncan lamented. "Alisdair promised to keep ye safe, and ye were not safe."

Fiona straightened her spine, her athletic form radiating defiance. "It is not the McClains' defenses that were lacking, but Sinclair deceit that prevailed. The warriors of both Clan McClain and Clan McAfee are without blame."

A flicker of pride crossed the laird's countenance at his daughter's spirited defense.

"Nevertheless," Duncan replied, "we must consider all possibilities. The safety of our kin is paramount."

Fiona's heart drummed a rhythm of protest, yet she held her tongue. She knew her father's mind battled between the love he bore for his daughter and the duty he owed to their clan.

"Let us not speak of blame now," she implored, her voice softening. "There are greater concerns ahead, and we must stand united."

His brow furrowed in thought, his eyes distant.

"Father," Fiona began. "I dinna ken Malcolm's treachery was his alone to bear."

Duncan's gaze returned from the horizon, settling upon his daughter with a solemnity that matched the gravity of their discourse. "Aye, Fiona. Malcolm acted without honor. But with the lad's passing, we're left with little but shadows and doubts." He rose from his chair, his movements deliberate, the tartan of his clan draping him in the dignity of his station. "And Arran Sinclair is no mere acquaintance. He is a friend, one whose word I have trusted for many a year. I cannot fathom him having a hand in such dark dealings."

Fiona watched her father pace slowly.

"Then what of Alisdair?" she pressed, the name of her betrothed carrying with it the hope of love entwined with the threads of political alliance. "Our union was to be a bond between our clans, a seal upon the peace we cherish."

"Indeed, it was… and mayhap still could be." Duncan halted his pacing, turning to face her, his expression an inscrutable mask carved from duty and concern. "But this incident casts a shadow upon the McClains' ability to safeguard their keep, let alone my daughter. I must ponder whether 'tis wise to entrust thee to such uncertainty."

"Father, I was the one who was out walking early in the morning before the sun was fully up. If I'd stayed inside the keep, where everyone thought I would be, then I never would have been taken.

The words struck Fiona like an unexpected squall against the cliffs, the idea of her marriage in jeopardy as unsettling as the ground quaking beneath one's feet. She felt the familiar stirrings of defiance. She had no desire to marry a man other than Alisdair McClain.

"Father, I ask you to weigh your decision with care. Not just for my heart's sake, but for the strength it would bring to both our clans." Her voice carried the gentle firmness of a calm sea that could turn tempestuous if provoked. "Ye ken the McClains would be important allies, as they are considered the strongest of all the Highland clans."

Laird Duncan nodded, a silent acknowledgment of the storm contained within his eldest daughter. "I shall consider it, Fiona. But know this—whatever my decision, 'tis for the good of our people and the future of the McAfees."

As he left the chamber, Fiona remained rooted to the spot, her mind whirling. She understood the precarious balance her father sought to maintain between personal desires and the inexorable demands of leadership. And though her heart yearned for Alisdair, she too was her father's daughter—a woman who would sacrifice her own happiness for the welfare of her clan, if need be.

Fiona joined her father later that day, hoping he'd made a decision about her marrying Alisdair. Fiona McAfee paced the length of the chamber. Her braid swung with the rhythm of her stride, a metronome to the tumult brewing within her heart.

"Father," she began as Laird Duncan entered the room, "I've given this matter much thought." Her eyes, the color of a stormy sea, met his steadfast gaze.

Duncan McAfee stood firm, his visage the embodiment of responsibility that had aged him beyond his years. "Aye, and so have I, Fiona. 'Tis a weighty decision."

"Weighty it may be," she countered, clasping her hands before her as if to steady herself. "But my heart has chosen its path. If ye stand in the way of my union with Alisdair, then I shall have no choice but to defy tradition and run off with him."

The air grew thick with tension, the words hanging between them like a drawn sword. Duncan's brows knit together, his lips thinning into a line of disapproval. "Would ye forsake your duty for passion? Think of what such recklessness would mean for our people!"

"Is it reckless to seek strength through alliance? To find love within the bonds of marriage?" Fiona's voice rose, her spirit as unyielding as the ancient oak that stood sentinel outside the keep.

"Love," Duncan scoffed, the word laced with a wariness born of experience. "Love can be as fleeting as the morning mist. 'Tis stability and honor that preserve a clan. I found love with yer mother, and we know what happened there. Then my next two wives were merely to be mothers to replace the one ye lost. Three wives I lost, and each left me with a daughter. Love is beautiful for the brief moment it lasts."

"Know this," Fiona insisted, "I shall marry Alisdair McClain, with or without your blessing, for I believe our union will bring love and strength to our clans."

Duncan studied his daughter, the spitting image of her late mother—headstrong and fierce. It was a staring contest with destiny, and in the depths of his heart, the laird knew he could not win.

"Three days," he conceded. "Ye shall have your wedding in three days' time."

"Thank ye, Father," Fiona replied, her tone softening.

ALISDAIR MCCLAIN STOOD before Laird Duncan McAfee, the stone floors of the grand hall echoing their somber footfalls. The air hung heavy with the lingering chill of dawn, a silent witness to the meeting of two formidable men.

"Laird McAfee," Alisdair began, his voice steady as the oak doors that safeguarded the hall. "I come before you—"

"Ye come before me having failed in your first duty as Fiona's betrothed." Duncan's words cut through the air, sharp and unyielding. "My daughter was taken on your watch. How can you claim to be the man fit to lead the McAfees if ye cannot ensure the safety of one lass?"

The accusation stung, but Alisdair's countenance did not

waver. "I take full responsibility, and I swear on my honor, it willna happen again. I will protect her with my life."

"Words are wind, lad," Duncan's gaze bore into him. "Actions speak louder than any vow. If yer to marry me Fiona, ye must prove yourself worthy. Not just as her husband, but as a leader for the McAfees."

Alisdair nodded. "I will do whatever it takes. My loyalty to Fiona—and to your clan—is unwavering."

Duncan held his stare a moment longer before nodding curtly, the matter settled for now.

IN THE PRIVACY of her chamber, Fiona McAfee sat with her sisters, Ailis and Moira, the only witnesses to her unbridled fury. Her hands trembled not with fear but with ire, her knuckles whitening as she recounted the tale.

"Those Sinclairs thought they could use me as a pawn," Fiona growled. "They underestimated the McAfees. And Father thinks that it is the McClains' fault I was taken from their land. He blames Alisdair when he should blame Clan Sinclair."

"Fiona, you're shaking," Ailis observed, her eyes reflecting the fire that blazed within her elder sister.

"Let her be, Ailis," Moira interjected softly. "She is shaking with righteous anger, not terror."

"Aye," Fiona confirmed. "It is not fear that makes me tremble but the wrath that comes from enduring the affront to our honor."

"The Sinclairs will pay for what they've done," Ailis vowed, her tone mirroring her sister's fervor.

"We'll stand beside ye, Fiona. In strength and in retribution," Moira added.

"First, we have a wedding to prepare for," Fiona declared. "And after, we'll show them who the McAfee daughters are, not as damsels in distress, but as vengeful spirits come to haunt them."

FIONA, HER BRAID swaying with each determined step, led her sisters Ailis and Moira into the midst of Clan McClain's warriors. The men paused, their swords momentarily still, as the daughters of Duncan McAfee approached.

"Good morrow, gentlemen," Fiona greeted. "We seek to train alongside you on this day."

A murmur rippled through the ranks, surprise etched on the weathered faces of the seasoned fighters. It was not custom for women to cross blades with men in the practice yard, yet none could deny the fire that burned in the eyes of these sisters.

"Ye have our respect, Lady Fiona," one of the McClain warriors responded, his grizzled features softening. "After what ye've endured, 'tis only right ye should wield sword and shield for your own defense."

With nods of assent from his fellows, the yard transformed into a mosaic of motion, steel clashing against steel. Ailis and Moira followed suit, their skill surprising the men who had underestimated them.

As the morning waned, sweat glistened upon furrowed brows. Men who had initially held back now engaged with earnest respect, recognizing the strength of the McAfee bloodline.

In the midst of the melee, Fiona caught sight of Alisdair, his broad figure commanding even in repose. His gaze followed her movements with an intensity that spoke volumes, admiration mingling with something deeper within the depths of his eyes.

"Alisdair," she called.

"Let us walk," he suggested, bearing the weight of unspoken words.

They strode across the grounds, the crunch of gravel beneath their boots punctuating their silence. Yet they were not alone. A McAfee soldier trailed behind them, his presence a constant reminder of the duty and watchfulness expected of Fiona's kin.

"Does he need to follow so closely?" Fiona asked, her frustration simmering beneath the surface.

"Aye, your father's orders," Alisdair replied, his jaw clenched as if the words pained him to speak. "He believes it prudent after… everything."

"Prudent or suffocating?" Fiona countered, her dry wit failing to mask the longing for freedom that echoed in her heart. She wanted to be alone with Alisdair. For with a witness, they couldn't kiss or touch.

"Both, perhaps," Alisdair conceded, his hand brushing against hers in a fleeting caress. "But we must bear it, for now. Duty demands vigilance."

"Then let us be vigilant together," Fiona declared, her resolve fortifying with each step. She felt the weight of the future pressing upon her, the delicate balance between love and leadership.

"Until the dawn breaks on our wedding day," Alisdair vowed.

"Until then," Fiona agreed.

FIONA STOOD ON the stone balcony, her gaze fixed upon the distant hills. The cool breeze whispered through the courtyard below, carrying with it the faint murmur of the McClain men as they retired from their training. She wrapped her arms around herself, a shiver creeping down her spine that had little to do with the chill in the air.

"Three days," she murmured.

The heavy sound of footsteps heralded Alisdair's approach. She turned to find him framed in the doorway, his broad shoulders casting a long shadow that reached out to her across the flagstones.

"Alisdair," she greeted.

"Ye shouldna be out here alone. The night grows cold," he cried, crossing the distance between them with purposeful strides. He wrapped her in his embrace, trying to warm her with his caress.

"Perhaps, but the solitude grants me time away from watchful eyes," Fiona replied.

"Even mine?" Alisdair asked.

"Especially yours," she teased, though her smile faltered as she regarded him. He was her chosen, yet even he could not shield her from the weight of expectation that clung to her.

"Ye ken I wouldna ever let harm befall ye, Fiona." He brushed a stray lock of hair from her face, the gesture achingly tender.

"I know," she whispered, leaning into him. "It is not your protection I doubt, but the freedom to live beyond its confines. I told Malcolm repeatedly that he should surrender to save his men, and that you and yours would best them. I was right, but his men died alongside him."

"Only a few more nights," he assured her, his thumb tracing the line of her jaw. "And then—"

"And then I am truly yours," Fiona finished. The words were a vow, an anchor amidst the uncertainty that had come to define her days.

"Truly mine," he echoed, his voice low with a reverence that matched the solemnity of the moment.

Their lips met in both affirmation and defiance. Time halted, the world narrowing to the point of their connection, the silent pledge of hearts entwined.

As they parted, Fiona's fingers lingered on his cheek, reluctant to break the contact that offered solace. "I cannot wait for the day when we may be together without the need for guards or permissions," she quietly confessed.

"Nor can I," Alisdair agreed.

He kissed her forehead gently before stepping back. "Goodnight, my fierce warrior," he crooned.

"Goodnight, my heart," Fiona replied, watching as he retreated into the keep, lingering on his retreating form until he vanished from sight.

IT WAS WELL past midnight when Fiona awoke to a sound from outside her room. She knew it could well be the guards her father had acting as watchmen for her and her sisters, but it felt off to her. Grabbing her dirk, she stepped outside the room, ready to protect herself if needed.

Instead of one of the guards, she spotted Alisdair standing outside her room, deep in thought. She turned one way and then the other before launching herself at him, wrapping her arms around him and holding him close. It was truly the first time she'd felt alone with him since the Sinclairs had taken her.

Alisdair took her into his arms and kissed her. No words were necessary.

Their kiss deepened, fueled by the intensity of their longing and the fear that had gripped them during Fiona's ordeal. Relief at her safe return mingled with a fierce desire for one another.

Fiona's hands roamed over Alisdair's strong frame, memorizing the contours of his body as if to ensure he was truly there with her. His caress set her skin ablaze, every brush of his fingers sending sparks of electricity through her veins. In that moment, nothing else existed but the two of them, lost in a world where duty and danger faded into insignificance.

Alisdair cupped her face, his thumbs tracing the line of her jaw before tangling in her hair. He deepened the kiss, pouring all his unspoken emotions into the fervent meeting of their lips. Fiona responded in kind, her heart pounding in rhythm with his as they clung to one another, the heat between them igniting a passionate flame that consumed all doubts and fears.

Their bodies pressed together, fitting like two halves of a whole as their kiss deepened, the world falling away around them. Desire coursed through Fiona. It was an overwhelming need to be closer to Alisdair, to feel every part of him against her.

Alisdair moved his hands from her face to her waist, pulling her even closer as he deepened the kiss, their breaths mingling in a heady exchange. Fiona melted into his caress, her fingers threading through his hair as she lost herself in the intensity of their connection.

The weight of the past days, filled with worry and uncertainty, lifted from Fiona's shoulders as she surrendered to the moment. Every caress from Alisdair was a promise of love and protection, a vow written in their bodily language.

As they broke apart for air, their foreheads resting against each other, they heard the footsteps of one of Fiona's guards coming toward them. After one more quick kiss, she returned to the room she shared with her sisters and her lonely bed.

As she fell back to sleep, her mind was full of her future husband and the way his caress burned her.

CHAPTER THIRTEEN

Fiona McAfee stood at a distance, arms crossed over her chest as she watched the training grounds of the McClains. A single strand of blond hair, rebellious as her spirit, danced upon her brow as her piercing blue eyes reflected the arcs of swinging swords.

"Again!" Alisdair commanded from the center of the men, his voice carrying over the din of combat. His gaze found Fiona's—a silent acknowledgment of her presence.

As the men around him continued their dance of mock warfare, Fiona's thoughts wandered, her lips moving silently in conversation with herself. She was tired of talking about wedding preparations. She'd already made these decisions for the day they were supposed to wed, and now she was having to make them all over again. Why couldn't her original decisions for the wedding still hold true?

She knew well that Ailis, with her keen eye and zest for such affairs, would revel in taking over the reins of wedding preparations.

"Brother," Alisdair called, his tone slicing through the air with practiced ease. Brodie, with the poise of an archer even on foot, approached, his eyes seeking instruction. "Take the men through the paces. I have a matter to attend to."

Brodie nodded, his demeanor calm as a still lake, his dark hair tied back in solemnity for the task at hand. There was trust there, a silent language spoken in the briefest of glances and the subtle shift of responsibility from one pair of capable hands to another.

With a final nod, Alisdair withdrew from the field, his movements deliberate, every step a measured advance toward Fiona. The world slowed its breath, the clamor of training fading into a distant thrum as he approached her. Fiona watched him come, her heart beating a rhythm akin to the warriors' drills, yet her posture betrayed none of the tumult that stirred within her.

"Ye find escape in the spectacle of battle, Fiona?" Alisdair asked. His low rumble was rich with the promise of shared confidences.

"Escape? Nay," she replied. Her reflective tone belied the storm of emotions that played behind her stoic facade. "Merely seeking solace in familiarity. 'Tis a comfort to see life continue unabated, as decisions for the morrow are made without my hand."

Alisdair's eyes captured hers in a moment of vulnerability. "Then perhaps ye'll allow me to offer a different kind of solace, away from prying eyes?"

Alisdair extended his hand. Without a word, Fiona placed her own in his. Even as she did, she knew her father would be displeased if he caught her. But at that moment, it was a great deal more important to caress Alisdair and be caressed by him than try to avoid her father's wrath.

They wound their way through the maze of tents and supplies, slipping past the vigilant eyes of the guards with the ease of shadows.

"Are we daring too much?" Fiona whispered, not wanting to be caught.

"Mayhap," Alisdair conceded. "But what is life without a measure of risk?"

They delved deeper into the woods, where the clamor of the keep was muffled by the dense embrace of the forest. Here among ancient trees, they found a haven untouched by duty's call—a rock veiled by overhanging branches and the dappled shade they offered.

"Here, we are but man and woman," Alisdair murmured. "Not pawns in the game of clans."

Fiona's breath caught as she gazed into his eyes, seeing there the reflection of her own yearning. She allowed herself this moment, this sweet surrender to desire, as if the world beyond these trees ceased to exist.

Seated upon the stone, Fiona sensed the solid weight of him, exploring the contours of his broad shoulders through the fabric of his tunic. Alisdair returned her fervor, his fingers threading through her hair, releasing it from her braid to cascade down her back.

Their lips met in a kiss that was passionate and thrilling to them both. He eased her onto his lap, stroking her back, one boldly coming around to cup her breast and toy with the nipple he found there. "The days leading up to our wedding are taking much too long," he whispered against her lips.

Their kiss deepened, a dance of longing and urgency that spoke volumes of the desire they shared. Fiona's hands roamed over Alisdair's warm chest, memorizing every ridge and muscle as if committing them to heart. His caress ignited a fire within her, a blaze that consumed any doubts or fears, leaving only the unquenchable yearning for more.

Alisdair's devotion was obvious in the way he held her, not with possession but with care, as if she were a precious treasure to be cherished. His lips trailed a path of scorching kisses along her jawline, down her neck, igniting a trail of fire. Fiona arched into his caress, gasping raggedly as she surrendered to the heady rush of sensation that enveloped them. She could feel the bulge of his member pressing against her from under his plaid, and she thought how easy it would be to lift both of their plaids and join together.

The world around them faded into insignificance as they lost themselves in each other. Their bodies moved in perfect sync as if they were two halves of a whole, destined to intertwine in a dance as old as time. The rustle of leaves above them whispered a secret melody.

For Fiona, every caress from Alisdair felt like an awakening, igniting a passion within her that she had long kept dormant. With his calloused hands, he traced patterns of desire along her skin, leaving trails of heat in their wake. As his mouth found hers once more, a fierce and unrelenting hunger rose within her.

She responded in kind, her kisses a symphony of longing and love, telling him without words the depth of her emotions. Their connection transcended the physical, delving into the realm of souls intertwined, bound by a bond that defied the constraints of duty and expectation.

The world beyond their secluded haven ceased to exist as they continued rubbing and kissing one another, laying bare their desires and vulnerabilities in the shared intimacy of that hidden sanctuary. Fiona's hands trembled with a mixture of anticipation and raw emotion as she sought to convey what words could never truly capture.

Alisdair's gaze held a fierce determination yet softened by the tenderness reserved only for her. In that moment, he was not just a warrior burdened by responsibilities. He was a man laid bare before her, offering himself.

As if guided by an unspoken understanding, Fiona traced the lines of his face, memorizing every contour with a delicate caress. Each mark told a story of battles fought and hardships endured, but to her, they were the map leading to the core of his being. In her eyes, those scars were not signs of weakness but proof of his strength.

Their breaths mingled in the space between them. Alisdair's chest beat thunderously beneath Fiona's fingertips, a steady drumming that reverberated through her and called to her. In the quiet of that secluded glade, she found a sanctuary where they could shed the expectations and burdens weighing upon them, embracing the passion that bound them together.

As Alisdair trailed fiery kisses down her neck, Fiona was ablaze. Her body arched instinctively into his, seeking ever closer proximity as if to merge their very beings into one. The warmth of his breath against her skin sent shivers of anticipation racing down her spine, awakening a hunger that had long simmered within her.

Their movements were a fluid symphony of passion, each caress a note in a melody of unspoken devotion and longing. Fiona surrendered herself wholly to Alisdair's body, her heart pounding in rhythm with his, two hearts beating as one. The world around them melted away, leaving only the heat of desire and their breathless whispers.

In this moment, time stood still. Fiona was on the precipice of something extraordinary—a leap into the unknown depths of passion that promised to flood her senses and redefine her understanding of love. She wanted to drown in the intensity of this connection. As Alisdair's hands roamed over her, leaving trails of fire in their wake, Fiona teetered on the edge of an abyss, ready to plunge into the depths of desire with no fear of what lay beneath.

"Ye shouldnae be here alone with him, milady." The voice was like a stone through glass. Startled, they turned to find the guard, his expression a mix of disapproval and concern etched deeply upon his weathered face.

It took Fiona a moment to comprehend his words, but when she did, she jumped up from Alisdair's lap, fixing her clothing.

"Forgive us, Aiden," Fiona began, her cheeks flushed with the embers of their passion now cooled by the chill of duty. "We meant no disrespect nor danger to ourselves."

"Respect or nae," Aiden replied sternly, though his eyes softened as they rested on Fiona, "it is for yer safety I am charged. The woods hold more than secret trysts. They harbor unseen threats that care not for love's embrace." He paused for a moment. "After what has occurred, ye should ken that better than anyone."

"Ye speak truly," Alisdair acknowledged, standing and offering a hand to help Fiona rise. "We'll not forget our station again."

AIDEN STRODE WITH purpose through the stone corridors of Castle McClain, the echo of his boots a somber prelude to the news he bore. His shadow stretched long and thin in the waning light that filtered through the arrow slits, as if it too sensed the gravity of his report. He found Laird Duncan in the great hall, hunched over scrolls and missives that spoke of alliances and feuds, the weight of leadership etched into his furrowed brow.

"Laird," Aiden began, his voice carrying the heavy burden of duty. "I must speak on a matter most urgent."

Duncan raised his gaze. "Speak, Aiden. What troubles have ye found?"

"Your daughter, the Lady Fiona..." Aiden hesitated, the words catching like thorns in his throat. "She has evaded my watch and sought the company of Alisdair McClain in the forest."

The air grew dense with silence. With measured calm, Duncan rose from his seat, the sash of his clan swaying gently. "So be it," he declared. "We shall return to our lands. The wedding is called off. If she cannae abide by the rules of her courtship, then there will be no more courtship."

As the laird summoned his daughters for their journey home, an unspoken understanding passed between them.

Alisdair McClain watched from a distance. His jaw set firm, his resolve unwavering. He would not forsake Fiona to the whims of fate nor the dictates of clans. With silent determination, he followed the procession to the keep of Clan McAfee.

Laird McAfee could not fault him for this—knowing well the protection their land provided, knowing too the stubbornness of young hearts. Alisdair's presence within their walls was a challenge to tradition, yet Duncan perceived the honor in his actions, even as the future lay uncertain like the untamed wilderness beyond their gates.

Within the keep, Fiona paced her chamber, her mind a

tempest of emotions. She yearned for Alisdair's embrace, for the freedom of their time together, yet she was bound by the cords of birthright and the looming specter of responsibility. Her once defiant spirit now grappled with the complexities of loyalty.

ALISDAIR'S SWORD MET the clanging of steel against steel, his muscular frame moving with a precision that spoke of many battles and skirmishes. The men of Clan McAfee circled around him, their respect for his prowess growing with every deft maneuver he executed. They had come to accept him, not merely as an outsider, but as one of their own, bound by the sweat of training and the camaraderie forged in shared exertion. He had trained with them every day since he'd come to stay with them a fortnight before.

Fiona watched from the shade of an ancient oak, her blue eyes tracing Alisdair's movements like a hawk tracking its prey. Her heart thrummed, not only from the thrill of his combat but from the knowledge that soon, they would escape the vigilant eyes for the seclusion of the forest.

"Ye fight well, McClain," grunted one burly McAfee warrior, clapping Alisdair on the shoulder as they took a moment away from their sparring. Silent acknowledgment passed between them.

Alisdair sheathed his blade and strode toward Fiona. Their fingers entwined, they slipped away, unnoticed by all. In the forest's embrace, passion bloomed anew, as if the very earth itself conspired to draw them closer. Lips met in fervent haste, hands exploring the familiar yet still exhilarating contours of each other's bodies.

She pulled back from Alisdair. "I must try to speak with my father again. We will be caught if we keep sneaking off this way."

Alisdair nodded. "Aye. I want to marry ye, not dally with ye in the forest."

Alisdair's words echoed in Fiona's mind as she gazed into his captivating eyes. The weight of his sincerity hit her, causing her heart to race with a mix of anxiety and longing. She knew she had to find a way to convince her father, Laird Duncan McAfee, to see things from her perspective.

As they walked through the lush greenery of the forest, Fiona grew determined. She needed to find the right words to sway her father's rigid beliefs. Ideas swirled in her mind like colorful leaves dancing in the wind, each one vying for attention.

They found a secluded spot near a bubbling brook, its melodious song providing a soothing backdrop to their conversation. Fiona sighed, steeling herself for what was to come. This moment could change everything.

"I believe I have a plan," she began steadily despite her fluttering stomach.

Fiona's gaze locked with Alisdair's, the intensity in her piercing blue eyes mirroring the gravity of their clandestine meeting.

"Alisdair," she began, "we have traversed beyond the boundaries set by tradition and duty." Her fingers brushed against the fabric of her kilt, straightening it unconsciously—a habit that emerged when her thoughts ran deep.

"Aye, we find ourselves entangled within the very heart of forbidden terrain," he replied, his posture reflecting both his acknowledgment of their transgression and readiness to stand firm beside her.

"Yet, 'tis precisely this boldness, this willingness to defy convention, that shall be the cornerstone of my appeal to my father," Fiona continued, her braid swaying slightly as she tilted her head, considering the path they must now tread. "I shall approach him with candor, laying bare our intentions and the depth of our commitment."

"Such a revelation will demand great courage, Fiona," Alisdair replied, though the glint in his eye showed his admiration for her tenacity. "The McAfee clan is steeped in principle, and your father—"

"Is a man of reason as much as he is of tradition," she cut in. "He cannot deny the strategic merit of our union. The alliance between McAfee and McClain would fortify our lands against any who dare encroach upon our sovereignty."

"Your words are as a fortress themselves, unyielding and formidable," Alisdair conceded. "And what of the contention such honesty may incite? Our families, bound by honor but divided by history, might not readily accept this breach of etiquette as easily as you foresee."

"Then it is upon us to present a vision of unity, one so compelling that even the staunchest opposition will yield to its promise," Fiona replied. "For what is a life without risk, and what is love if not the greatest venture of all?"

"Indeed," Alisdair murmured. He stepped closer, the space between them charged with the tension of their intertwined fates. "Ye speak of duty and sacrifice, yet I see in your eyes the flame of personal desire. I'm willing to do whatever it takes to get yer father to trust me again."

Their hands met, fingers intertwining. The moment held the fragility of a truce on the eve of war, yet it was strengthened by the unspoken oath that pulsed through their clasped hands. In the quiet that enveloped them, time itself bowed to the inevitability of their bond.

She spoke of their shared values, their aspirations for a peaceful future together, and the undeniable connection that bound them together as one.

Alisdair's eyes softened with each word, his admiration for Fiona growing with every impassioned argument she presented. He perceived the fire in her soul, the fierce determination that lay beneath her composed exterior.

She finally fell silent. A moment of stillness enveloped them like a protective cloak. The brook continued its gentle song, a reminder of the passage of time and the eternal flow of nature.

"Do ye think he'll listen?" Fiona asked nervously.

Alisdair sighed. "I hope so. I'm ready for ye to be my wife."

They wandered back to the castle, hand in hand, her mind working through the arguments she'd prepared to present to her father. Surely, he would listen. He'd promised to hear her out on prospective suitors.

"Father," Fiona began, "I must speak with ye."

Duncan sat behind the great oak desk that had borne witness to countless decisions shaping the destiny of their clan.

"Speak, lass." His eyes met hers. He'd obviously been expecting her to come with all the reasons she should be allowed to marry Alisdair, which made her forget the reasons she'd prepared.

"Alisdair and I wish to marry. We both want more than a political alliance, and naught shall sever the bond we share," Fiona declared, lifting her chin in defiance.

The laird regarded her, the silence stretching into eternity before he finally responded. "Then he must prove himself worthy of ye, Fiona—worthy of being the laird of Clan McAfee."

"And what if he does not?" Fiona whispered.

"Then ye ken yer duty," Duncan replied, his voice soft but irrevocable.

"Would ye have me choose between my heart and my clan? I'll run away this very night to marry him, if that's what it takes," she threatened, her fierce spirit flaring.

"Ye would have already left if ye truly meant to," Duncan countered, his eyes revealing a depth of understanding. "Ye are your mother's daughter, through and through."

Fiona emerged from the keep, her stride brisk as she crossed the dew-kissed courtyard to where Alisdair awaited her. The cool morning air did little to soothe the fire of annoyance that blazed within her chest. Her heart beat a fierce rhythm against her ribs, echoing the turmoil that churned in her thoughts.

"Alisdair." Her voice carried the edge of her vexation. Her braid swayed with each determined step she took toward him, the escaped strands framing her face like the tendrils of her growing frustration.

He faced her, his blue eyes piercing through the facade of her composure. "Ye've spoken with yer father, then?" he asked, his voice calm and even, betraying none of the urgency he felt.

"Aye, and he demands ye prove yerself worthy of my hand, as if I were some prize to be won at the end of a trial," Fiona retorted bitterly. She watched as his jaw tightened, the subtle shift of muscle beneath the skin revealing his own inner struggle.

"Perhaps he is right," Alisdair conceded. "I was remiss in allowing ye to be taken from McClain land. It falls to me now to show that I can protect ye—that I am fit to stand by yer side."

For a moment, Fiona could only stare at him, her mind grappling with the weight of his agreement. The idea of Alisdair acquiescing to her father's demand stirred a torrent of emotions within her. She had expected resistance, but instead, she found a man willing to shoulder the burden of proof.

"Then what are we to do?" she asked, the fierceness of her spirit not yet quelled. "Shall we dance to the tune he plays for us?"

"Nay, Fiona," he replied, stepping closer to her until the space between them was but a whisper. "We shall not push for this wedding. Let us lay aside the mantle of expectation and simply be together."

The simplicity of his proposal gave pause to the tempest in Fiona's soul. To enjoy stolen moments without the shadow of duty looming over them—it was a temptation sweet and inviting.

"Very well," she agreed with a small smile. "We shall spend time in each other's company, and let the morrow bring what it may."

Together, they walked, veering away from the prying eyes of the keep and into the sanctuary of the forest. The world around them fell into a hush, as if nature itself held its breath in reverence to their plight. Here, among the ancient trees and the soft carpet of fallen leaves, they found solace in the quiet embrace of the woods.

Their time was their own, a precious commodity they hoarded greedily. With every kiss, they made many sweet memories.

◆━━◆━━❈━━◆━━◆

CHAPTER FOURTEEN

ALISDAIR APPROACHED THE imposing stone structure that housed the McAfee clan. Today, he would meet with Laird McAfee in secret.

Alisdair rehearsed the words he meant to say, the promises he was prepared to make. The heavy oak door before him swung inward at the caress of his calloused hand, revealing the proud, graying figure of the laird, peering out the window.

"Laird McAfee," Alisdair began, "I come before ye to offer my fealty and my word. I am willing to do whatever it takes to prove meself worthy of marriage to yer daughter, Fiona."

Duncan regarded him with eyes that weighed the very essence of his being, the corners of his mouth hinting at a smile. "Ye are bold, Alisdair McClain, to seek my blessing thus. Tell me, what makes ye deem yerself worthy of my eldest, who is both warrior and heir?"

Alisdair's gaze did not waver as he responded, "It is not just in battle that I have proven myself, but in the care and leadership of my clan. I vow to protect and honor Fiona, to stand by her side, and to support her ambitions as she will undoubtedly lead the McAfees to further glory."

The laird nodded slowly, pondering the weight of Alisdair's words. It was then that the sound of laughter drifted through the open window, drawing both men's attention to the courtyard below.

There, Fiona stood with her sisters, Ailis and Moira, their

heads thrown back in mirth. Alisdair observed from above, a silent sentinel to their camaraderie. Ailis teased Fiona with a mischievous glint in her gray eyes, while Moira playfully tugged at the end of Fiona's braid, eliciting another burst of laughter from the trio.

The sight filled Alisdair with an unexpected warmth. He witnessed the bond of loyalty and support between the sisters. It was a bond he longed to be part of, one he yearned to fortify with his own unwavering dedication. He had it with his brothers, but that was something that had followed from childhood. He wanted the same thing now that he was an adult, no longer living with his brothers.

"Yer daughters share a kinship that is rare and beautiful," Alisdair remarked respectfully.

"Aye, they do," Laird McAfee replied, his eyes softening as he watched them. "And it is that very bond, that unity, which has seen our clan through the darkest times. Any man who wishes to join our family must understand and honor it."

"I understand more than ye may realize," Alisdair spoke quietly.

"Then perhaps," Duncan replied, "there is hope for ye yet, Alisdair McClain."

Hope indeed, Alisdair thought, as he watched Fiona throw her head back once more, her laughter echoing like a promise.

ALISDAIR LINGERED IN the shadow of the grand archway, his gaze following Fiona as she knelt beside a small boy whose sobs fractured the stillness of the castle's courtyard. The child, an orphan cared for under the protective wing of the McAfee clan, clutched a ragged doll to his chest, his cries piercing the air with their plaintive resonance.

"Ye needn't worry, little one," Fiona cooed. With deft hands, she smoothed back the tousled hair from his brow, her fingers as gentle as the first thaw of spring. "This clan is yer family now, and we will stand by ye."

Alisdair held a profound respect for the woman who wielded both sword and solace. Her compassion was not a mere act of obligation but a sincere outpouring from a wellspring of empathy deep within her heart. He watched, silent and unseen, as the boy's tears subsided, his sniffles giving way to a quivering smile under Fiona's comforting ministrations.

"See there, all is well," Fiona whispered, her blue eyes cradling the promise of security. Alisdair marveled at the strength that lay beneath her nurturing spirit—a strength that fortified the very essence of the McAfee legacy.

As the orphan scampered away, Fiona rose to rejoin her sisters. Ailis and Moira moved to her, their arms linked in solidarity, and began to recount tales of yesteryears fraught with trials and tribulations. The sisters spoke of seasons marked by harsh winters and meager harvests, of the sacrifices they had made—sharing cloaks and going without—to ensure none in their clan felt the biting sting of cold or hunger.

"Remember when Da fashioned wooden swords for us to practice with?" Moira's voice, bright as the glint of dawn, cut through the heavier memories. "We would spar for hours, determined to protect our people."

"Even then, ye showed the heart of a lioness, Fiona," Ailis added.

Alisdair listened, captivated by the fierce love that bound them together. In their words, he discerned the pulse of the McAfee clan—a resilient beat that had weathered storms and stood defiant against adversity. Their loyalty to one another was the bedrock upon which their future was built. It was this very foundation that Alisdair sought to become a part of.

Alisdair understood the gravity of his desire to join their ranks. It was not merely a union with Fiona he sought, but an allegiance with a family whose honor was etched into every corner of their land. A family that had sacrificed much yet remained unbroken.

"Ye have my vow," Alisdair murmured to himself, "to honor and uphold the sanctity of this bond."

Alisdair McClain stood before Laird Duncan McAfee in the great hall, where the air was thick with the weight of history.

"Leadership is naught but a series of choices, each one heavy with consequence," Alisdair began steadily as he met the laird's piercing gaze. "It demands a man to put the needs of his clan above his own desires."

"Aye, it does," Laird McAfee replied, searching Alisdair's countenance for sincerity. "The mantle of responsibility is oft a burdensome one, and not all men are fit to bear it."

"Yet I find that burden lightened by the support of kin and the unyielding bonds of family," Alisdair countered, remembering Fiona's unwavering compassion and the steadfast loyalty among her sisters.

"Family is the stronghold from which a laird must draw his strength," Laird McAfee acknowledged.

Alisdair sensed the moment ripe to address the heart of the matter. "M'lord," he ventured, a note of solemnity lacing his speech, "I ken well your concerns regarding my ability to safeguard your daughter and your people."

Laird McAfee's brow furrowed, a subtle nod encouraging Alisdair to continue.

"Ye know of my victories in battle, of the strategies I have woven to protect my own kin." Alisdair's blue eyes burned with fervor. "But beyond the prowess in combat, 'tis my dedication to Fiona and to the McAfee clan that I pledge. Her safety and her happiness shall be of utmost importance to me."

A silence settled between them, dense as the mist that clung to the highland moors. Laird McAfee's face remained inscrutable. Yet his expression softened, a sign perhaps that Alisdair's vow had reached the depths of the father's protective heart.

"Ye speak with conviction, Alisdair," the laird finally replied, his voice resonating with the unspoken gravity of his position. "And I see the fire in yer eyes that tells me ye mean what ye say."

"Upon my honor," Alisdair intoned, bowing, "I will stand vigilant. Not just as a suitor to your daughter, but as a son to this clan. This, I swear."

"Then let us walk together, Alisdair." The laird gestured toward the open doorway. "For there is much to prepare if ye are to join our ranks."

They stepped outside and followed a path away from the training soldiers and toward the forest.

"Alisdair McClain," Duncan began with the regal timbre of a laird born and bred, "ye ken what pledging fealty means to Clan McAfee?"

"Ye are to serve as shield and sword to our kin, to uphold the honor of our name." Duncan rested his hand upon the hilt of his dirk. "And most importantly, ye must place the needs of this clan above yer own."

Alisdair's gaze met Duncan's with an intensity that spoke of his commitment. "I understand, Laird McAfee. And I swear on my life, my allegiance is unwavering."

"Good." Duncan's lips quirked in a rare smile, the creases at his temples softening. "For the bond of loyalty is sacred, not to be forsaken."

"Aye," Alisdair replied.

"I would like ye to take on more responsibility, so I can take yer measure and be certain ye are the man I want married to Fiona. There have been so many missteps in this courtship that I have trouble believing it is meant to be."

"I understand," Alisdair replied softly.

"Starting tomorrow, I would like ye to be the one to train my men. I watched ye with yer father's men back in McClain territory, but these men haven't been raised to believe ye are their leader. I would like to see how ye do with them."

"It's a responsibility I take on gladly." Anything to marry Fiona. Anything.

THROUGH THE GRAND hall of the McAfee stronghold, laughter echoed off stone walls as Alisdair's deep voice melded with the lighter tones of Fiona's kinsfolk. He stood among them, a towering figure whose presence commanded attention, yet whose smile softened his warrior's mien. The flickering hearth light danced upon his features, casting shadows that played upon the scars of battles past—marks that enhanced rather than marred his rugged handsomeness.

"Aye, 'tis no mere beast could frighten yer Ailis when she wields her knitting needles," Alisdair jested, his eyes twinkling with mirth as he recounted an anecdote of a wolf encounter during his last visit.

"Och, and would ye face down a wolf with naught but yarn and wit?" Moira returned with a playful arch of her brow.

"Perhaps not," Alisdair admitted, "but I'd like to think my sword arm and quick thinking could match Ailis's deftness with her... weaponry." The room erupted with laughter.

When Fiona grew tired, she excused herself with a nod toward Alisdair, who followed with a discrete grace. They slipped away, their departure barely noticed amid the genial chaos of the great hall.

The cool evening breeze greeted them as they stepped outside, the moon casting a silver glow over the untamed landscape that surrounded the McAfee home. Alisdair offered Fiona his arm, which she accepted, her fingers resting lightly upon the sturdy fabric of his sleeve.

"Ye spoke well to my father," Fiona remarked with gratitude. "It means much that ye understand the mantle ye seek to bear."

"Your father is a man of honor, much like my own," Alisdair replied, lingering on her profile—the determined set of her jaw softened by moonlight. "I would be remiss if I did not recognize the depth of his concerns, for they mirror mine. To protect, to serve, to cherish—it is all that I am."

"Yet there is more to ye, Alisdair," Fiona countered gently, pausing to face him. Her blue eyes searched his. "Ye have a heart that sees beyond duty, a spirit that yearns for more than just obligation."

"Perhaps," he conceded, his fingertips brushing a stray lock of hair from her face. "But without duty, what are we? It is the compass by which we navigate this life."

"True," Fiona murmured, leaning into his caress. "But even a compass needs a hand to guide it, and a heart to follow its direction."

"Then let us be each other's guide," Alisdair whispered. In that moment, the world beyond the walls of the McAfee stronghold ceased to exist. There was only them, two souls bound by the pull of shared destiny.

Fiona closed the distance between them. Their lips met in a kiss that sealed their promise—a vow of unity against the ever-shifting tides of clan politics and the demands of leadership. Duty and desire entwined, forging a bond that no force on earth could rend asunder.

THROUGH THE MIST and murk of early dawn, the training field stretched before Alisdair. It was his first day leading the McAfee men in their training, and he could see already that the idea of obeying him was filling the soldiers with turmoil. His broad frame cut a formidable silhouette against the backdrop of clashing swords and the cries of men. Alisdair's piercing blue eyes surveyed the melee with calculated precision, his mind as sharp as the blade he wielded.

He had divided the McAfee soldiers into two armies, and they were fighting one another, with him commanding one, and one of the other trainers leading the other.

"Fall back!" he commanded. But the soldiers of Clan McAfee hesitated, their movements sluggish, untrusting of this outsider's lead.

"Ye ken not what yer doin', McClain!" barked a grizzled veteran, his face smeared with dirt and blood. Murmurs of assent rose among the ranks, questioning glances exchanged between breaths.

"Obey or die," Alisdair retorted, not with malice, but a cold necessity. He parried an enemy blade, stepping over a fallen comrade with a grimace. "I fight for your lives, for our victory!"

The battle raged on, a relentless tide of violence and steel. Yet, amid the chaos, some soldiers began to mimic Alisdair's tactics. Their survival testament to his strategic acumen. Slowly, begrudgingly, respect was forged in the fires of combat.

DAYS LATER, UPON the practice fields, Alisdair's presence commanded a different kind of battlefield. Here, the clang of sword against shield rang methodically under a sky brushed with billowing clouds. Alisdair demonstrated a complex maneuver, his movements deft.

"Watch and learn," he instructed, the lines of his face set in fierce concentration. The soldiers, sweat gleaming on their brows, echoed his steps with varying degrees of success.

"Like this?" a young soldier ventured, emulating Alisdair's stance, his eyes eager for approval.

"Almost," Alisdair acknowledged with a curt nod, correcting the lad's grip. "Again."

They drilled for hours, muscles aching and spirits tested. But as the sun dipped below the horizon, they developed camaraderie. Laughter mingled with the groans of exertion, and even the most skeptical among them could not deny the skill woven into Alisdair's every command.

"Ye might just make warriors of us yet," conceded a veteran from the battlefield, a grudging smile breaking through his weathered face.

Alisdair allowed himself the ghost of a smile, a rare slip of emotion. He saw the potential for true unity, a force that could stand against any foe. For now, he would temper them into the soldiers he knew they could be, soldiers worthy of both McAfee and McClain.

THE MORNING AIR held a crispness that hinted at the approach of autumn, and with it, the promise of the challenges to come. Alisdair McClain drilled the soldiers of Clan McAfee on the field below, his presence a steady beacon in the middle of clashing swords and shields.

His commands sliced through the din of metal and men, each syllable a testament to unwavering authority. The soldiers moved as one, a phalanx of bodies trained to perfection, their previous insubordination a ghost of the past. They had become an extension of Alisdair's will, every man stepping forward in precise harmony, their obedience as sure as the dawn.

"Shield wall!" he bellowed. Instantly, a barrier of wood and iron formed, impenetrable and resolute.

It was a dance of war, each movement calculated and deliberate, honed through relentless repetition until doubt had no room to breathe.

There was a subtle shift in Alisdair's stance as he surveyed his men, pride etched into the lines of his face, though he would never boast of it.

The weight of duty pressed upon his broad shoulders. He had forgone personal desires for the sake of his clan, his every action steeped in the tension between love for his people and the harsh necessities of politics.

"Advance!" Alisdair's next command unfurled across the field. The soldiers responded with immediate compliance, their trust in his leadership as deeply rooted as the ancient oaks that lined the edges of the McAfee lands.

The rhythm of their boots thudding against the earth was steady and slow, a measured march toward an unseen enemy, a testament to their readiness for whatever trials lay ahead. Not one man faltered, their faith in Alisdair's command absolute.

As the morning melded into afternoon and the drills continued without respite, Alisdair realized that the men were working in unity, where every soldier obeyed without question, and every heart beat to the drum of Alisdair McClain's indomitable spirit.

ALISDAIR STOOD AT a respectful distance, his arms folded across his broad chest, watching with a keen eye as Fiona moved among her kin. Clad in a garment that melded the practicality of a warrior with the grace of a lady, she commanded the room not by voice alone but by her very presence. Her piercing blue eyes surveyed the gathered McAfees, each member poised to heed her counsel.

"See here," Fiona began, "The winter stores are less than generous this season. We must ration carefully and seek aid from our neighboring clans under terms that benefit us all." Ailis nodded somberly. Fiona lowered her voice. "But not the Sinclairs. I have no trust for them, and I would rather deal with a trustworthy clan."

Alisdair couldn't help but admire Fiona's strategic mind. Evidently, her leadership extended well beyond the battlefield. It was woven into the fabric of her daily life, ensuring the survival and prosperity of her clan.

As evening descended upon the highland estate, the McAfee family gathered within the warmth of the great hall. The crackling hearth cast a golden glow upon their faces as they settled in for a time-honored tradition—the telling of tales. Alisdair took his place beside Fiona, their shoulders brushing in silent camaraderie.

"Tonight, we share the saga of the Silent Boar," announced Laird Duncan. As the laird told the tale of a ghostly white boar that granted prosperity to the clan that could track it without uttering a word, Alisdair observed Fiona's face. Her eyes sparkled with the magic of the story, reflecting the same enchantment he felt in her presence.

When it came time for the meal, servers passed around platters of game and vegetables. Alisdair found himself immersed in the simple yet profound act of breaking bread with the McAfees. He sat beside Fiona, their hands occasionally brushing as they reached for their food—a caress that spoke volumes more than words ever could.

"Ye ken," Fiona whispered to him between bites, "we've always believed that sharing a meal binds us closer than any oath."

"I am beginning to understand the depth of that belief," Alisdair replied. The feast continued, punctuated by laughter and the clinking of goblets, but amidst the revelry, Alisdair found his thoughts returning again and again to Fiona's earlier display of leadership.

As the evening waned and the shadows grew long across the grand hall, Alisdair rose from his seat at the head of the McAfee table. The feast had dwindled to shared tales and the soft strumming of a lute in the background. He caught Fiona's piercing blue gaze steadying him.

"Laird Duncan, ladies Ailis and Moira, and all kin of Clan McAfee," Alisdair began. "I find myself humbled by the warmth and generosity ye have shown me within these walls. Your trust is not a gift I bear lightly."

He turned slightly, ensuring each member of the family understood the weight of his gaze. "To you, Laird, I vow my sword and my strength. To your daughters, my steadfast protection."

His eyes softened as they met Fiona's once more. "And to ye, Fiona, my entire being, now and for all days to come."

A respectful murmur rippled through the hall. Alisdair's stature was that of a warrior pledging fealty, offering not just a vow but a sacred promise.

As the fire crackled, Alisdair retreated into the recesses of the chamber. There, he allowed himself a moment of reflection.

In the quiet solitude, the echoes of laughter and camaraderie from the McAfee family filled him with an unexpected sense of belonging. He considered the depth of their bonds, forged through trials and sacrifice, much like the steel of his own blade.

Alisdair thought of Fiona's leadership, both nurturing and fierce, guiding her kin with the certainty of a seasoned chieftain. Each memory etched itself upon his heart.

With a renewed sense of purpose, Alisdair acknowledged the path before him, one fraught with challenges yet bright with the promise of unity.

"By the morrow, we forge ahead," he mused, envisioning his future alongside Fiona. "Together, we shall rise."

Alisdair McClain stepped back into the light of the great hall, ready to face whatever the fates might put in his path, his allegiance to the McAfee clan unwavering.

CHAPTER FIFTEEN

LACHLAN AND BRODIE arrived with a contingent of soldiers from Clan McClain. Quickly, the soldiers began bickering with the McAfee soldiers about the kidnapping.

"Alisdair," Fiona began, "the discord 'twixt our kin grows thicker than ever. We must forge a passage through this looming tempest ere it rends us apart."

"Aye, Fiona," Alisdair replied. "Our families turn to us for guidance, yet little do they ken how we strive to quell the storm that threatens to engulf us all. Your father and his men blame the McClains for your kidnapping. My men believe that your father's men should have paid better attention. Since it was the McClains who rescued you, they believe your father should be more forgiving." He shook his head. "I dinna want animosity between the two clans."

The morrow brought with it the clamor of dispute, a cacophony that rose from the heart of the glen as two members of their respective clans crossed swords over a simple argument. Fiona stepped between them with Alisdair by her side, a united front in the middle of the fray.

"Enough!" Her command sliced through the clatter of swords. "Shall blood be shed over bygones? Naught can change the past. Let reason be our ally this day."

"Your words ring true, Fiona," Alisdair agreed. "Let us parley and find accord in shared prosperity."

Yet even as the pair paraded the virtues of peace, mutters of dissent wove through the gathered crowd like serpents through grass. The clansmen, upset by weeks of enmity, regarded each other with suspicion sharpened on the whetstone of history.

"McAfee speaks of peace while her warriors train at dawn," sneered one.

"McClain's olive branch hides thorns," retorted another.

Despite Fiona's fervent appeals and Alisdair's measured counsel, the chasm grew wider, fueled by ancestral grudges that no mere words could heal.

In the quiet that followed the failed mediation, beneath the same oaks that had witnessed their secret vows, Fiona and Alisdair regarded each other with weariness.

"Why are hearts so fraught with hate that love seems all but lost?" Fiona murmured, more to herself than to him.

"Perchance 'tis our lot to bear this burden, to strive 'gainst the tide until the morrow grants us a reprieve or oblivion," Alisdair replied.

Fiona and Alisdair resolved to press onward. For within their grasp lay not only their affection but the promise of unity for their people—a future worth every sacrifice laid upon the altar of peace.

FIONA SOUGHT THE shelter of the weeping willow. Within this secluded glade, she found Ailis. Her sister's presence was as soothing as the gentle brook that murmured nearby.

"Oh Ailis," Fiona quavered, "the chasm 'twixt our kin and the McClains deepens with each passing day. I fear what this discord may yet keep us apart."

Ailis, perceiving the tumult in Fiona's soul, took her sister's hands. "The path of peace is fraught with thistles and thorns, yet tread we must," she counseled. "Mayhap, a festival—a celebration of common ground to remind both clans of shared joys and sorrows long past."

Fiona considered the proposal, the seed of hope sprouting. "Aye, a gathering under guise of merriment might serve to soften hardened hearts."

Before they could speak more, a clash of voices disrupted the tranquility of the grove. Fiona and Ailis hastened toward the source of the commotion, where Laird Duncan McAfee stood face-to-face with Lachlan McClain.

"Would ye dare to claim honor when yer kin seeks naught but to undermine mine own?" Duncan's words thundered across the clearing.

"Yer pride blinds ye to reason, McAfee," Lachlan retorted, his stance unyielding as the oak that towered behind him. "We seek not dominion, only respect and fair dealing."

The air grew thick with the scent of impending conflict. Fiona's heart clenched at the sight of her beloved father, his countenance a storm of wrathful resolve, opposite Lachlan, whose charm now lay buried beneath the gravity of the moment.

"Father, pray, allow cooler heads to prevail," Fiona implored. "This discord serves none but those who would see us both weakened." *The Sinclairs*. Her father would never believe it.

Duncan turned to study his daughter, his expression softening ever so slightly. "Child, ye ken not the depth of treachery that festers within the hearts of men."

"Yet if we do not extend the branch of trust, how shall we ever reap the fruits of peace?" Fiona pressed, her resolve as steadfast as the ancient stones that ringed their homeland.

FIONA BRUSHED AGAINST the parchment, a symbol of hope that now appeared as fragile as the morning mist clinging to the heather-laden hills. Beside her stood Alisdair. Together, they had crafted an invitation, a call for unity from the brewing tempest of clan discord.

"Shall we set it forth?" Alisdair asked.

"Aye," Fiona replied, her gaze fixed upon the wax seal that bore the entwined emblems of their houses. "If our kin but see the merit in discourse, peace may yet flourish where strife has long taken root."

"Brothers, sisters," Fiona began, "we stand before thee, not as foes, but as kindred spirits yearning for harmony."

Murmurs rippled through the assembled crowds like wind through barley, carrying skepticism and hardened pride. Eyes that once held warmth now regarded them with the chill of doubt. Alisdair stepped forward, commanding attention.

"Let us break bread as one family under the vast sky," he proposed, "and forge a path not marred by the sins of our forebears."

The resistance was palpable, a wall built not of stone but of mistrust. Laird Duncan McAfee rose, his visage as stern as the craggy cliffs that bordered their lands.

"Peace is a noble pursuit," he conceded, "yet how shall we lay down arms when betrayal lurks behind every smile?"

"Talks have been had, promises made and broken," a seasoned clansman declared. "What assurance have we that this time shall be different?"

As dusk painted the sky in hues of fading gold and crimson, Fiona wandered the outskirts of the glen, Alisdair's silent form at her side. The air was still, as if the very earth held its breath, awaiting the outcome of a struggle too long endured.

"Are we but dreamers, Alisdair?" Fiona murmured. "Seekers of a dawn that may never break upon our clans?"

Alisdair turned toward her, his gaze piercing through the encroaching twilight. "Perhaps," he admitted sorrowfully. "But 'tis a dream worth cherishing. Without it, what remains but endless night?"

"Yet even dreams must yield to the immutable truth," Fiona lamented. "Our feelings, though true as the north star, may falter 'neath the weight of enmity. Our clans have never been enemies, but with the Sinclairs spreading lies, it's hard to see that."

"Then let it not be said that we shied from the challenge," Alisdair declared, taking her hand. There, their fingers intertwined—a silent pact between hearts that refused to yield to the cold march of destiny. "For I would rather brave the storm with ye than seek shelter alone."

Fiona lifted her chin, the lines of her face etched with resolve that mirrored the steadfast hills surrounding them. "Together, then, we shall face the morrow, come what may."

The distant clamor of steel upon steel roused Fiona from her reverie, the harsh clangs a discordant symphony that set her heart racing. She rose swiftly, her gaze piercing through the mist-shrouded moors as she sought the source of the disturbance. Beside her, Alisdair tensed, his warrior instincts awakening like a slumbering dragon roused by the scent of smoke.

"An attack?" Fiona murmured, her fingers brushing the hilt of her dirk—one she'd taken to wearing since she was taken captive.

"Mayhap," Alisdair growled. He clenched his jaw, scanning the horizon with the precision of an eagle sighting its prey. "But 'tis not our own kin—it comes from the borderlands, where neither McAfee nor McClain lay claim."

Together, they hastened toward the tumult, their footsteps a silent pact forged in urgency. As they crested a hillock, the veil of uncertainty lifted, revealing a skirmish that turned their blood cold. A band of rogues, bearing no colors to honor, laid siege upon a caravan.

"There!" Fiona pointed to the crest beyond, where figures emerged, clad in the familiar tartans of both McAfee and McClain. Her breath caught as she witnessed clansmen, once divided, now rushing as one toward the fray.

"Can it be?" Alisdair forgot his previous enmity in the face of shared peril.

"Come," Fiona called. She drew her blade, its edge glinting with the promise of protection. "We must aid them, for their cause is just, and our purpose clear."

Side by side, they charged down the slope, their clans' rivalries lost in the clash of arms. Fiona leaped into the melee with the grace of a hunting cat, her strikes true and deadly. Alisdair fought with the ferocity of a storm, his presence a bulwark against the tide of violence.

As the battle waned, the rogues retreating like shadows at dawn's approach, Fiona and Alisdair stood in the middle of their kinsmen, breathless yet unbroken. For a moment, no words were needed—their unity spoke volumes.

"Let us seize this fleeting truce," Alisdair declared. His gaze met Fiona's as they turned to survey their gathered brethren. "Our foes lie vanquished, but 'tis the war within that we must now address."

Fiona nodded, her spirit buoyed by the glimpse of harmony. "We shall parlay with our kin, ere the warmth of battle fades from their hearts."

They found Ailis and Lachlan among the throng, their faces etched with the weariness of conflict, yet alight with the sparks of hope. Together, the four retreated to a secluded glen, where the murmurs of nature provided a tranquil backdrop for their council.

"Brother," Lachlan began, "what if we host a feast? A celebration of this day's valor, inviting both clans to break bread beneath one roof."

"Aye," Ailis chimed in. "And let us tell tales of bravery shared, forging legends not of McAfee or McClain, but of kinship newly sprouted."

"Such a gathering could mend the enmity," Fiona conceded, her mind alive with possibilities. "If we can unite in battle, why not in peace?"

"Then it is settled," Alisdair declared. "We shall extend our hands, not in challenge, but in fellowship. Let this feast be but the first step toward a future where our love need not be shadowed by strife."

Fiona stood at the forefront of her clan. "Today, we stand not as rivals, but as allies. Our unity is our might. With it, we shall face the foe that threatens our lands."

Alisdair raised his sword, its blade catching the somber light, a silent echo to Fiona's call. Together they advanced, a united front against the encroaching threat that sought to exploit the fissures of ancient enmities.

The rivals, who wore the plaid of no clan, met them at the threshold of the moor. Shouts pierced the heavy air as the two forces collided, the clash of steel resounding like thunder rolling over the Highlands. Alisdair's tactical mind orchestrated their movements, a dance of war that weaved through the chaos, each step measured, purposeful.

Fiona fought with the ferocity of a tempest, her sword a blur as she parried and struck with precision. She moved through the melee, her heart torn between the call of duty to her clan and the whispered promise of a passion that dared to breach the chasm between her world and Alisdair's.

Around them, the battle raged, a vision of violence and valor. The McAfees and McClains, once adversaries, now fought shoulder to shoulder, their combined strength a bulwark against the oncoming tide. Each cry in the fray was a note in the symphony of their resolve, each fallen foe a vow of their shared will to protect what they held most dear.

In the thick of the struggle, Fiona spotted Alisdair dispatching an opponent with a swift, decisive blow. Their eyes met across the battlefield, a fleeting moment of connection. It was a silent vow reaffirmed, a pledge that their joint efforts would not be in vain, that their sacrifice would forge a path for peace.

As the sun began its descent, the enemy's vigor waned. The relentless assault by Fiona and Alisdair's unified force bore down upon them until, at last, the rival clan faltered, their numbers dwindling under the steadfast onslaught.

In the wake of the conflict, the realization settled upon friend and foe alike: the day was theirs. The union of the McAfee and McClain clans had not only endured but triumphed, their bond cemented in battle.

Fiona stood with shoulders squared, heaving measuredly. Around her, the remnants of the rival clan yielded, their will to fight dissipating. The stoic faces of her kin bore the marks of battle, yet in their eyes shone a glint of something more profound than victory alone—a glimmer of hope for harmony.

Beside her, Alisdair surveyed the scene with a gaze that showed both relief and resolve. His blade, now cleaned and returned to its sheath, had been an extension of his will throughout the fray. Together, he and Fiona had turned the tide, their unity a beacon in the turmoil.

"Ye have fought bravely," Fiona proclaimed, "not for glory nor vengeance, but for peace. This day shall be remembered not for the blood spilt but for the future we have secured."

Alisdair nodded, stepping forward to join her. "Aye, the bond between McAfee and McClain has been sealed by our common cause. Let us look to tomorrow, when our children may live in a land not carved by feuds but shaped by fellowship."

Swords were sheathed, and hands once raised in enmity now extended in aid as the wounded were tended, and the fallen honored.

As twilight descended upon the Highlands, casting a celestial glow upon the loch below, Fiona and Alisdair sought solace in each other's presence away from the watchful eyes of their followers.

"Look at what we have accomplished, Alisdair," Fiona murmured, her blue eyes reflecting the dying light.

"Indeed, Fiona. But the cost..." Alisdair trailed off.

"Every choice bears its weight," she replied, her hand finding his, their fingers entwining. "Yet I would bear it a thousandfold for the chance at peace... for the chance to be with ye."

"And I with ye, my fierce warrior."

They shared a kiss, soft and lingering—a seal upon their commitment to each other and the path they had forged through courage and sacrifice.

FIONA STOOD UPON the battlements, her gaze sweeping across the land. Below, the members of both clans moved together, their actions no longer dictated by discord but by a shared purpose. With tools in hand where once swords had prevailed, they began the arduous task of mending what had been broken.

The air, laced with the scent of earth turned anew and wood being sawed for repairs, carried a different sound—a hopeful note that promised of better days to come. Alisdair worked shoulder to shoulder with her father and his brother Lachlan.

"See how they labor as kin, not foes," Ailis remarked, joining Fiona. Her words held the weight of wonder.

"Aye," Fiona replied reverently. "It is as if the very soil beneath our feet yearns to nourish the seeds of peace we have sown."

"Yet the path ahead will test us, sister," Ailis replied. "Can the bond formed in adversity hold fast?"

"Adversity has forged us, Ailis. We shall not falter." Fiona's determination was as steadfast as the mountains. "We must stand vigilant, guiding our people with hands joined in unity."

Ailis nodded, her faith in Fiona's leadership unshaken. The sisters watched as children from both clans played amidst the bustle, their laughter a sweet melody that soared high above the ramparts. It spoke of innocence reclaimed.

CHAPTER SIXTEEN

A HUSH FELL upon the gathered kin as Alisdair stepped over the threshold into the keep of Clan McAfee. He scanned the assembly, seeking out the one whose favor he must earn.

Laird McAfee stood at the head of the long table. He regarded Alisdair with scrutiny. The hum of whispered speculations from his kin did little to unnerve the imposing figure who now approached him with measured steps.

"Ye honor us with yer presence," Laird Duncan began.

"An honor it is, Laird McAfee," Alisdair replied. "I come before ye with a heart laden with sincerity." He paused. "It is for Fiona's hand I ask, and I pray that this time you will consider everything, including our feelings and all the time and effort I've put into training with yer clan. I have done everything ye have asked and more."

Alisdair continued, "I pledge to protect her and bring her as much happiness as a person is capable of feeling. I vow to cherish her."

Laird Duncan regarded the young man before him, his face a mask. Yet behind those age-tempered eyes flickered the flame of a father's love for his daughter.

Fiona, standing a step behind her father, bore witness to the unfolding scene. Her heart thrummed. She prayed her father would agree to the wedding. After two tries to get married already, she felt that he should be more amenable, as he'd gotten to know Alisdair as well as they all had. She understood well the dance of desire and decree.

"Ye come before us with promises of devotion," Laird Duncan began, "but love is but one facet of a union. What of protection? The world is no stranger to turmoil. My Fiona is strong, but still needs protection. Can ye offer her the type of protection she needs to remain safe?"

Alisdair McClain regarded the laird. "Laird Duncan," he answered calmly, "I am no child brandishing a sword at shadows. I have led my clan in battle many times, and I have done so with the respect of all who follow me. I have led yer clan in battle, and they respect me as well." He spoke then of skirmishes won, of alliances forged with honor, of whispered oaths fulfilled beneath the silent witness of the moonlit sky. He did not boast, but quietly affirmed his life spent in duty and defense.

Two worlds vied for dominion within Fiona's heart. Her gaze flitted between her father and her suitor, each man a pillar of strength.

Alisdair nodded. "The hearth is more than stone and timber, my laird. It is the sanctuary of kin and memory. To protect Fiona is to protect the essence of the McAfee clan, for her spirit is indomitable, and in it, I see the future—a future I will defend with my life."

A hush fell upon the assembly, the gravity of Alisdair's vow hanging in the air. Fiona caught her breath, her pulse echoing the silent cadence of hope and fear that danced upon the edge of possibility.

Within the heart of the McAfee stronghold, amid the tapestry of expectation and yearning, the scene unfolded—an intricate ballet of words and wills, where the prize was the melding of destinies.

Ailis stepped lightly forward. Her movement beckoned attention, and her voice rose—soft as the heather on the hill—with an intention to soothe the tempest of wills before her.

"Father, might I speak on behalf of Alisdair?" she entreated Laird Duncan, her gaze lit with the gentle fire of conviction. "For in his courage, I have witnessed not merely the heart of a warrior but the essence of a protector who values heart above glory."

"Alisdair has shown a dedication unwavering," continued Ailis, painting pictures of valor. "When bandits took to our roads, it was he who stood sentinel over our trade routes, ensuring safe passage for kin and commoner alike. And when the cries of the downtrodden reached our ears, it was Alisdair who championed their cause without thought for his own gain."

It was then that Moira stepped forth with a playful twirl of her skirts—a stark contrast to the weighty discourse that had preceded. Her voice cut through the tension.

"Aye, Father," she chimed in, smiling mischievously as she cast a sidelong glance at Alisdair, "if the man can single-handedly fend off a horde of brigands, surely he can handle the likes of us." A ripple of laughter coursed through the assembly.

"Besides," Moira added, her eyes twinkling, "I daresay he could prove useful in our annual contest of wits and strategy. 'Tis a rare occasion indeed when Fiona's hand is bested."

Laird Duncan, caught between the earnest advocacy of Ailis and the irrepressible humor of Moira, allowed himself the ghost of a chuckle—a small surrender to the levity.

Alisdair turned his attentions to Ailis. With the grace of a seasoned diplomat, he inquired after her well-being, his voice low and resonant, echoing through the tapestry-draped hall.

"Moira," he greeted, "I've been forewarned of your prowess in matters of wit and strategy. Might there be room in your escapades for a humble warrior such as myself?"

Moira tilted her head, regarding Alisdair with a playful scrutiny. "If humility is your cloak, then I fear it may be a guise ill-suited for the adventures that seek me out." Her laughter, a silvery peal, cut through the tension.

Their exchange was lively, a dance of words that skirted the edge of propriety yet never overstepped. Alisdair parried Moira's jests with ease, his humor unexpected yet sincere, revealing glimpses of the man beneath the mantle of leadership.

Laird Duncan watched from his seat at the head of the long table. The lines etched by years of rulership softened. He lingered on the interactions before him.

In Alisdair's earnest efforts, Duncan discerned the stirrings of genuine regard for Fiona and her sisters. The sight coaxed the shadows from the laird's mind, prompting the consideration of possibilities.

"Father," Fiona began, her voice ringing with a clarity that matched the steel in her spine. "I stand before ye not as a child seeking indulgence, but as a woman who knows her own heart." The room hung suspended on her words, each syllable weaving through the air like threads of fate drawing together. A hush had settled over the gathered crowd, a collective breath held in anticipation. "Alisdair," Fiona continued, "is a man of honor, of strength, whose love for me is unwavering. He has proven his valor, not just in battle, but in the tenderness with which he regards those he cherishes. Grant him the chance to show that his intentions are pure."

"Perhaps," he uttered at last, "a chance may be afforded."

"Laird," Alisdair assured him, "I ken the weight of yer concerns, for they are now mine own to bear." The eyes of those who dwelt within these walls bore witness to his pledge, their breaths held in anticipation. "With the heavens as my testament, I vow to safeguard Fiona—yer bonnie daughter—and all kin of McAfee with my very life."

Alisdair's gaze met Fiona's. "Her joys shall be my joys. And should peril ever dare encroach upon this hallowed ground, I shall fight it to my very death."

Duncan stared at the younger man, and his face was softer, as if he was relenting. "While the heart may war against the mind, 'tis clear ye hold my daughter's love and loyalty in high regard."

Duncan paused as his gaze moved between his eldest daughter and Alisdair. "Ye have my blessing," he declared. "May this union between McClain and McAfee herald a time of peace and prosperity for our clans."

At those words, Fiona ran across the room and threw herself into Alisdair's arms. He caught her to him, holding her close. He would keep her safe.

With no command, the servants in the hall began to stir with the preparations for a feast. They hurried out of the room, returning with food to fill the tables that filled the great hall.

The McAfee clan gathered at the long oak table, its surface gleaming under the flickering candlelight. Laird Duncan took his place at the head, his chair slightly askew as if reluctant to assume its role in this evening of camaraderie. Ailis and Moira flanked their sister, their presence a bulwark against the uncertainty that lay beyond the stronghold's walls.

Alisdair joined them, his seat among the McAfees a symbol of the alliance newly formed—a blending of clans, of hearts, and of destinies entwined. With each shared glance and clasped hand, the atmosphere swelled with unity and acceptance.

As the feast unfolded, the clatter of cutlery and the murmur of voices filled the hall with life. Each shared dish, each raised cup, wove the fabric of their collective story tighter, binding them with threads stronger than any force that might seek to divide them.

As the meal wound down, musicians took their places within the hall and music was played. Understanding his role, Alisdair got to his feet and offered his hand to Fiona, who took it with a smile.

Together they danced. Slowly the room was filled with others dancing around them, but Fiona saw no one but Alisdair. Finally, they were to be married!

After the dance, Fiona took Alisdair to the kitchens to finally meet her grandmother, the most important woman in her life.

Fiona navigated the stone corridors with a purposeful stride. The hem of her gown brushed against the cool flagstones as she led Alisdair through the familiar labyrinth of her ancestral home. Her piercing blue eyes softened with a hint of vulnerability as they approached the kitchen, the hearth and heart of her grandmother's domain.

The heavy wooden door creaked open, revealing the warmth of the fire and the rich aroma of stewing herbs and meats that enveloped them like an embrace. Fiona's grandmother, the matriarch whose wisdom had steered the McAfee clan through seasons of both scarcity and plenty, stood at the center of this sanctuary of sustenance. Silver strands laced her hair, each one a testament to a life steeped in duty and sacrifice.

"Granny," Fiona began, "I present to you Alisdair McClain." Her gaze flitted to Alisdair, seeking affirmation in his steady presence beside her.

The old woman turned, her eyes crinkling as she regarded the man before her. "So, ye are the lad. I wondered if I'd ever get to meet the one Fiona had chosen as her husband." Her tone was laced with both curiosity and mirth.

Alisdair bowed his head respectfully. "It is an honor to stand before you, my lady," he replied, his voice rich and measured. His piercing eyes met those of the elder with a glint of reverence. "I am grateful for the welcome into your kin."

As Fiona observed the exchange, she grew proud. Here stood the two pillars of her past and future, the wisdom of generations meeting the promise of the ones to come. Yet, in this union, an undercurrent of tension hummed—a silent acknowledgment of the political responsibilities and alliances that their marriage represented.

In the steadiness of Alisdair's gaze and the knowing glint in her grandmother's eyes, Fiona found an unspoken understanding. They were all bound by the same creed of duty, all willing to make sacrifices for the good of their clans. It was in this kitchen, amid the simple grandeur of daily life, that personal desires yielded to the greater call of legacy and unity.

Fiona understood her choice was more than a match of hearts. It was a merging of destinies, intertwining the fates of the McAfee and McClain clans.

⚜

CHAPTER SEVENTEEN

THE FOLLOWING MORNING, Alisdair dispatched Brodie with news that would spread through the clans swiftly. The air was crisp, and the morning mist clung to the earth as if reluctant to release its embrace. With solemn purpose, Brodie mounted his gelding and galloped toward Clan McClain to inform the clan of the upcoming nuptials and where they should be to witness them.

Alisdair watched his brother's figure diminish into the distance, the weight of his decision anchoring him to the spot. The keep of McAfee would soon become his home.

Hours later, alone in his chamber, Alisdair was interrupted by an unexpected voice.

"Ye've stirred the nest with this one, brother," Boyd chided with a grin, perched precariously on the windowsill as though he belonged there. He relayed their mother's joy, a sentiment that warmed Alisdair's heart even as he frowned at the recklessness before him.

"Ye shouldnae be here, Boyd. It's nae safe beyond our lands," Alisdair admonished.

"Ah, but what's life without a wee bit of adventure?" Boyd chuckled, his departure as sudden as his arrival.

Alisdair knew that Boyd would soon be home, but he also knew their mother would be worried when he disappeared as he did. Boyd was well known in the family for disappearing when he wanted, and he always returned.

The atmosphere of the keep shifted when Caitlin and Fearghas arrived. Fiona observed from a respectful distance as the two patriarchs, Laird McClain and Lair McAfee, convened for the first time under truce and tentative kinship.

"Ye ken this binds us closer than ever afore," Fearghas spoke. "Clan McAfee will be in capable hands." Though Fearghas hated the idea of his eldest son moving away from the clan, he understood that Alisdair had always been destined to lead, and he could not lead the McClains.

"Aye, it's a new dawning for us all," replied Laird McAfee, his eyes filled with the promise of shared fires and future feasts. "The alliance with McClain shall forge a bond as strong as the one yer clan has held with the Campbells these many years."

A silence fell, heavy with the unspoken acknowledgment of the sacrifices made in the name of unity. Alisdair's gaze met Fiona's across the room, their understanding unvoiced yet resounding. She knew the mantle of leadership weighed upon him, his desires secondary to the mantle he was about to assume.

As the men continued to deliberate, Fiona allowed herself a moment of reverence for the path they were all now bound to tread. Duty, sacrifice, and the tension between personal yearnings and political necessities entwined like the intricate braids of a bridal plait.

AMIDST THE FLURRY of wedding preparations, Caitlin McClain found a quiet corner with Fiona. With an affectionate gaze, Caitlin reached out, her fingers light upon Fiona's arm.

"Ye are truly the daughter I've always yearned for," she murmured.

Fiona's eyes met Caitlin's, the weight of years without a mother's embrace hanging between them. "My own mother passed giving me life," Fiona began on a melancholy note. "My father's heart had scarce time to mend before he wed again, seeking a mother for his newborn bairn. And a son. He wanted a son to take his place someday. Twice more did death visit our doorstep. Each time a new wife bore him a child, the cruel hand of fate took her from us. It was my grandmother who helped Father raise Ailis, Moira, and myself." Fiona paused, her gaze distant. "But the love of a mother has long been a void in my heart."

Caitlin's hand tightened gently around Fiona's. "Then let it be so no longer," she whispered.

As they parted, Fiona carried the warmth of their exchange like a cloak against the chill of the keep. But time was a relentless foe, sweeping Alisdair away to train the McAfee men.

Later, in the dimming light of the day, Fiona sought the counsel of her grandmother. The elderly woman's keen eyes studied her granddaughter, wisdom etched into every line of her face.

"Tell me, child," her grandmother asked, "Are ye still a maiden?"

A blush crept over Fiona's cheeks, betraying her calm exterior. "Alisdair and I have known moments of closeness," she confessed, her voice barely above a whisper. "Once we nearly surrendered to our passions but were discovered ere the act was done."

"Ye need not fear the marriage bed," her grandmother counseled reassuringly and frankly. "What lies between husband and wife is a dance of love and trust. In time, ye shall find joy in the union of your spirits and bodies alike."

FIONA STRODE INTO the great hall, her athletic frame moving gracefully among the high stone walls that had borne witness to countless gatherings of her clan. The air was cool and still, carrying the faint scent of peat from the hearth, where embers glowed with the promise of warmth. Her piercing blue eyes surveyed the scene before her, finding Caitlin McClain first, seated at the head of the aged oak table, quill in hand.

"Good morn, Caitlin," Fiona chirped.

"Good morn, Fiona," Caitlin replied, her smile gentle as she prepared to transcribe the details of their discussion.

Granny was laying out an assortment of jars and vials upon the table, each containing herbs and spices essential to Highland cuisine. "We must have neeps and tatties," Granny declared, her green eyes sparkling with anticipation. "And a venison pie thick enough to satisfy a chieftain!"

Ailis, her wavy auburn hair cascading softly around her shoulders, nodded in agreement, humming a tune that spoke of joyous times. "Oh, and do not forget the bannocks, Granny. 'Tis a feast for celebration, after all." Though Granny was only Fiona's grandmother, she was also called Granny by her sisters.

"Indeed," Fiona replied. She turned her gaze toward Moira, whose fiery red locks were a stark contrast to the serene tapestry that hung behind her. Moira leaned forward with characteristic liveliness, gesturing vividly as she described the decorations.

"Imagine, Fiona, garlands of heather and thistle twining 'round the room, and candles flickering like stars come down to dance with us!" Moira's voice danced with excitement, but Fiona sensed the undercurrent of duty that anchored the festivities.

"Write down every flower and flame," Fiona instructed Caitlin, watching as the quill scratched across the parchment. She paused, the dry wit that so often laced her words replaced by a sobering frown. "But there is one matter that weighs heavy on my heart."

All eyes fixed upon her, a collective breath held within the ancient walls. "I wish not to see a single Sinclair cross the threshold on that day," she declared. "After what they did to me, they have no right to eat McAfee food or enjoy our hospitality."

"Da says they must attend," Ailis interjected gently.

"Malcolm's deeds are his own, not of his kin," Granny insisted. "Unless ye have proof otherwise, and I ken ye do not, or ye would have shared it."

"Father believes it was solely Malcolm's doing," Fiona conceded reluctantly. "Yet my heart harbors unease at the thought of their presence at our celebration."

"Your father speaks of peace," Caitlin reminded Fiona, her motherly tone infused with understanding. "It is a sacrifice, perhaps, but one that may heal old wounds." She covered Fiona's hand with hers. "I understand it will be difficult for Alisdair to have them there as well, but as the laird's eldest child, ye must keep what the clan needs in mind. And the clans all need peace."

Fiona grappled with the duality of her wishes and her obligations. It was a delicate balance between personal desires and political responsibilities.

"Very well," Fiona conceded with a nod. "Let the Sinclairs be guests, for the sake of unity and my father's wishes."

With that, the planning resumed, the steady rhythm of voices and quill strokes crafting the blueprint of a wedding that would be etched in the annals of the clans for generations to come.

ALISDAIR APPROACHED HIS father with a solemnity that matched the gravity of the impending nuptials. The great hall of Clan McAfee, usually alight with roaring fires and the boisterous laughter of warriors, held its breath, as if the very stones understood the significance of the moment.

"Father," Alisdair began, "might I request a boon?"

Laird Fearghas, whose presence commanded attention even in silence, regarded his son with an inscrutable gaze. He nodded for Alisdair to continue, his expression betraying none of the concern that lay heavy on his heart.

"Would you grant leave for my brothers, Lachlan and Brodie,

to stay with me in McAfee lands for a time after the wedding? Their counsel and companionship would ease the transition as I learn the ways of Fiona's people."

The laird's eyes softened slightly, the lines around them deepening with contemplation. "Aye, they shall stay with you," he consented. Pausing, Fearghas leaned closer. "But be warned, son. The winds of change sweep through the Highlands. Our clan may soon find itself in troubled times."

Alisdair absorbed his father's words, a frisson of unease threading through him. He bowed his head in gratitude and respect before turning to make preparations for the journey ahead.

As evening descended upon the keep Fiona stealthily joined Alisdair in the gardens. Each attempted escape for solitude had been thwarted, their paths intercepted by well-meaning kin or diligent retainers. But tonight, fortune favored them, granting a reprieve from prying eyes. They walked side by side beneath the moonlit canopy.

"Alisdair," Fiona whispered fiercely, as "Ye must ken that I will stand beside ye, not behind ye. My voice shall carry equal weight in our rule."

He glanced at her, the silver light reflecting in his eyes, revealing a depth of understanding. "Aye, Fiona. Ye are the heart of Clan McAfee, a warrior the same as me."

"And ye will listen to my words and we shall both be equal rulers?" She knew they'd had this discussion before, but now that the wedding was getting close, she wanted to confirm he still felt the same way.

"Aye. Ye ken yer clan better than I do. We will share the responsibilities of leadership. Ye will be my equal. My wife."

In the seclusion of the night, their conversation wove between the practical matters of leadership and the tender admissions of their hopes for the future. Alisdair listened intently, his nods and affirmations acknowledging the wisdom in Fiona's words.

"Anything ye deem necessary for our clan, I shall heed," he vowed. "Together, we shall lead as one."

THE SUN HAD barely crested the highlands when Fiona found herself astride her sturdy chestnut mare, the crisp morning air filling her lungs. Today's hunt was not for sport. It bore the weight of tradition and necessity, a final contribution to the morrow's wedding feast where she would stand beside Alisdair as his bride.

The party divided into pairs as Granny's insistent words echoed in Fiona's mind—two deer, three if the gods be kind. Fiona's heart swelled with pride as she watched her sisters, Ailis and Moira, stride confidently alongside Lachlan and Brodie. The seam between the two families was mended further with every shared glance and hushed word between them.

With Alisdair at her side, Fiona led her mount into the dense thicket, her eyes keen for the telltale signs of their quarry. Alisdair's presence was both comforting and commanding, his own gelding moving in harmony with the rhythms of the wild.

Fiona noted the way Alisdair's blue gaze mirrored the intensity of the sky, his focus never waning as he surveyed the landscape for movement. Her own warrior instincts honed to sharpness, she mirrored his vigilance. Together, they were a formidable pair, their connection unspoken yet palpable in the quiet of the hunt.

In the distance, Ailis and Lachlan moved through the woods, laughter occasionally floating back to Fiona's ears. Ailis's smile was like a beacon in the dim woods, her voice mingling with Lachlan's. Fiona felt a surge of gratitude that her sister had found comfort in the company of such a man, one who could appreciate Ailis's nurturing spirit.

Her gaze then shifted to Moira and Brodie, now comrades on this prenuptial quest. Brodie's calm stability was the perfect counterbalance to Moira's fiery energy, his silent strength a grounding force as they traversed the uneven terrain. Fiona's lips curved in a tender smile, knowing that Moira's adventurous heart was well matched by Brodie's observant nature.

As the morning gave way to noon, the tension of the hunt mounted. Fiona's thoughts returned to the impending ceremony, the union of clans, and the expectations resting upon her shoulders. She was the bridge between two legacies, her marriage a symbol of alliance and future prosperity. In the quiet companionship of the hunt, these responsibilities weighed heavily, yet she found solace in the duty she was about to fulfill.

A rustle in the underbrush captured her attention, and she signaled to Alisdair with a slight nod. They readied their bows in unison, the draw of the strings taut against the silence. Fiona sighed slowly, her piercing blue eyes narrowing as a majestic stag stepped into the clearing.

"Steady," Alisdair rumbled. Fiona held her breath, her fingers steady despite the storm of emotions within her. Duty and desire merged in that suspended moment—a warrior's heart beating in time with a lover's soul.

As the arrow flew true, the promise of the morrow solidified. Tomorrow, she would offer more than venison pies. She would bring unity and strength to her people. As she watched the gentle ease between her sisters and Alisdair's brothers, Fiona understood that this marriage was not merely an arrangement of convenience but a joining of clans that would strengthen them all.

CHAPTER EIGHTEEN

THE GRAND HALL of Clan McAfee's keep brimmed with the chaos of a proud Highland gathering. Fiona, wearing the rich tartan of her clan, stood beside Alisdair before the gathered assembly, their hands clasped. The air thrummed with the pulse of bagpipes, and the scent of pine from the surrounding forests seeped into the stone walls, bearing witness to this union.

"Ye are now bonded, one flesh, one heart, one clan," proclaimed the priest as he bound Fiona's and Alisdair's wrists with an embroidered cloth. The throng erupted into cheers.

Duncan McAfee offered a nod that held the gravity of a thousand silent blessings upon his daughter. Fiona met her father's eyes, understanding the unspoken pledge to uphold the legacy of their line.

"Let us feast and revel in honor of the future Laird and Lady McAfee!" Duncan boomed.

As the celebration unfolded, plenty of meats, venison pies, and honeyed mead graced the tables. Laughter and tales of valor swelled around them, yet Fiona remained vigilant, scanning the faces around her. She caught sight of the Sinclair laird, whose claim of ignorance regarding his son's misdeeds hung between them. His eyes, shrewd and calculating, skirted away from hers, but not before she discerned the flicker of something concealed within their depths.

"Father," Fiona murmured to Duncan, "I trust not the Sinclairs' word."

"Keep yer friends close and yer enemies closer still, lass," Duncan replied. "We shall be watchful."

The night waned as the newly joined pair led the dance, their movements a harmonious blend of strength and elegance. Each turn and step they took echoed the rhythm of two hearts learning the measure of each other's beat.

A hush descended upon the revelers when the moon hung heavy. It was time. Fiona and Alisdair, guided by tradition and expectation, withdrew from the warmth of the hearth and the company of their kin.

Ascending the staircase to their chamber, the door closed behind them with a solemn thud, sealing away the cacophony of celebration. The revelry would last long into the night, but Fiona and Alisdair had waited long enough. They were alone at last, their breaths mingling in the cool silence of their sanctum. The weight of their titles, the expectations of their clans, lay outside those sturdy oak doors. Here they were simply man and wife, and they desired one another greatly.

Fiona faced Alisdair, much more nervous than she'd expected. In the quiet of their chamber, the clamor of duty receded, leaving room for the tender unfolding of a shared life just beginning.

Alisdair's fingertips, calloused yet gentle, brushed the tear from her cheek, and their eyes met in the flickering candlelight. The language of longing, unspoken but palpable, filled the space between them.

"Fiona," he breathed his wife's name like a benediction. "Finally."

In that moment, Fiona knew she could entrust herself to this man—a man who saw past his place in her clan and found the woman beneath. Slowly, as if unfurling the petals of a delicate flower, Alisdair undressed her, his gaze never wavering from her eyes, his every caress imbued with reverence and tenderness.

Alisdair's caress ignited a fire deep within Fiona's soul. The layers of her clothing slipped away, leaving her clad in only the fabric of her underdress, the tartan of her clan cascading like a waterfall around her. She stood before Alisdair, her heart pounding in rhythm with the distant beat of the drums, vulnerability and desire intermingling in the air around them.

Alisdair's hands caressed her skin with a gentleness that contradicted his fierce exterior. With each featherlight stroke, he unraveled the layers of armor she had worn for so long, exposing the raw beauty of her longing and affection. Fiona's breath hitched as he uncovered a breast, leaning down to place a tender kiss upon the soft flesh, his lips warm against her skin.

She cried out when he took the nipple between his teeth and gently suckled it as would a bairn. She wasn't sure if it was right for him to nibble her that way, but she didn't argue. Nay, it felt too good for argument, and she felt heat shoot straight through her to her core.

Fiona's fingers trembled as she reached out to Alisdair, hesitating for a moment before tracing the contours of his chest, sensing the steady thrum of his heartbeat beneath her palm. The firelight danced in his eyes, reflecting a desire that mirrored her own, a primal need to fully surrender to the pull drawing them together.

As she trailed lower, she explored the planes of his body with a curiosity born of newfound intimacy. Alisdair groaned softly against her skin. The glorious sound resonated deep within her. The weight of their responsibilities melted away, leaving only the intoxicating blend of want and adoration swirling in the air around them.

As her palm trembled, she tentatively brushed against the plaid still covering his manhood. Her eyes widened at the sight of the hardness beneath, a testament to the depth of his desire. Fiona's breath caught in her throat, a mix of awe and desire swirling within her.

With a gentle caress, she began to uncover him, her fingers shaking with a mixture of excitement and apprehension. Alisdair watched her with a mixture of awe and desire, his eyes never leaving her face.

As Fiona's fingers reached the sensitive skin beneath, Alisdair's breath hitched. Fiona's heart pounded, the rhythm of her emotions mirroring the pounding of the drums outside. She could feel the heat of his arousal through the plaid, a raw and primal connection that threatened to overwhelm them both.

The air was thick with anticipation as Fiona finally fingered the delicate skin covering Alisdair's erection. She felt the longing and desire coursing through his body. Her gaze met his, and she saw a storm of emotions in the depths of his eyes—a mixture of vulnerability, desire, and a fierce need for her that she had not realized before.

She held his member, stroking it softly, and heard him groan. "That is not a good idea. Later, you can caress me all you want."

Fiona's heart swelled with love and longing. A new courage surged through her veins. She knew that this was the moment of truth, the moment when they would either surrender to the fires of their passion or retreat into the safety of their titles and duties.

Alisdair reached out and gently cupped her face, his thumb brushing away the last tear from her cheek. Their lips met, and the kiss was as passionate as it was tender. It was a culmination of all the emotions and desires they had been suppressing for what felt like a lifetime.

As they kissed, Fiona was finally able to break free from the shackles that had bound her heart for so long. She could sense Alisdair's care and desire for her, a warmth that radiated from his body and enveloped her in a cocoon of safety and longing.

Their bodies pressed together, and a new kind of fire ignited within Fiona. It was a fire born of love and desire, a fire that burned bright and true. She wrapped her arms around Alisdair's neck, pulling him closer, savoring the feel of his hard muscles against her soft skin.

Alisdair's hands roamed over Fiona's body, exploring every inch of her with a tenderness that took her breath away. His caress was gentle yet passionate, and the fire in his eyes burned brighter with each stroke. Fiona's heart swelled with love and longing. She was finally where she belonged.

As their lips met again, the passion between them intensified. Their tongues danced together. Fiona could sense his erection, hard and straining against her.

With a low growl, Alisdair broke their kiss, his eyes burning with a fierce need that Fiona had never seen before. He gazed intensely and possessively at her as he slowly pushed her back onto the bed.

Fiona gasped as she felt the cold, hard surface of the bed beneath her, but she understood what was coming. Alisdair's eyes never left hers as he positioned himself between her legs, his erection throbbing against her thigh.

"Are ye ready for me?" he growled, sending shivers down her spine.

"Aye," she whispered, her eyes locked on his.

With a possessed expression, Alisdair slowly lowered himself onto her, their hips coming together. Fiona moaned as his hardness overwhelmed her.

"You feel so good," he murmured, his lips brushing against her ear.

Fiona's hands gripped his shoulders, her nails digging into his flesh. "I want you," she breathed.

Alisdair began to move. Their bodies glided against each other in a slow, sensual rhythm that built to a frenzy. The air was thick with the scent of their desire. Fiona's breath hitched with each thrust, her body responding to Alisdair's caress in ways she had never before imagined.

His eyes never left hers as he drove into her, the fire in his eyes intensifying with each stroke. The tension between them built, the desire coursing through their veins like wildfire. They moved in perfect sync, their bodies a testament to the passion that had been building between them for so long.

Fiona clawed at Alisdair's back, her body arching to meet his every thrust. The pleasure was unlike anything she had ever experienced before, a raw and primal connection that took her breath away.

Alisdair's lips found her neck, his teeth gently grazing her skin as he continued to move inside her.

Their bodies moved in a perfect rhythm. A fire ignited within Fiona at every thrust. Her breaths came in short gasps, and her heart pounded wildly.

But even as the pleasure consumed them, they never lost sight of each other. Their eyes locked.

Afterward, she lay in his arms for a long while before reaching out and exploring him.

Her mind was only curious about one part of him, and that's where her hand went. Her fingers wrapped around his hard length, her fingers brushing against his sensitive skin. She gazed at him, her eyes filled with a combination of fear and desire.

Alisdair moaned softly, his eyes never leaving hers. "Ye can caress me," he whispered lustfully.

Fiona's hand tightened around his erection, her grip firm but gentle. She stroked him slowly, her fingers gliding over the silky skin.

Alisdair groaned, his eyes closed for a moment as the sensation washed over him. He opened his eyes and gazed intensely, lustfully, and lovingly upon her. "Ye should never be afraid to explore," he reminded her, his voice deep and full of promise.

Fiona bit her lip, her heart racing as she continued to stroke him. She held control over him. But there was also a vulnerability in her, a need to be cared for and cherished.

Alisdair raised his hand and gently cupped her face, his thumb brushing against her cheek. "Ye are beautiful," he whispered in awe.

Fiona's eyes filled with tears, her heart swelling with love for him. She leaned forward and kissed him. Their lips met in a fervent embrace.

Alisdair groaned, gripping her hips as their tongues danced and their breaths mingled. Fiona felt the warmth of his body against hers, the fire between them burning brighter with each passing moment.

As they kissed, Alisdair slowly eased her on top of him, their bodies locking together. Fiona felt him fill her even fuller than before. She didn't know what to do, but she figured it out as she slowly began to move atop him.

Fiona's eyes fluttered open, her face flushed with desire as she gazed at Alisdair. The air around them shimmered with their passion, the scent of their lovemaking lingering in the air.

Alisdair's eyes met hers, his gaze filled with a mix of awe and tenderness. He leaned down, his lips brushing against her ear as he whispered, "Ye make me wild, lass."

Fiona's heart swelled for him, her body trembling. She reached up and gently cupped his face, brushing against his strong jawline. "Aye," she breathed.

Their eyes locked, their hearts beating in unison as they savored the moment. But the fire between them still burned, their desire for each other too strong to ignore.

Fiona let her hands wander, tracing the lines of Alisdair's body as she explored every inch of him. Her caress was gentle, yet possessive, as she reveled in the feel of his skin beneath her fingers.

Alisdair groaned softly, his body arching toward her as she continued to stroke him. His heart pounded wildly, his desire for her growing with every passing moment.

Alisdair's intense, lustful eyes met hers. "Ye are mine," he moaned softly.

Fiona's breath hitched at his words, her heart swelling with a possessiveness that mirrored his own. "And ye are mine."

With that, he rolled her onto her back. "Ye are moving too slow!" They continued to move in time, the rhythm faster and more intense than it had been. Fiona's caress became more insistent, brushing against his sensitive skin with a featherlight touch that sent shivers of pleasure coursing through him.

"Our bodies are connected," Fiona whispered. "And our

hearts are one."

Alisdair's breath caught in his throat at her words, closing his eyes for a moment as he reveled in her caress. "Aye," he agreed, his voice thick with emotion.

Their passion continued to build, the fire between them becoming an inferno that threatened to consume them both. Fiona traced a path from his chest to his abdomen, her stroke filled with intensity. She could feel the heat radiating from his body, the desire that burned within him matching her own.

Alisdair's heart pounded wildly, gasping as he met her caress. "Ye drive me mad, lass," he whispered lustfully.

Fiona smiled wickedly as she traced the edge of his waistband. "And ye drive me wild."

As their passion continued to build, Fiona and Alisdair lost themselves in the moment. Their bodies moved in perfect harmony, their desires melding together in a symphony of fire and desire.

The air around them shimmered, the scent of their lovemaking thick and intoxicating. Fiona's heart pounded wildly, trembling as the full force of her desire for Alisdair became clear.

Alisdair groaned softly, his body arching toward hers as her caress set his skin on fire. The fire between them was all-consuming, their bodies locked together in a dance of pure desire.

Fiona gasped as she was overwhelmed by the power of their passion. Her eyes met his, her heart racing with love and longing as they surrendered to the inferno that threatened to engulf them both.

Their bodies moved in perfect sync, their desires melding together in a fiery symphony that shattered the very air around them. Fiona traced the lines of his body, her caress both tender and intense. Alisdair's heart pounded wildly, his desire for her growing with every passing moment.

As their passion reached its peak, Fiona and Alisdair lost all sense of time and place. Their bodies moved as one, their desires melding together in a perfect harmony of fire and desire.

The air around them shimmered. Fiona's heart pounded wildly, her body trembling with emotion as she felt the full force of her desire for Alisdair.

Fiona's breath came in ragged gasps as fell back against the bed, not quite believing what she and Alisdair had just done to one another. One thing was certain. Granny had been right about this. It was pleasurable.

As Fiona closed her eyes to sleep, she could still hear the revelry from the great hall drifting through the open window. For a moment, she wondered if she should be down there with her guests, but then she decided it didn't matter. She was where she belonged. In the arms of her husband.

❧

CHAPTER NINETEEN

Laird Arran Sinclair convened with his remaining sons. The air was thick with the scent of peat smoke and the undercurrent of anticipation that always preceded his councils of war.

Aaran addressed Malcolm and Ian with a voice that resonated through the vaulted ceilings. "The time for action is now," he declared, the lines on his face deepening. "Alisdair McClain is a thorn in our side that must be plucked out. Should blood fail to secure our future, then marriage shall bind it."

There was a subtle shift in Ian's stance, an unspoken movement of both ambition and apprehension. He was the elder, the heir apparent, whose shoulders bore the burden of future leadership. Beside him, Callum's eyes held a gleam of steely resolve.

"Which of you will deliver us from this impasse?" Laird Sinclair's question hung in the air, a gauntlet thrown.

Ian stepped forward, his voice steady as the ancient pines that crowned their highland home. "Father, 'tis I who shall seek Alisdair and challenge the fate that binds us to his will. If by the sword we cannot unite our clans, then by the heart I shall endeavor."

Callum nodded, a silent sentinel conceding the strategy to his brother. For in their world, the ties of blood were second only to the bonds of allegiance.

"Before the leaves fall and winter's chill embraces the glen, we must have victory or alliance," Laird Sinclair declared, his words etched with the frost of necessity. "The clan will not survive the winter without the McAfees' food stores." He shook his head. "Ye lads should not have encouraged all men to become warriors and hunters, for the clan needs farmers and the food they grow to be healthy."

The brothers stared at one another. Malcolm had been the one who had taunted any lad who spoke of being a farmer. He had been the one to lack foresight, not them, but it would do no good to tell their father that. Nay, Da was convinced that Malcolm had been the smartest and strongest of his sons. He was wrong, but that didn't change his mind about it.

Ian and Callum convened with the chosen men of their clan. The great hall was dimly lit by the flickering flames of torches, casting elongated shadows that danced upon the walls like restless spirits. Anyone with eyes could see the brothers had heavy weights upon their shoulders.

The gathering was an assembly of strength, where destinies would be changed forever. Ian, his stance firm and authoritative, addressed the warriors. Callum stood nearby, his presence equally commanding though tempered by the patience of one who knows his part in the grander scheme.

"Ye ken what is at stake," Ian's voice resounded through the hall. "An alliance must be forged, by blood or bond."

The two warriors selected nodded, their expressions unreadable masks of fealty. These men were not just soldiers. They were extensions of the Sinclair will, their loyalty unwavering.

"Ye shall don these." Callum presented the plaids that bore no crest. The fabrics were like the mist of the moors—elusive and without allegiance. It was a guise necessary for the task ahead, one that required the erasure of identity so that their mission might be shrouded in secrecy. "A contingent of soldiers will be sent with ye, men who have never gone to McAfee land. They will distract others, and the two of ye will attack Alisdair at the same time, killing him and getting him out of the way."

The plaids were exchanged in silence, the gravity of the moment akin to the solemnity of a sacred rite. As the fabric settled upon the warriors' frames, they were transformed—no longer sons of Sinclair in the eyes of the world, but phantoms dispatched on a perilous quest.

Ian's hand clasped the shoulder of one warrior, a gesture that spoke volumes of the trust placed in these men. It was a silent impartation of responsibility, the understanding that failure was a luxury they could ill afford.

"Return to us with triumph," he began, his voice a low thrum of conviction.

"Or not at all," Callum added, his tone tinged with the harsh reality of their grim undertaking.

THE MORNING MIST hung heavy over the Sinclair encampment as Ian strode with purpose through the ranks of warriors. The air was chill, but the fire in Ian's breast burned hotter than the midsummer sun. Today, a contingent of Sinclair men would ride against the McAfees, disguised in plain red plaids, and the weight of his father's expectations bore down on him.

"Brothers," Ian's voice rang out, steady and clear. "This day, ye face our foes with valor and strength. Twenty of ye will ride with Gavin and Logan to the field of honor."

The men shifted, their leather armor creaking, eyes filled with excitement at the prospect of battle. None questioned the summons. To be chosen by Ian Sinclair was to be marked for glory. Yet behind the pride in their eyes, uncertainty flickered like shadows cast by an unseen flame.

"Ye ken what awaits us," Callum called. He did not mention Alisdair McClain by name. Only Gavin and Logan knew the true mission. "We are Sinclairs, each one bound to the other. Our cause is just, our arms strong."

The warriors nodded, clashing gauntlets against breastplates in assent—a loud metallic sound heralding their readiness. But Ian stood silent, his gaze piercing each man as if to etch their visage into his memory. They were pawns in a grand game of thrones and swords, and though his heart balked at the sacrifice, duty anchored him like stone.

A collective breath was drawn, and as it was released, so too was the specter of distraction. There was only the mission, the blood oath of the Sinclair Clan, and the understanding that some might not return. In the hushed reverence of the moment, Ian saw the reflection of his own resolve mirrored back at him, twenty-fold.

In truth, the men who went with their chosen champions were but sacrifices to the clan's needs. They did not need to be told so, for fear they would desert.

Thus, with hearts girded and blades unsheathed, the Sinclair men readied themselves to march toward destiny, where the looming shadow of Alisdair McClain awaited.

THE FIRST LIGHT of dawn had yet to penetrate the thick tapestries that adorned the walls of the bedchamber. Alisdair and Fiona lay entwined in a cocoon of warm linens and shared breaths, the sacred cocoon of new marriage where days and nights blurred into a continuous thread of intimacy and whispered confessions.

Fiona, with her warrior's senses never fully at rest, stirred at the faintest change in the air—a prelude to the intrusion that was about to come. She nestled closer to Alisdair. Their chamber bore silent witness to the merging of two souls, neither time nor duty had breached its doors since vows were exchanged and kisses sealed their union.

It was on the tenth morn of their marriage when the reality of life beyond their threshold came crashing down. A loud knock rattled the heavy wooden door, curt and insistent. Fiona's eyes snapped open, the piercing blue orbs reflecting a sudden alertness, her body tensed like a bowstring. Beside her, Alisdair's slumber was shattered by rude summons. With a grunt of annoyance, he rolled from the bed, his warrior's physique casting a large shadow in the dimly lit room.

"Who dares?" Alisdair's voice was a low growl, rumbling through the space between them and the unwelcome caller.

"Riders, m'lord," came a voice from without. "More men in pure red kilts."

"Red kilts," Fiona murmured to herself, speaking her worries into existence. The men in the red kilts were cowards, sacrificing themselves for the clan or clans they were a part of. Her belief was they were all from Clan Sinclair, there to finish what Malcolm had started.

She watched as Alisdair donned his kilt, his movements deliberate and efficient, the embodiment of a leader called too often away from moments of peace. Fiona rose as well, her long blond hair cascading over her shoulders, hastily tying it back with practiced hands.

"Stay here," Alisdair commanded softly, though his eyes betrayed his reluctance to leave her side. His gaze lingered on her for a moment longer before he strode toward the door, each step heavy with the weight of responsibility.

"I will stay because I understand the necessity of it, not because you commanded it," she replied.

Alisdair turned to her. "I forget myself. Please stay here, and we will deal with the intruders on our land."

Fiona brushed against the cool metal of her sword's hilt, an anchor in a suddenly shifting world. From the narrow slit of the window, she could see the stark contrast of red against green, a line of men dotting the landscape where the McAfee clan's territory began.

"Men in red kilts," she repeated to herself, her tone now hardened with resolve. The men were there for evil purposes. She could feel it inside her.

Descending the staircase to the great hall, Alisdair's boots echoed off the ancient stone, each step amplifying the urgency that gripped him. He found his brothers, Lachlan and Brodie, already gathered below. Their faces were etched with the same anger that hardened his own. Without the need for many words, they came to a swift decision. Together, with their McAfee kin and the remnants of Clan McClain's warriors, they would confront the threat that dared to encroach upon their lands.

The three brothers stepped out into the chill of dawn, where the men had assembled, a sea of tartan against the backdrop of their ancestral home. Brodie's fingers absently brushed the fletching of the arrows slung across his back, while Lachlan's hand rested on the hilt of his sword, scanning the horizon with the sharpness of a hawk.

"Today, we stand united," Alisdair proclaimed. "We shall turn back these intruders, for they cannot fathom the strength of those who are born of this land."

The men responded with a rumble of assent, the sound rolling like thunder over the fields. With Alisdair at the fore, they advanced toward the border where the ominous line of red kilts awaited, a scarlet stain upon the earth that had known only peace for a long while.

The men awaiting them were shadows without a banner, a riddle wrapped in an enigma, cloaked by the anonymity of their garb. The clash of steel rang out as the two forces met, the shrill cries of battle piercing the serenity of the glen. Alisdair fought with the ferocity of a mountain cat, his blade an extension of his will, driving back the faceless marauders.

The din of battle rang through the air, the sound familiar to Alisdair and his brothers.

Two warriors of the clanless men slipped closer to Alisdair with purposeful intent, their eyes fixed upon him as hawks upon a hare. Their blades glinted in the waning sunlight, drawing nearer with each breath. These interlopers clearly sought to ensnare the man, to close in like wolves circling their prey.

Alisdair stood strong, flanked by adversaries unknown, his broad form exuding an aura of unyielding strength. He parried and feinted, a dance of death under the open sky, his movements showing the years of discipline and mastery he'd put into his training.

"Who has wrought this treachery?" Alisdair demanded, voice booming above the sounds of battle, even as he dispatched a flurry of strikes that forced one assailant back. His question hung unanswered in the cool highland breeze.

"From where do ye hail?" he pressed on. The men offered naught but silence, their grim resolve unshaken as they renewed their assault.

Alisdair turned the tide, his blade singing through the air, a dirge for those who dared challenge him. She knew well the burden he bore, the mantle of leadership that demanded he place duty above all else, even when faced with enigmatic foes.

With a swift and decisive motion, Alisdair's sword found its mark, and the first challenger crumpled lifelessly to the earth. The second man, witnessing the fate of his comrade, fought with reckless abandon, yet Alisdair met him with calm precision.

"Reveal yer master, or share his fate," Alisdair demanded. Though he knew the man would never reveal who had sent him, it was only fair to give him a chance.

As if in response, the final foe lunged with desperation, only to be met by Alisdair's unrelenting force. Alisdair dispatched the man quickly.

Alisdair surveyed the aftermath, his piercing blue eyes searching for further threats. Yet amid the strife, there was a strength about him, a reminder of the unwavering commitment that defined both his legacy and her own.

The fallen would remain, their secrets entombed with them, a chilling testament to the ever-present shadow of conflict that loomed over the highlands.

Returning to the keep, with the echo of battle still ringing in his ears, Alisdair's thoughts turned to Fiona. Her plea for passion over lineage resonated within him, fueling the fire of his determination. For her, for their future, he would fortify their borders, safeguard their lands, and stand vigilant against the waves of men who sought to engulf them. It was his duty, his sacrifice, and his unwavering commitment.

Alisdair's strode through the stone corridors of the keep. His mind, still ensnared by the fray, sought solace within the sturdy walls of his new home.

Laird Duncan stood before the hearth, his gaze fixed upon the flames that danced with wild abandon, ignorant of the world's troubles. Alisdair approached, his presence soon acknowledged with a nod as somber as the mood that enshrouded them.

"Laird, we must consider who these attackers might be," Alisdair began, his voice carrying the weight of his unease. "The Sinclairs have ever been ambitious, and their appetite for power knows little restraint. They are known for using their army to take what they need instead of working for it themselves. They do not value farmers or any other type of workers, only warriors and their hunters, who are often warriors as well."

Duncan turned, yet his expression remained unreadable. "Nay, lad. I ken your concern, but the Sinclairs are bound to us by honor. It is not their way to strike from the shadows."

"Yet, something lurks within those shadows, something that seeks to undo us," Alisdair argued. "We cannot dismiss any possibility, no matter how uncomfortable it may be."

"Enough!" Duncan's voice was a thunderclap, jolting the silence. "I will hear no more of this. We shall remain vigilant, but I will not accuse without cause. That is not our way."

Alisdair's jaw tightened, the taste of unsaid words bitter on his tongue. With a curt nod, he conceded the point, though his heart rebelled against the dismissal of his fears.

Seeking respite from the tension that clung to him, Alisdair found Fiona in the courtyard. She turned at his approach, her blue eyes piercing through the encroaching dusk.

"Join me on a hunt?" he asked. Ever the leader, he refused to simply go on a stroll with no purpose, even with his wife. He used his time wisely, and not a man alive could call him lazy.

"Of course," Fiona replied, her voice a balm to his chafed spirit. They gathered their bows and set out beyond the keep's walls.

Through the forest they moved, united in purpose, until at last, a stag graced their path—a creature proud and noble, unaware of its role in the day's convergence of fate. Alisdair's arrow flew true, and together, they claimed the prize that would sustain their people.

After they did their duty, they gazed into each other's eyes. Within moments, they were shedding their garments.

Fiona's fiery spirit met Alisdair's roughness with a fierce passion that matched his own. Alisdair's stroke was firm and commanding, igniting a hunger within Fiona.

The scent of crushed pine needles mingled with their shared breaths, creating an intoxicating blend of musk and nature as they surrendered to each other.

In that fleeting moment, their individual burdens melted away, consumed by the all-encompassing blaze of their union. Each gasp, each shared heartbeat, wove a tapestry of unspoken promises between them, binding their souls in a silent vow of devotion.

As the last vestiges of daylight faded into twilight, they clung to each other with a desperation born of longing. Fiona's skin tingled under Alisdair's caress, every calloused fingertip leaving a trail of fire in its wake. She welcomed his roughness, the raw intensity of his desire mirroring her own.

Alisdair gazed at Fiona with a hunger that transcended mere physical need. His eyes, usually so sharp and guarded, now held a vulnerability that echoed the depths of his soul. With each kiss, each caress, he sought solace in her embrace, finding a refuge from the turmoil of his duties and the weight of his responsibilities.

Fiona responded to him with a fierce passion, her own desires laid bare in the press of their bodies and their shared breaths.

They moved with a passion that mirrored the primal forces of nature around them, giving and taking with equal fervor. Alisdair found solace not in the solitude of contemplation, but in the shared breath and beating pulse of the woman he had vowed to protect.

Alisdair and Fiona made their way back to the keep, the stag on Alisdair's shoulders. "Two men," Alisdair's voice broke through the quiet that had settled between them, his tone grave, "they came for me in the chaos of the battle. It was no mere skirmish we found ourselves in today—it was an orchestration, a deathly assault meant to end with my life snuffed out."

His words were measured, each syllable heavy with the weight of revelation. Fiona's eyes mirrored the solemnity of his confession.

"An attempt on your life," she mused. "But why? And who would dare?"

"Questions that need answers," he acknowledged, a muscle in his jaw tightening. Alisdair's gaze stayed forward, fixed on the crenelated ramparts of the keep. "I believe it was Sinclairs, but your father is still defending them."

Fiona reached out, her hand briefly brushing against his arm—a gesture full of strength and reassurance. "We will find those responsible."

"Aye," Alisdair replied, allowing himself a momentary glance at her, noting that her braid had come undone while they'd trysted on the forest floor.

ALISDAIR STOOD UPON the ramparts of the keep, his gaze sweeping over the landscape that encircled the McAfee ancestral lands. The mist clung to the ground like a shroud, and the air was heavy with the scent of impending rain.

"More guards," he murmured. "We need eyes on every pass, every thicket where danger might lurk." His words were not questions but commands, given to the men who stood at attention behind him—loyal soldiers who would heed his will without hesitation.

As the first rays of sunlight pierced the fog, a horn sounded in the distance. Alisdair's taut expression softened for just a moment, a silent acknowledgment of the sacrifices made by those who would now stand sentinel over their home.

The clatter of hooves against stone heralded the approach of an entourage, and Alisdair turned to witness Laird Sinclair's arrival. The older man dismounted with a grace surprising for his years, his presence commanding even in the still of the courtyard.

"Alisdair McClain," Laird Sinclair began, his tone laced with formality. "I come bearing a proposal—a union that could fortify our clans against any who would dare threaten us."

Alisdair listened, his mind already weighing the implications of such an alliance. Yet it was not his decision alone to make. He watched as Laird Duncan emerged from the great hall, his figure exuding an aura of indomitable strength.

"Arran," Duncan acknowledged with a nod to Sinclair, though his eyes remained impassive. "These are trying times. Our focus must be on safeguarding our people, not on forging ties through marriage."

Sinclair's gaze hardened, a flicker of impatience crossing his features as he countered, "And yet, if our houses were joined, would we not present a united front all the more formidable? Think on it, Duncan. Your daughter Ailis wed to my son."

"Enough," Duncan interjected, his voice devoid of warmth. "There is no time for this now. We are beset on all sides, and I will not have my hand forced while uncertainty looms over us."

A tense silence fell, the kind that spoke volumes more than words ever could. Alisdair watched the exchange, a silent observer of the delicate dance of power and diplomacy.

Laird Sinclair inclined his head, the merest hint of concession.

"Very well. But consider my words. Strength lies in unity—in bonds forged not just by blood, but by shared purpose."

With that, he signaled to his men, and they departed as swiftly as they had come, leaving behind a ripple of disquiet that lingered long after the echo of their departure had faded.

"I do believe they are after an alliance, and they will do whatever it takes to get it." Alisdair briefly explained how he had been the target of the attack the previous day.

Laird Duncan shook his head. "It cannot be them."

Alisdair said nothing more, but he knew the truth, and he suspected Laird Duncan did as well.

IN THE QUIET of the great hall, Fiona approached her father. "Father," she began, her voice steady despite the tempest within, "I must speak on behalf of Ailis and Moira." She paused, searching his face for signs of the compassion she knew him to possess. His eyes, like storm clouds, met hers with an intensity that spoke of battles fought and burdens borne.

"Ye ken the times are dire," Duncan replied, his words heavy. "Alliances through marriage can be as strong as steel, securing peace and prosperity."

Fiona held her ground, her gaze unwavering. "But at what cost?" she implored. "I have been fortunate to marry for love, to lie beside a man whose heart beats in tandem with my own. Should not Ailis and Moira be granted the same chance?"

Laird Duncan's expression softened, just a fraction, but enough for Fiona to continue. "Love has fortified me, given me strength beyond measure. It is a force that no alliance, however politically astute, can replicate."

A silence stretched between them, fraught with unspoken fears and unyielding duty. Fiona's hands, which had clasped together of their own accord, trembled slightly, betraying the fervency of her plea.

"Ye speak from the heart," Duncan conceded, his voice a low rumble. "And I would see my daughters happy. But a laird must look beyond the present joy to the future of his clan."

"Then let us forge our own path," Fiona countered. "Let us show that love and loyalty can triumph over adversity, that they too can be the bedrock upon which alliances are built."

Duncan's eyes searched his daughter's, fierce and unyielding. In them, he saw not only the fire of her convictions but also wisdom. He let out a breath, the weight of his decision visible in the set of his shoulders.

"Very well," he answered, the words slow and deliberate. "I will consider your words, Fiona. For the love you bear your sisters, and for the peace of this family, I will ponder the path we should take."

CHAPTER TWENTY

THE GREAT HALL of McAfee Castle was filled with tension as
Fiona walked toward the long, oak table at the room's
center. Beside her, Alisdair matched her pace, his broad shoulders
squared in readiness for the confrontation ahead.

"Father," Fiona began, her voice betraying none of the
tempest that brewed within her, "we must parley with the
Sinclairs."

Laird Duncan stood firm, his gaze lingering on his eldest
daughter, the very image of stoic leadership. Yet in his eyes
flickered a flame of reluctance. "It is against my better judgment,"
he conceded, but with a nod, he signaled his acquiescence to the
will of those who would one day lead.

No sooner had the Sinclair party been ushered into the hall
than Laird Arran, flanked by his sons Ian and Callum, wasted no
time in voicing their intent. "An alliance, forged through
marriage," Arran proposed with diplomatic finery, his eyes
landing upon Ailis, who stood beside her sister.

Fiona's brow furrowed, worried her father would agree. She
knew the offer for what it was—a bid for power, not partnership.
"Our clans share a bond, but it shall not be strengthened by
binding Ailis against her will," she replied.

Undeterred, the Sinclairs shifted their proposition, this time
suggesting a union between Callum and Moira. The suggestion
hovered in the air.

"Moira, too, shall choose her own path," Fiona declared, the refusal clear and irrevocable.

Alisdair watched the exchange, his eyes sharp as an eagle's, taking the measure of the men before him.

The flickering torchlight cast a somber glow upon the stone walls of the great hall, where the heavy tapestries absorbed both warmth and sound.

"Let us speak plainly," Laird Duncan began, his voice resonating through the hallowed space with the gravity only years of leadership could bestow. "An alliance forged in trust is as strong as the mightiest fortress, but what Malcolm has wrought upon my daughter's peace has rent a fissure in that stronghold."

Laird Arran met Duncan's gaze, his own eyes betraying none of the turmoil that surely roiled beneath. "It was Malcolm who erred grievously, not the Sinclair clan. He acted alone, and for his transgressions, he has died." He turned to Alisdair. "By your hand, I presume?"

Alisdair nodded. "Aye, by my hand and no other. A man raised with honor would never kidnap a woman who has done nothing wrong."

Fiona watched as Alisdair stepped forward, his muscular frame poised with the confidence of a seasoned warrior addressing his equal.

"Where, then, did Malcolm find the men to aid him in such treachery?" Alisdair asked, but Arran had an answer for everything.

Laird Arran's lips thinned into a line of practiced composure. "I know not," he replied, his voice steady. "For none of our warriors are unaccounted for."

The statement bore the stain of untruth—a shadow lurking just behind the eyes of the man who uttered it. Fiona's intuition whispered to her of the deception nestled within those carefully chosen words.

In the silence that followed, the air became thick with unspoken suspicions, each breath drawn a testament to the delicate balance between duty and honor. The future of their clans was now a precarious thing that remained on the edge of extinction.

As the conversation turned to matters of restitution and reparations, Fiona's thoughts lingered on her father, wondering if he saw the deception as clearly as she did. She understood that the preservation of their people came above all else, even if it meant dealing with alliances tainted by betrayal.

Duncan's eyes moved over the brothers Sinclair—two branches of an ancient tree that now bore poisoned fruit.

"Brothers," Duncan remarked, "your countenances speak volumes more than your tongues." Ian and Callum shifted uncomfortably under his scrutiny, their guilt a cloak too heavy upon their shoulders.

Laird Arran, sensing the shift, cast his net once more into turbulent waters. "We seek to mend what has been torn asunder," he began, seeking to soothe his old friend. "Let us join our houses, not through force, but through the gentle ties of matrimony."

Duncan regarded Arran with the wariness of a seasoned commander. "Aye," he conceded, wanting to heal the wounds of the past. "If one of yer sons wishes to court my Ailis, so be it. But know this—" He raised a hand, forestalling any premature triumph, "she is her own woman, free to choose her path. No alliance shall be forged with chains, only with the willing consent of her heart."

Around the great table, the assembled leaders waited with bated breath for the response from the Sinclair brethren. Young Ian rose swiftly to his feet. His voice, scarcely tempered by the gravity of the moment, rang clear and eager.

"Then it shall be I," he declared. "I will seek to earn fair Ailis's favor."

Duncan regarded Ian with an intensity that might have withered a lesser man.

OUTSIDE THE FORTRESS walls, Alisdair and Fiona found solace in nature and one another. Their steps fell in rhythm with the pulsing heart of the earth, their path winding through the whispering grasses. Here, they could lay bare their thoughts, unshackled from the confines of expectation.

"Every word they utter weaves a web of deceit," Alisdair confided, his tone laced with the frost of conviction. "The Sinclairs are entangled in this dark plot more than they dare admit."

Fiona walked beside him, her mind racing with concern over what her father had agreed to. "Aye," she replied. "Malcolm's treachery is but a piece of the evil they concoct."

Alisdair halted, turning to Fiona. "I will have Lachlan guard Ailis closely," he intoned solemnly. "If the Sinclair wolves circle our fold, they shall find the fangs of the McClain hounds ready."

THE GRAND HALL of McAfee Castle was aglow with the soft light of a hundred candles as Fiona and Alisdair returned from their twilight sojourn. The Sinclairs awaited them with bread and salt at the ready—a peace offering for the meal to come. As they all seated themselves around the heavy oak table, the air was fraught with the scent of roasted meats and freshly baked loaves.

Ian Sinclair leaned close toward Ailis, his words spilling forth like fine ale—frothy and plentiful. Callum, with an easy charm, directed his attentions to Moira, whose laughter tinkled through the hall like the chime of bells.

Fiona observed their antics with a wary eye. Alisdair shared her sentiment. His jaw was set in a line that spoke of his distrust. When he finished his meal, he drew Lachlan and Brodie away from the merrymaking.

"Stay by Ailis's side," Alisdair instructed Lachlan in a tone that brooked no argument. "And Brodie, keep Moira within sight."

Both men nodded, understanding the gravity beneath their brother's command.

As the evening wore on, the gathering shifted from jovial feasting to the somber matters that lingered between the clans. Duncan and Arran, once the closest of friends, stood apart from the crowd, their voices low but laced with the venom of old grievances.

"What stirs the embers of discord?" Fiona asked, her gaze shifting between the two elders.

Laird Arran's laugh cut through the tension, though it held little mirth. "A tale as old as time." A wistful note threaded his words. "I once sought the affections of Lady Eileen, your mother. But she chose Duncan over me."

Duncan responded with a steely glare, but before he could continue, Arran waved a dismissive hand. "Ah, but history has shown us that the better man did not win her heart."

Alisdair considered Arran's words, his thoughts obscured behind a veil of duty. Fiona felt the undercurrent of rivalry and regret that colored the room, a reminder of the sacrifices made at love's behest and the relentless march of obligation that cared not for the desires of the heart.

LAIRD DUNCAN SUMMONED the McClain brothers to his side with a gesture that brooked no argument.

"Brothers McClain," Duncan began, his voice a deep rumble, "the events of yestereve have left a shadow upon my trust for the Sinclair clan."

Alisdair, Lachlan, and Brodie stood before the laird, their postures rigid with attention. It was Alisdair who spoke first, his tone laced with the authority of one accustomed to command. "We stand ready, Laird McAfee. What is it ye ask of us?"

Duncan's gaze swept over the trio, lingering on each face

before settling on Lachlan. "Lachlan, I charge ye with the protection of Ailis. Let not shadow nor doubt cross her path without your intercepting hand."

Lachlan's lips quirked upward in a knowing smile. "It would be my honor to serve as a shield to Lady Ailis," he declared, his voice smooth and confident.

"And ye, Brodie—," Duncan continued, turning to the youngest brother. "Ye shall guard Moira with the same vigilance that ye would guard yer own daughter."

Brodie nodded, as if accepting a sacred trust.

A chuckle escaped Alisdair's lips. "I find myself a step ahead, for I've already tasked them with these duties." His glance at his brothers was filled with camaraderie and unspoken understanding.

Laughter, soft and warm, wound through the chamber, easing the tension. Duncan joined in, the sound rich and unexpected.

"Then we are of one mind. For in unity, we find strength."

THE SUN ROSE on a new day, painting the skies with hues of promise and peril. As the clansmen went about their morning tasks, the peace was shattered by the clamor of conflict—a band of red-kilted warriors descended upon the McAfee lands, their intentions clear.

Alisdair's hand rested on the hilt of his sword, scanning the field. Beside him, the Sinclair men—Arran and his sons—stood, their own weapons drawn.

"Let us join you," offered Ian Sinclair, gripping the pommel of his sword with a warrior's eagerness.

Alisdair's jaw set firm, his gaze unwavering. "Nay, Sinclair. We know not the measure of your strength nor the manner of your fight. Stand back."

The refusal hung between them, a chasm of trust yet unbridged. And as the clang of metal rang out, the Sinclairs could only watch as the McAfees and their kin clashed with the invaders.

The battle was short-lived, lasting only an hour before the attackers ran away in defeat.

THE SINCLAIR MEN, who had been forced to the role of idle spectators, stepped forward.

"Ye ken our men would not raise arms while we are on McAfee soil," Arran Sinclair asserted, his voice carrying the weight of unwavering conviction. "This brazen attack—it could not have sprung from our men."

Alisdair, standing tall amid the carnage, turned to the Sinclairs with a measured scrutiny. "Indeed, Laird Sinclair," Alisdair responded, his tone deliberate, "no accusation has been cast upon yer kin."

A shadow of doubt changed Alisdair's stern features for a moment. His eyes narrowed slightly, the cogs of his mind turning with a strategist's precision. He perceived the unsolicited defense as a crack in the Sinclair armor—an unwitting revelation most telling.

"Yet here you stand, offering denials unbidden," Alisdair continued, his stance resolute. "One might wonder at the eagerness to disavow deeds unspoken."

Arran Sinclair's jaw clenched, and his sons shifted uneasily beside him as if the very earth beneath their feet had become uncertain. The air, thick with the coppery scent of spilled blood, constricted around them.

"I wonder what gives ye a guilty conscience and makes ye deny something ye were not accused of doing," Alisdair remarked, glaring at Laird Sinclair.

Arran offered no retort. Alisdair's gaze lingered on the Sinclairs for a moment longer before he turned and walked away.

CHAPTER TWENTY-ONE

TWO FIGURES EMERGED from the morning mist that covered the hills of McAfee land. Ailis, her brown hair a softened halo in the muted light, spared only fleeting glances at the Sinclair men who trailed behind her and Moira like shadows bound to their heels. The Sinclair brothers, earnest in their pursuit but lacking the spark that could ignite the sisters' affections, were met with courteous nods and polite smiles, but they were truly uninterested in the Sinclair men, and not only because they believed their clan was behind their sister's abduction. Trailing mere yards behind the Sinclair men were Lachlan and Brodie, taking their duties seriously as they carefully watched the two men.

Beyond the courtyard, Fiona and Alisdair stood with an air of growing command. With each passing day, Laird Duncan entrusted more of the clan's governance to his daughter and son-in-law, preparing them for the leadership of the clan.

The transition of power was not without its ripples. Fiona observed the subtle shifts in her clansmen's demeanors, the way they hesitated before following Alisdair's directives, still unaccustomed to his voice carrying the weight of authority. Yet, with measured patience and firm resolve, Alisdair began to earn their trust, his strategies and judgments proving both sound and just.

At the periphery of Fiona's vision, Brodie and Lachlan maintained their vigilance, ever watchful over the safety of her sisters. Their loyalty brought a great deal of peace to Fiona's mind because it meant her sisters were never alone with the men who had betrayed them. It brought reassurance to Fiona, knowing that even as her responsibilities grew, her sisters would be guarded by fierce warriors.

Fiona let her gaze drift back to the Sinclairs, observing the interplay of courtship from afar. Ian and Callum carried themselves with a veneer of confidence, yet beneath it lay a hunger that spoke of needs beyond the marital alliances they sought. The cessation of attacks from the clanless marauders coincided all too conveniently with the Sinclairs' frequent visits, a detail that did not escape Fiona's notice.

"Something troubles you, my sister," came Ailis's gentle observation, her voice drew Fiona's attention away from worries filling her mind.

"Merely the weight of impending leadership," Fiona replied, allowing herself a moment of vulnerability before her middle sister. "And the ceaseless dance of politics that ensnares us all."

Ailis offered a knowing smile, one that spoke of shared burdens and the silent promise of support.

"Well, well, what secret plans are being hatched now?" Moira teased, a knowing smirk playing on her lips as she nudged Fiona with an elbow. "Don't tell me you two are conspiring to take over the world next."

Fiona couldn't help but crack a smile at her younger sister's antics. Moira's infectious energy was a stark contrast to the worries on Fiona's mind. Alisdair's deep chuckle rumbled in his chest, his stern facade momentarily melting away.

"Let the Sinclairs dance alone." Moira giggled, her eyes filled with mischief. "Our hearts are not so easily won, nor our minds so quickly swayed by pretty words and empty gestures."

Fiona couldn't help but share in her youngest sister's mirth. There was truth in Moira's jest for neither Ailis nor Moira could see the Sinclair men as potential suitors.

"Aye," Fiona agreed. Her heart never failed to skip a beat when her eyes met Alisdair's.

In the calm of the morning, with the Sinclair brothers persisting in their futile endeavors and the clan gradually bending to Alisdair's emerging leadership, Fiona felt the delicate balance of her world shifting. Duty and desire, sacrifice and love.

Fiona stood beside Alisdair as they presided over the clan's evening repast.

Ian Sinclair approached, always staying for supper whether invited or not. With a courteous nod, he sought the attention of the new laird and his lady, his voice a low thrum that carried with it the weight of purpose.

"Lady, Laird," Ian began, inclining his head toward Fiona and Alisdair respectively. "With respect to your honored house and the ties that bind our clans, I come before you to request the hand of the fair Ailis in marriage."

A hushed silence fell upon the gathered assembly, and all eyes turned toward Fiona and Alisdair. Fiona's gaze met Ian's with a steadiness that contradicted the turmoil churning beneath her composed exterior. The man was confident in himself, that was for certain. He wouldn't have dared broach the subject in front of others otherwise.

"Ye honor us with yer request, Ian," Alisdair spoke, his voice resonating with the timbre of authority. "Yet in this clan matters of the heart are not dictated by the will of others. Ailis must be free to make her own choice in this union."

Fiona nodded in agreement, her thoughts adrift to the bond she herself shared with Alisdair—a bond not yet sealed by the talk of love she so deeply craved. It was a whisper of longing that wound its way through her heart, unspoken but fervently felt.

"Aye," Fiona added, her words echoing the sentiment of her husband. "Ailis shall have her say, for no alliance can be forged without the consent of both hearts. Ask her, then if she agrees, talk to us again, and we will decide if ye are worthy."

Ian dipped his head once more, a subtle flush crossing his features before he masked it with a practiced smile. It was the only way he showed his anger, but he had truly made it obvious to those around him that he was unhappy with the answer he'd been given. He retreated, leaving behind a trail of speculative whispers among the onlookers.

As the evening waned and the chamber emptied, Fiona found herself alone with Alisdair. Their fingers entwined, a silent testament to the unity they presented to the world. Yet the space between them was vast. It *seemed* he loved her, and that was true, but without him speaking the words, she could never be certain.

Fiona's gaze swept over the man she had wed, the leader who now stood at her side, guiding their people with wisdom and strength. She longed to hear the words that would bridge the distance between duty and desire—to confirm that their marriage was more than an alliance, that it was a joining of two hearts.

She studied the planes of his face, noting his handsome face, strong demeanor, and the eyes that held the secrets of his heart. The love she bore him was a fierce flame within her, yet she remained silent, bound by the belief that it was his place to voice such tender truths first.

In the stillness of their chamber, with the embers of the fire dying to a soft glow, Fiona wrestled with the tension that lay at the core of her being—the yearning for love's confession and the solemn vows of a lady born to lead.

"Goodnight, my lady," Alisdair murmured, his voice a gentle rumble that stirred the quiet of the chamber.

"Goodnight, my husband," Fiona replied, moving across the bed to lay in his arms. Even without love, his caress brought her great joy.

THE WOODS WERE silent but for the twang of a bowstring and the whispered flight of an arrow. Fiona, her grip steady and eyes fierce with the focus that had become as natural to her as breathing, watched as the projectile found its mark with deadly precision. The deer, startled, bounded away only to collapse moments later amidst the bracken.

"An impressive shot," Alisdair remarked, emerging from the shadow of the towering pines, his own bow slack in his hand.

"Thank you," Fiona replied, though the usual spark that lit up her words was dimmed by the weight of her thoughts. She turned to him, the man she had pledged her life to, yet still felt a chasm of uncertainty between them.

"Is something amiss?" Alisdair asked, sensing the shift in her demeanor.

As they walked toward their quarry, Fiona's gaze lingered on the forest floor, a tapestry of copper and gold leaves crunching beneath their boots. "I cannot ease my mind," she confessed, her voice low and troubled. "We know not the true nature of these clanless warriors, nor can we trust the motives of the Sinclairs who now hover about Ailis and Moira like vultures."

"Is there more?" Alisdair prodded gently, taking note of the furrow in her brow that spoke volumes more than her words.

She hesitated, the raw vulnerability uncharacteristic of the normally indomitable lady. "And I... I find myself adrift, unsure of your sentiments toward me."

Alisdair's expression shifted, a mixture of disbelief and dawning understanding crossing his rugged features. He set down his bow and took her hands in his.

"Fiona," he cried, his voice filled with a fervor that surprised even him, "I thought my actions had spoken for themselves. My pursuit of you, my desire to unite our lives—it was not solely for the alliance of our clans."

She sought the truth within the depths of his gaze.

"Love is a luxury often denied to those who bear the burden of leadership," Alisdair continued, his thumb tracing circles over her knuckles. "But I love ye, Fiona, in a manner most unfitting for a warrior. I would risk placing ye above all else—even the very clan I have sworn to protect."

The breath caught in Fiona's throat. The confession she had so desperately craved now hung in the air between them. Her own heart clamored against the walls she had built around it, and the words spilled forth unbidden, "I love ye too, Alisdair."

In that moment, with the rustle of leaves and the distant call of a hawk overhead, they embraced. It was a union not just of two bodies, but of two hearts—each recognizing the other as their chosen equal in the dance of power and passion.

For now, the matters of clan politics and mysterious adversaries could wait. In the circle of Alisdair's arms, Fiona found solace and strength. And within her embrace, he discovered the courage to face whatever trials lay ahead, knowing they would do so together.

ALISDAIR AND FIONA returned from their hunt. With practiced ease, they hoisted their quarry—two sturdy deer—from the backs of their mounts, the fruits of a day spent in nature. A sense of accomplishment filled the air.

"Come, let us inform Granny of our success." Alisdair led the way into the stone edifice.

Fiona followed, her steps echoing softly in the grandeur of the castle halls. She found Granny in the kitchen, where she was always working at this time of day.

"Granny," Fiona announced with a fond smile, "we've brought venison. Two stags."

"Ah, that'll do nicely for supper on the morrow, and we will salt some for the winter. The two of ye are singlehandedly saving the Clan from starvation." Granny never ceased her work, even as she spoke.

Content with Granny's approval, Alisdair and Fiona strode back to the courtyard, intent on retrieving the deer for the larder. Yet, upon their return, the air stilled. An ominous quiet settled over the space where once two carcasses had lain. Now, there was but one.

Fiona's hand flew to her mouth, a gasp escaping her lips. Beside her, Alisdair tensed, scanning the perimeter for any sign of intrusion or theft.

"By the saints…" Fiona murmured, her voice barely a whisper against the encroaching silence.

Alisdair shook his head. "I'm certain it was the Sinclairs," he declared, the surety in his tone betraying no doubt. "Their hunters are not as good as the hunters of our clan, and almost all of their clansmen are warriors or hunters. They have few farmers because they do not respect farmers."

Fiona nodded, her own suspicions mirroring his. The Sinclairs had sown seeds of mistrust within the walls of her home. They could easily have spent the day hunting as she and Alisdair had, but instead, they took what was not theirs to take.

"Such an act reeks of desperation," Fiona remarked, her voice steady despite the turmoil churning inside her.

"Aye," Alisdair agreed, his jaw set. "It is a brazen move, one born of necessity, perhaps, but folly nonetheless. It shall not go unanswered." He shook his head. "Everything they do is from a place of desperation, including courting yer sisters."

With a shared expression of resolve, the pair turned back toward the castle, their thoughts now consumed by the implications of this latest affront.

In the waning light, the castle stood tall and unyielding—a bastion against the chaos of the world outside. And within its walls, Fiona knew she could find the strength to stand beside Alisdair, united in purpose and heart.

Fiona leaned against the cool stone of the parapet, her gaze on the darkening forest beyond. The stolen deer was but one more enigma in a series that had begun to unfold the day she and Alisdair had started to court. "It seems," she mused to her husband, who stood by her side, "that these mysteries are entwined with our very union."

Alisdair's hand found hers, firm yet gentle, as if he sought to anchor her to him through the uncertainty. "I cannot fathom their purpose or design," he murmured, "but I vow we shall see them unraveled."

"Perhaps it is the test of our bond," Fiona replied, her fingers tightening around his. "A trial set before us to prove our resolve."

"Then together, we shall face it," he assured her. His resolve matched her own.

Fiona and Alisdair retired to their chamber for the night. The weight of the day's events still hung heavily on them both, but within the sanctity of their shared space, they allowed themselves to lay aside the burden of leadership, if only for a moment.

In the quiet intimacy of their bedchamber, with only the flickering light of a single candle casting shadows upon the walls, Alisdair drew Fiona into his arms. He whispered words of devotion into her ear, each one laden with the depth of his love, and with each utterance, her heart swelled.

"Ye are the compass that guides me, Fiona," he confessed, his breath warm upon her skin. "In ye, I find the courage to lead, the strength to protect, and the warmth to soothe the chill of doubt."

Fiona nestled closer, her head resting upon his chest, where she could hear the steady beat of his heart—a rhythm that soothed her restless spirit. "And ye, my love," she responded, her voice barely above a whisper, "are the beacon that lights my way. With ye, I am whole, unafraid, and ready to face whatever trials may come."

SHADOW STRETCHED ACROSS the Sinclair encampment as the two young men, burdened with the weight of a freshly killed stag, made their way toward the central fire where Laird Arran sat. His gaze, sharp and assessing, followed their approach, noting the proud lift of their heads—a triumph in their stride that spoke of more than a successful hunt.

"Father," Ian began, breaking the evening's stillness with his announcement, "we've brought home a stag, taken near the McAfee keep."

"Two were there for the taking," Callum added, a note of pride threading his voice. "We doubted one would be missed."

The air grew taut as Laird Arran rose to his full height, his expression darkening like the gathering clouds above. The glow from the flames cast an ominous light on his features as he surveyed the prize before them.

"Ye act without foresight," Arran chastised. "To steal from the McAfees now, when we stand on the precipice of alliance, is folly." He shook his head. "At least Malcolm knew not to do things quite so foolish."

"Father, it was but a single stag," Ian protested, the shadows dancing across his face revealing a flicker of uncertainty.

"Even so," Arran added, "our actions must be beyond reproach. Tell me, how fares your suit with Ailis McAfee?"

Ian shifted, discomfort clear in the tense set of his shoulders. "I have asked for her hand, as you commanded. Yet, they insist I must gain her favor first."

"And have ye?" Arran prodded.

Silence hung heavy between them before Ian squared his jaw, resolve hardening his stance. "I have yet to find the opportune moment. But make no mistake, Father—I shall have her consent. With Ailis as my bride, our clans will unite, and our larders will be filled once more." He sighed softly. "Two of the McClain brothers follow Ailis and Moira everywhere they go. We are never truly alone with them."

Arran studied his son, the lines of worry softening as he considered the determination etched into Ian's visage. "Then let us hope for a swift courtship," he declared, his voice a mix of command and encouragement. "For the prosperity of our clan rests upon your shoulders, my son. The Sinclairs will rise, and through this union, we shall triumph."

And there, amidst the stark reality of their ambition, the Sinclair men stood united under the mantle of dusk, each heart beating with the promise of power and the peril of desire intertwined with duty.

EPILOGUE

Many years later

ALISDAIR AND FIONA stood in the middle of the Highland chapel, smiling happily. Alisdair McClain's broad frame, adorned in ceremonial tartan, stood like a silent sentinel beside his wife Fiona.

Their gazes were fixed upon their daughter, her hand clasped in that of a man deemed worthy by both love and lineage. The soft murmur of Gaelic blessings filled the air as vows were exchanged with a solemnity befitting the sanctity of the moment.

In the quiet recesses of their hearts, Alisdair and Fiona reminisced about the days when their three sons, now stalwart leaders with families of their own, had been but mischievous lads chasing through the heather. The eldest, prepared to inherit the lairdship of Clan McAfee, bore the same gaze as his father, while his brothers provided strength and unity to their clan.

As the couple reflected on the journeys that had led them here, their reverie was broken by the exuberant cry of their youngest grandchild. A wee lad scampered toward them, his arms flung wide and his face lit with the joy only a child can possess. His voice rang out clear and true, piercing the dignified silence of the aftermath of sacred oaths.

"Granny! Granda!"

Alisdair bent down, his joints protesting only slightly and swept the boy into his arms. Fiona chuckled softly, the sound mingling with the whispering breeze, as she smoothed a stray lock of hair from the lad's forehead.

"Granda," the boy repeated, his small hands patting Alisdair's cheek with innocent affection.

"Ye are a braw lad," Alisdair remarked, his eyes twinkling with unspoken pride. Fiona reached over, her fingers intertwining with those of her husband, a silent acknowledgment of their shared journey.

For a timeless moment, as they watched their kin exchange jubilant congratulations and begin the festivities, Alisdair and Fiona stood anchored in the realization that in the middle of the intricate dance of duty and sacrifice, their lives were woven into a tapestry more perfect than they could have ever envisioned. It was a moment of profound clarity—a reflection of the enduring legacy they had built together, rooted in the rich soil of the Highlands.

Later, at the feast, Fiona and Alisdair stood side by side. The sun dipped low over the horizon, casting a warm glow on the gathering of clansmen who had come for the ceilidh they threw to celebrate the marriage of their youngest child.

"Alisdair," Fiona whispered, "do ye ken they will be happy?"

He nodded solemnly. "Aye, or I never would have agreed to the alliance," he responded.

As they presided over the feast at the huge oak table, they watched their daughter, seeing her sneak kisses with the man she'd just married. It made Fiona remember her own wedding day, which had taken so long to arrive, but she now realized had been merely the blink of an eye.

"Do ye remember when we felt like Da would never agree to our marriage?" she asked softly.

Alisdair smiled, taking her hand and kissing her fingers. "I remember. It felt like forever. But it feels like Cait's engagement, though longer than ours, flew by in moments."

She nodded, grinning at him. "I was thinking the same."

After the meal, people took turns wishing the newlyweds well.

"Tonight, we celebrate not only the union of our clans but the prosperity we've experienced as a clan under the leadership of yer parents, Cait," someone called—a respected elder whose opinion held sway among the McAfees. "Ye will do well in life if you but follow their example."

"Slàinte mhath," came the chorus of voices.

As the music of pipes and drums filled the air, Alisdair extended his hand to Fiona, leading her into the throng of dancers. Held in his arms, she still felt the same as she had when they were first married. They would never have enough time alone to suit her.

About the Author

USA Today bestselling author Kirsten Osbourne knows how to write. Each book is an experience that transplants the reader, indulging them in decadence, intense emotion and sweeping love.

Kirsten was born in Wisconsin, and now lives in Idaho, but she's lived in Minnesota, Texas, and Louisiana along the way.

She writes contemporary and historical romance, venturing into the realm of paranormal romance and women's fiction. She invites you to join her in her world of fantasy, love, and make believe, no matter the location, where there is always a happily ever after at the end.